SMALL CHANGE

SMALL CHANGE

Stanley Middleton

HUTCHINSON
London

The right of Stanley Middleton to be identified
as the author of this work has been asserted by Stanley Middleton
in accordance with the Copyright, Designs and Patents Act, 1988

First published in the United Kingdom in 2000 by Hutchinson

The Random House Group Limited
20 Vauxhall Bridge Road, London SW1V 2SA

Random House Australia (Pty) Limited
20 Alfred Street, Milsons Point, Sydney,
New South Wales 2061, Australia

Random House New Zealand Limited
18 Poland Road, Glenfield
Auckland 10, New Zealand

Random House South Africa (Pty) Limited
Endulini, 5a Jubilee Road, Parktown 2193, South Africa

Random House Group Limited Reg. No. 954009
www.randomhouse.co.uk

A CIP catalogue record for this book
is available from the British Library

Papers used by Random House
are natural, recyclable products made from wood grown in
sustainable forests. The manufacturing processes conform to
the environmental regulations of the country of origin.

ISBN 0 09 180110 9

Typeset in Times by MATS, Southend-on-Sea, Essex
Printed and bound in Great Britain by
Mackays of Chatham PLC, Chatham, Kent

I

Small, fast-moving clouds irregularly patched the blue of the sky. A breeze ruffled the hair of the walking man. June, he thought, and warm with it, but more like Spring. He smartened his step, the sun to his left, and cheerfully wished good-morning to an old lady waiting at a bus stop. She nodded, staring at him with a sour suspicion. He made his way downhill. The road, almost free of traffic, spread wide. Each one of the gardens in front of the brick-built houses was incredibly neat, and, he judged, incredibly dull. The owners had embarked on a competition to keep grass short, shrubs controlled and flowers unobtrusive, but would not draw attention to themselves and their efforts at the expense of those of their neighbours. He grinned at his fanciful conceit and turned right. The side road ran uphill for a hundred yards and then began to dip deeply towards the main traffic-thoroughfare in the valley, which hummed and banged with cars and racing lorries. He imagined the scene a hundred, no, perhaps as little as seventy years back. This hill would be grass-covered, with sheep, or darkly ploughed, and a new railway, Marylebone to Manchester, would run in a cutting, just out of his sight, before it plunged into tunnels and emerged at the city's Victoria Station. Now the line had been closed, the rails ripped up, the cutting filled, and new houses obliterated the route.

As Colin Turnbull marched on, still pleased with himself, the morning's weather, his prospective call on his brother, the road became steeper. At the bottom he paused until the traffic had cleared when he scuttled over to the grassy central division where he stood looking now to his left until he deemed it safe to cross. As he waited he noticed that the road almost opposite was barred with red and white tape and a police notice. A small, sharp policewoman questioned a man on the corner then signalled him forward with one finger. A large unmarked van and three police-cars were lined up in the carpark of the Fox Inn. By the time Colin had crossed the second part of the main road the policewoman

1

had turned her back on him and made her way towards three male officers. As soon as he appeared in her road, she swung round and from a distance of four yards called out,

'The road's closed.'

'Oh?'

'You can read, can't you?' She pointed at the notice.

'I thought that applied to cars only.'

She shrugged at the assumption and straightened her hat.

'It doesn't. Where did you think you were going?'

'Along this street and then to Templeton Avenue.' He pointed the direction out.

'You can't. You'll have to go round by the next.' She performed her own finger-wagging routine.

'But you let him through.' He nodded towards the back of the still retreating man.

'He lives there. We can't keep him out of his own house.'

'I'm just going straight along to the top. I shall be under your observation all the way.'

She shook her head.

'Next street, please. Then we don't need to observe you at all.'

'Can I get round that way?'

'I expect so.'

'What's the trouble?' he asked. 'Or is it just an exercise?'

'For real,' she answered, and turning strutted back towards her colleagues. He stared hard at her jaunty progress, waited until she had joined the others and then wheeled about to make a reluctant exit towards the next street, unknown territory. His good humour had evaporated. The clouds moved as skittishly over the blue; the breeze touched his face, but his pleasure had dissipated itself.

The street he now embarked on ran in parallel to, and looked almost a copy of, the one from which he was exiled. Nobody came out. One van rattled fussily past. The road appeared dusty compared with its neighbour. He knew that to be untrue. The houses were in much the same style, brick-built semis, but he knew the other place, had grown used to the unusual features, porches, or concreted car-spaces, garages, hedges, painted fences. No one made an appearance. Often in the next street he had stopped for two minutes' chat with a householder leaning on his gate, a stocky man, with powerful tattooed forearms, but who breathed with difficulty, wheezing, denying the strength of those arms. The man

2

patted his chest as if to excuse his coughing. He spoke about his army service in Korea.

'By God, it were co'd. And they didn't issue us with the proper kit. We were frózzen. The Americans, they was different. You should have seen the stuff they got. Padded coats, fur collars, the lot. And us. Well.'

Again he held his chest as if to contain the disease there. Soon he'd be back in his garden, slowly mowing his lawn, tying up his hollyhocks, tending lanky delphiniums.

Colin Turnbull turned at the top of this Godforsaken road, walked leftwards towards the original route, taped off at the junction, with a further police-car in attendance. He looked along the length of the forbidden road. Empty. Police at either end, doing nothing. He made for Templeton Avenue.

He rang his brother's door-bell, unwilling to try the back way. Linda, his brother's wife, appeared after his second push at the bell.

'Colin,' she said. 'Sorry I was so long. I was upstairs.'

'In bed?' he asked facetiously.

'Don't be daft. It's my day for the bedrooms.'

'You do them every week?'

'Yes. And I bet Anna does, too.' His wife. 'You just don't notice.' She smiled, a strong woman, tall, willowy but strong, invited him in. 'Aren't you at work this morning?'

He ignored her question. If she wanted an answer 'why' she should ask it accurately. She could see he wasn't at work.

'Sit down,' she said, pulling a chair for him from under the dining-room table. 'Terence's at the shop. Can I get you a cup of tea? Or coffee?'

'No, thanks. He wanted to see me.'

'About what?'

'You tell me,' Colin answered. 'Money, I expect.'

'You know, then,' she said.

'Why should I be asking you if I know already?'

'Why should you call in here? You know he'll be at the shop.'

She stood behind his chair, very close. Suddenly, but softly, she put her arms round him over his shoulder. Her breasts rested on his head. He sat quite still, saying nothing for a time, enjoying her proximity, the embrace. Even on this working morning Linda was perfumed, tactfully, half ready, it seemed for erotic emergency.

'Come on,' then he said, rather dismissively, 'tell us all about it.'

3

Linda ruffled his hair, then smoothed it before rounding the end of the table to sit half-facing him. She frowned as if searching for her introductory words, but seemed in no way troubled. In a low voice she began her account. Terence, her husband, had a new scheme. He wanted to enlarge his first shop to sell a new line in electrical machinery. Some firm had badgered him, Moss-Langley of Stoke and Derby. He had the necessary room, well, with some minimum building, which he had already costed, but the new department would demand an extra employee.

'He's got the man who'd run the additional improvements, but he'd need to be replaced, not very expensively on the ordinary counters. And all this needs money.'

'Which I provide?' Colin said, politely mocking.

'He's been branching out in the television department, and he sells up-to-the-minute computers. There are more than a dozen people working for him now, in the three shops. But you know all this.'

'And he hasn't the cash to hand?'

'No. He has to borrow it from somebody.' She laughed. 'He thought he'd try you first.'

'Suppose I said "No", would he go ahead?'

She murmured sounds of ignorance or doubt before she answered,

'I don't know. He's cautious.'

'Terry's sixty next birthday. Why does he want to expand? He ought to be thinking of retirement.'

'You know the answer to that as well as I do. He's a worker and while he's doing the job he'll do it as hard and successfully as he can.'

'Then all he's got to do if this new venture's going to be as profitable as he thinks is to walk along to the bank and arrange a loan.'

'You're not going to lend it to him, then?' she asked.

'I didn't say that. How much is it going to cost?'

'I've seen all the papers, but I don't exactly remember. It wasn't very large. Somewhere over a hundred thousand, in the first place.'

'It's not peanuts.'

Linda pushed her right little finger into her mouth, and gently sucked the end, comforting herself, aware perhaps that she had not argued her husband's case well. Colin Turnbull leaned back,

4

hands on the edge of the table, balancing his chair on its back two legs. He closed his eyes, a man thinking or praying.

He had no perplexity over the problem. Terence his brother was twelve years older than he, and like him had attended the grammar school. Terry had done moderately well there, but had no difficulty in making up his mind to leave after School Certificate. Apprenticed as an electrician with the National Coal Board he'd made progress, was promoted, travelled abroad, but then at the age of thirty-five had set up on his own in the electrical business. In that year he had married Linda Crich, aged twenty-three, four days older than his young brother, Colin. Over the last twenty-five years he'd laboured at his business, cautiously expanding, providing himself with a decent standard of life. He had twice moved house at his wife's behest, each time to advantage. His present home, with four spacious bedrooms, stood in a large garden, his wife's main interest. Their only child, Henry, had read mathematics and architecture at the local polytechnic, now a university, and worked, somewhat mysteriously to his parents, at first just outside Paris and now in London. Linda had mentioned a French fiancée, and though she had twice been over to England, Colin had not met her.

'I hope to God she'll bring her children up to speak English,' Terry had grumbled to his brother.

'You're a bit ahead of yourself,' Linda, passing, had intervened.

'They're living together, aren't they? Cohabiting?'

'Well?'

'That means sex. And sex means children.'

'Not always.' Linda bustled from the room, laughing. Terence, at least in public, adopted this bluff, quarrelsome tone with his wife. In private, he adored her, pleased her every whim, not that there were many, and attributed his success to her.

'If it had been left to me,' he'd pronounce, 'I'd still be living in a tent in Titchfield Park.'

'Did you ever do that?' Colin had teased.

'Do what?'

'Live in a tent?'

'You bloody well know I didn't.'

Terence admired his young brother. Colin was a man apart, different, brilliant. He'd studied mathematics and economics at the university, achieved a First, refused blandishments for a Ph.D., had immediately begun to qualify as an accountant with

5

Price-Waterhouse, had qualified with honours and two prizes, and had joined Meyer's, a very large local firm. Kuno Meyer, a Berliner by origin, had tested him, found him worthy, promoted him, made him a partner before he was thirty, by which time he had married Kuno's daughter, Anna. By Colin's fortieth birthday, both men had expanded their offices, branched out extraordinarily, had made themselves by far the largest accountancy concern in the East Midlands and the North East of England. Moreover, both had amassed substantial fortunes by their investments. Meyer lived in considerable style in Ashby, one of the outlying villages where he had bought, comparatively cheaply, the manor house, on which he had spent a great deal bringing it to a modernity which his wife considered convenient, comfortable and tasteful. His son-in-law existed more modestly in the town still, in a large house with private grounds.

Anna expressed her doubts about her father's pretensions.

'I don't know why he wanted to buy a place that size,' she had often said. 'It's not as if he had a huge family to accommodate.' She was the only child. 'I think it makes him feel like a real Englishman.'

'That's what he looks and sounds like.'

'I said "feel".'

Kuno Meyer had fled Nazi Germany with his parents. At the time he had been fourteen, and though he still spoke fluent German his accent in English was that of a native. They had been taken into his home by his father's brother, an eccentric bachelor, who in spite of the economic difficulties of the Thirties was making a comfortable living in the rag-trade. The two brothers did well during the War, providing Army uniforms and accessories and by the time Kuno had come out of the Pioneer Corps father and uncle were well-to-do. The young man trained in accountancy, married an English girl, the daughter of his employer, left London and began his successful career in the Midlands. Now, seventy-seven years of age, tall, handsome still, retaining his elegant figure, he strolled about his estate in smart tweeds and polished brogues, swinging his ash walking stick, the picture of health, master of his fate. At the age of seventy he and Colin, his son-in-law, had sold off part of his accountancy interests to a large corporation. He had consulted his son-in-law closely about the change.

'You're sure,' he muttered, 'that you'll have enough to occupy yourself with? After all you're not much over forty, and that's no age for giving up work.'

'I'll have plenty to do, don't you fret yourself.'

'I do worry, Colin. You're like me, a workaholic. You need a job. That's why I had a consultancy for you written into the take-over.' In fact, Colin had insisted on it. They didn't need to talk much; they shared the same aims. Each had married the boss's daughter, and they appreciated this as a marvellously apposite joke. There, they laughed, good fortune had begun for them. Kuno had every confidence in his son-in-law. If he retired at forty-odd from accountancy, it wouldn't be long before he was doing well, or better, at something equally profitable. It was already the case. The two men had walked out from the balustraded terrace of the manor house into the small park talking about big money. Kuno's stick flashed in the sunlight, and the son-in-law wondered why, if the older man regarded English life and customs so highly, he had never changed his name, Kuno Meyer to, say, Kenneth Major or Keith Marshall. You never quite fathomed the old man.

Linda sat, gently smiling at her brother in law. He would have done well to have accepted the cup of coffee, as he was clearly in no sort of hurry. She kept silent, waiting for Colin to give himself away.

'What do you want me to do?' he asked.

'What's that to do with it?' she answered.

'Look. Terry's nearly sixty. Don't you want him to ease down a bit?'

'Why should I?'

'You'd have the time for leisurely holidays, a house in France, long cruises, flights to China or Australia.'

'You think that's what Terry wants?'

'I'm sure he doesn't. But you can teach him. All he can think of now is some different way of expanding his business. That's all he's been doing for twenty-five years. He's good at it, and he enjoys it, but he ought to think of something else. It's not large enough for a lifetime occupation.'

'Where will ye spend eternity?'

'Say that again.'

'Where will ye spend eternity? It's a hymn we used to sing in Sunday school.'

'Bloody hell.'

'I hope not.'

They laughed together, enjoying the exchange. Colin had not realised that she had attended Sunday School. He had hardly known her when she was young, though they had lived not a hundred yards from each other, and had been in the same class in the infant and junior school. Her family had moved to a superior house and she had attended a girls' grammar school before training as a teacher, and then she had made this reappearance at the age of twenty-two as Terence's fiancée. He had been taken slightly aback. He recognised her at once, but she seemed, on show before the Turnbull parents, demure, diffident, neatly unobtrusive. He had shaken hands with her. Her eyes were light blue.

'What did you think of her?' his ailing father had asked Colin.

'She was in my class at school.'

'So you knew her?'

'Years ago.'

'Will she suit our Terence?'

'I've no idea. He's sensible, and should know what he wants at his age.'

'Ay. He's thirty-five. It's a big year for him. He's just set himself up in his own business and now he's got married. Next it'll be children.'

'Is she pregnant, then?'

'I hope not. Though owt's possible these days. I don't think of our Terry as a husband, you know. He's too serious.'

'Isn't marriage serious then?'

'You're too sharp for your own safety, my lad.'

His father, a self-employed builder, occasionally used to corner him for these small conversations. The son had no idea how significantly his Dad took these question-and-answer sessions, but he guessed his mother had pressed her husband: 'Have you asked our Col about it?' Since he had spent a week of his summer holidays from university reorganizing the accounts and billing of his father's business, and had instructed both parents how to employ the new system, his mother had regarded him as an oracle.

'Our Col'll know,' she'd say.

'He's still wet behind the ears,' he'd argue. His father had only a year to live.

'Don't you be so sure.'

Now, this bright June morning, Linda and Colin sat at smiling ease.

'How's the garden?' he asked.

'Just about at its best.'

'Then I'll take a stroll and look, if it's permitted.'

'Have you the time? I thought you had to see Terry.'

'I'll give you five minutes to show off your work.' He liked her ironical tone. 'You know what will happen. When I arrive at the shop I shall find Terry's gone out to do a job that he can't trust anybody else to do properly.'

They walked out through the French window. The garden blazed with flowers, the air heavy and sweet with *buddleia alternifolia.*

'In these days of 'phones and faxes I don't know why you have to go to see Terry. I thought your office was full of electronic stuff.'

'It is. But you don't get much physical exercise out of a fax machine.'

'You look well enough.'

'Because I leave my car behind. Most days now. That's the beauty of doing as I like. If Meyer and Turnbull want a job done they can usually put it through to my office at home. I don't need to go winding in and out of lines of lorries and buses.'

Linda put her arm through his. They walked closely like young lovers and under the shade of a sycamore tree they kissed.

'I never see you these days,' she complained.

'That's why I came round this way.'

They walked on until they reached a kind of classical temple with pillars and statuary which stood behind a pond, large enough for a swimming pool, surrounded by steps. The temple had been built by her husband, and a bricklayer, in his spare time, based on a photograph in a Sunday magazine.

'I'm not so sure I can do it,' Terry had told Linda.

'Are you willing to try?'

'I shall do my best for you. Our Colin got me a scale plan of this place.'

'You told him about it, did you?'

'I did. And he was round next day with a plan. We'll measure up. And I'll cut it down to a suitable size, and before I start any bricks and mortar I'll show you how much of this bottom end of your garden it will take up.'

'We've plenty of room. And it'll look marvellous with a cypress or two about, really Italianate.'

9

'Let me get my thinking cap on.' He frowned. 'It'll be bricks and breeze-blocks with plaster, not stone, y'know. But I don't want to make a fool of myself.'

Now Linda and Colin sat in the pavilion-temple. It had taken her husband nearly two years to complete, but it was excellent, tasteful, exactly suited to the size of the garden.

'I feel very safe here,' she said, 'with you.'

'You shouldn't.'

II

Anna, Colin Turnbull's wife, was keeping an eye on her father's mansion while her parents were abroad. She had promised to call in once a week, to pay the housekeeper's assistant who did three full days, and the gardener who did five. Curtains were half-drawn against the sun, and the large drawing room gave the effect of a Jane Austen setting on TV, spacious, but not too much so, with a slight fading of colours of wall-paper and fabrics as if to prove the place was well lived in. The valuables had been packed away in the bank for the whole of July and August while the Meyers were on the continent. Her father confided to her that this convenience cost him almost nothing; he had done a former manager a favour, and the man had suggested this in return. When a later official informed him that the bank proposed to charge him their usual, eminently reasonable, fee for the service, Kuno had immediately called in and threatened to remove his money, and that of his firm. He'd pay an addition, in accordance with inflation, to the small amount which had been agreed to make the original transaction official.

'It will hardly cover insurance,' the manager argued.

'You make a great deal of money out of me,' Kuno said, always calm, never less than lucid. 'I've had the containers made to your specifications. It's only for two months of the year. It gives you no trouble.'

Her father liked such arguments, Anna thought, and went out of his way to indulge in them. The manager backed down. Kuno came out and sent his wife and daughter shopping for themselves. They cost him more than the bank scheme, but he did not care. He had the money, and his own way. A competitive man for all his gentlemanly mannerisms, Anna told Colin.

As she stood on the terrace and looked over the lawns, the gardener passed on his mower, raising a grimy hand. He'd been paid, and he loved machinery so that this morning of sunshine pleased him; his cap was pushed to the back of his head, and he

11

smiled with large yellow teeth. Anna moved back into the drawing room where Mrs Johnson straightened the covers over the furniture.

'When I've done,' Mrs Johnson had once confided, 'I sit here and look out of the window, at the trees and the clouds.'

'As if you lived here?' Anna had ventured.

'Yes. Without the responsibility. I relax. If I lived here I'd be worrying myself to death about the expense of keeping the place up to date and heating it.'

'All houses cost you money.'

'Yes, but this has nine bedrooms, all immaculate.'

'Does my mother insist?'

'I'd say it's more your father. He doesn't believe in moth-balling rooms that aren't in use.'

'But they don't have many visitors.'

'No. But he's adamant.'

Mrs Johnson gave the impression of flaunting an education. She had been a teacher in a grammar school somewhere in the west of England, Trowbridge or Taunton, Anna could not remember, had retired up here, had suddenly to pay out a great deal of her money to rescue her son's business and so had taken this job of cleaning and supervising the manor house. If anything happened to Anna's mother, Mrs Johnson would permanently move in as housekeeper. She, unlike her assistant and the gardener, was not paid in cash but by standing-order into her account. There was nothing formidable about her; she was smooth-tongued and efficient, but Anna had never found out what subjects she had taught in her school. Her mother had guessed that she was nowhere near sixty years of age, but her husband had died soon after they had moved to the village four years ago. He had not left her much, he was a wine-salesman with ideas and tastes above his station, and Nancy Johnson had to ravage her own savings soon after the funeral to salvage her son's business. She never complained, but lived independently in a pretty cottage ten minutes' walk away from the manor house. She spoke as an equal to Hilda or Anna, or as Kuno, the expert on army affairs said, an experienced major might speak to a youngish lieutenant-colonel. Anna, for reasons she could fathom for herself, wished she knew the woman better, and made a point of talking to her.

'You don't think my father's foolish, do you? Spending money like water on the house here?'

'No, I don't. It's what he wants. If he spent it on horse-racing or model railways or world cruises nobody would criticise. As long as the money's there.'

'You wouldn't do it, though?'

Mrs Johnson raised her eyebrows.

'I never had the opportunity.'

'But if you had?'

'Most people prefer leisure pursuits that take them away from home.'

'He has both.'

This morning Mrs Johnson seemed rather more forthcoming than usual. She spoke of her son, and his extravagant wife, and the one grandchild, spoilt beyond belief. The son's business seemed now to be doing well, but none of the profits came back her way. She had lived in comparative poverty to prop her boy's ambitions, and it availed her nothing now that he had begun to thrive. She seemed not to mind. It was proper for the old to tend the young. They had ambitions and needs; she had by-passed the glories of the world and as long as she could keep warm and dry and eat one decent, cooked meal a day that was enough.

'Are you calling in on Mr Norman today?' Nancy Johnson asked.

'Yes. Just for a few minutes. Have you seen him lately?'

'Not at any length. Just a few words. He's complaining with all his old gusto.'

Frank Norman had taught Anna Meyer at the local grammar school before Kuno (or Hilda, who knew?) had sent her off to complete her sixth-form studies as a boarder at a prestigious public school, now prevailed on to take girls into its higher reaches. Anna had not objected, had thoroughly enjoyed the experience and had gone on to read English at Oxford, but had come back to the Midlands to teach. She had, moreover, married her father's partner and had borne him their two children, Thomas and Alice. Kuno had expressed his pleasure at the marriage, but Hilda had sometimes wondered if Kuno would not have been better pleased to see his daughter married, let us say, to a baronet's heir, who needed subsidising. Colin, Anna's husband, could, for all his modest style, have bought out his father-in-law these days.

'I look forward to leaving my house to Anna and Colin,' Kuno had once said to his wife. 'He'll have the money to keep it up.'

'He's more likely to sell it,' she had answered.

'Do you think he will?'

'If he has any sense.'

'I shan't mind in my grave. I shan't know anything about it.'

'What if it turns out there's an after-life? And you have to sit there watching him auctioning the place off and putting the money to all sorts of nefarious uses?'

'I shall share the joke with God.'

'You'll be nowhere near Him, my friend.'

He and Hilda laughed, with a little bitterness, together.

Anna left her car at the manor house and walked through Ashby village to Frank Norman's home. The church, St Michael and All Angels, stood close to Kuno's, with the graveyard on the far side. The old vicarage, ivy-covered Victorian, stood near the road though the vicar now lived in a modern house at the far end of the village. She passed the pub, the post-office, a row of cottages, the vestiges of the green, below the road, on her left, with two seats, a lime and three silver-birches. Nothing happened officially there now, no cricket, no barbecues, no dancing round the maypole; Kuno would have encouraged such events, but nobody bothered now. New bungalows tastefully took their subservient place among the large houses which stood far back behind hedges with well-kept verges.

Frank Norman lived on the right side of the road, in the end house of an unusual terrace of six. These were substantial, stone-built Victorian with gothic doorways, and if they could have been properly viewed through a screen of a high hawthorn hedge would have looked like a section of decent lower-managerial houses plucked up from a street on some northern manufacturing town and placed here to look blackly out at fields, trees and high clouds.

Anna negotiated the wooden gate, the two levels of rising path divided by six steps and handrail and stood, in the porch in front of the dullness of the stained glass door. She had rung the bell, but knew that Norman took time to reach the front of the house. Turning her back on the place she faced the sunlight, but could see little of the village. She seemed to stare out over a small, irregular but well-kept forest. Cars occasionally hummed past, barely glimpsed, on the hidden road. A shimmer of breeze disturbed the tips of sycamores.

She heard the bolts being pulled and watched the door

grudgingly open. Frank Norman squinted out at her. He finally undid the chain.

'Uh,' he said. 'I didn't expect you.'

'Good-morning. I rang you yesterday to say I'd be in the village, and you invited me to call. At about eleven. That's the time now.'

The old man looked at the watch on his right wrist, seemingly unconvinced. He edged back, stumbling.

'You'd better come in,' he said.

She stepped forward.

'Good morning, Mrs Turnbull.' He used her married name with a kind of irony.

'Good morning, Mr Norman.'

'Where would you like to sit?'

'Anywhere that suits you.'

He signalled her into the drawing room, with its huge bay-window.

'Sit down. I'll get you a cup of coffee.'

'No, please don't. I can't stay long. But I was looking over my father's house, and so I thought I'd check up on you. I rang you about it yesterday.'

He opened a diary, produced from the inside pocket of his jacket.

'I hadn't put it down,' he confessed. He frowned. 'No. This is the wrong diary. This is my book of anniversaries.'

'Is every day filled in?'

'No. Not so.'

'Is today's interesting?'

He fiddled with, then opened the book. He peered, clumsily turning over a page or two.

'Yes,' he said.

Anna waited, said a thing or two about the Meyers' house and grounds.

'Where are they now?' he asked.

It was her turn to produce and consult a diary.

'Vienna,' she said. 'I'm never sure. They have changes of schedule. But Vienna's the centre of activities for this part of the month.'

'They'll enjoy it?'

'Oh, yes. And Daddy likes speaking German.'

'German, yes. German.'

15

Norman attempted to straighten the collar of his jacket. He'd pulled it on in a hurry when he heard the door bell. He'd not tucked in the front of his shirt properly, and one of his coal-black braces was twisted. Grey hair peaked uncombed, but his face, pink and smooth, had been shaved.

'The egregious Johnson was there?'

'She was.'

'What had she to say for herself?'

'That she'd seen you once or twice, but you hadn't talked together for long.'

'Thank God.'

He stared out of the high windows, but not to observe. Again he fumbled in his pockets and extracted the diary. Again he searched it, flicking awkwardly at the pages.

'I'm all thumbs this morning,' he said. 'I don't see eye-to-eye with her.' He tapped the open diary which he held on his left knee. 'Today my father died.'

'I'm sorry,' she said. He looked carefully, suspiciously at her as if for guidance, or hidden meaning behind her remark.

'It was long enough ago,' he said. Anna did not reply. 'I was a schoolboy. Fourteen years of age. Sixty-five years ago.'

'What was it?'

'Cancer. Carcinoma. Internal. It had spread.'

'Was he ill for long?'

'Adults didn't unburden themselves to boys in those days. But a year or two, I'd guess. Pain. Lavatory difficulties. Bleeding. They didn't comment openly at the time. Dad had been to the doctor's. That sort of thing was all they said. He didn't complain. Perhaps a bit more tetchy than usual, towards the end. I remember him ticking some boys off for fooling about on somebody's allotment. If he'd have been well, he'd have just have told them to clear off and not be nuisances. But he tore a savage strip off them this day, threatening all sorts of dire consequences. He said he'd go down and see their parents and their schoolmaster and the police. Quite unlike him.'

'Was he in pain?'

'Yes. Considerably so. I guess. I don't know for certain. They hadn't mastered the art of dying in comfort then. Not that they have yet. Even when they can kill pain, you can be humiliated by your nausea or incontinence or weakness. Not pleasant.'

'No. I suppose not.'

16

'His death came quickly. He walked into the hospital on Thursday, carrying his own case; they operated on Friday and he died on Saturday morning. His cancer was inoperable, they said. They just sewed him up again, and presumably the shock of the operation or the doses of morphia they gave him proved too much for his heart.'

'He was in a coma when he died?'

Norman looked at her as if he resented her curiosity, but he answered plainly.

'No, he was not. He was conscious right up to the end. My mother was there, and my sister. He said to the staff-nurse, "She's been a good wife to me". That was typical. He'd far rather praise than blame.'

'That was lovely,' she said.

'Lovely? Doesn't count for much these days.'

'You'd sooner carp, would you?'

'I didn't inherit his saintly character, of that I am sure.'

'How old was he?'

'Middle-fifties. That seemed old to me at the time, but when I reached that age I was at the top of my form. I'd plenty of energy; I still found my work interesting and had learnt to do it pretty well. It's not the time to die, that I can tell you. You're interested in what's going to happen. My father never knew that I went to university, something I think he wanted.'

'But the onset of pain and discomfort may alter that,' she objected.

'It's possible. My guess is that he hoped that he'd recover. If anyone deserved to do so, he did.'

'Did it affect you badly?'

'It's difficult to say at this distance. I was sad, but I was also a teenager, beginning to rebel. And I'd other things to occupy myself with. I used to play the piano with a violinist. And just at this time we were doing an early Beethoven sonata. A major, one of Op 12. It was dedicated to Salieri, of all people. And I busied myself with that.'

'And did you feel that was wrong?'

'In what way?'

'I thought perhaps you felt your grief for your father should have been greater.'

'I didn't; that's all I know. I was sorry. But I was beginning to be a bit bolshy. Teenagers were, even in those innocent days. He

17

was a better man than I have ever been, I don't doubt. And I tell you another thing I noticed at the time.' He paused, clearing his throat, to make sure she was listening. 'When I met people in the street, they seemed embarrassed, ill-at-ease, as if the death had come between us. I've wondered about it often enough since. Perhaps they expected me to break down or something. Or was it that I read my own unease into their behaviour? But if I stopped and talked ordinarily for five minutes, they became normal and chatted about school or weather and the like. It was odd.'

Anna said nothing, as he, writhing in his chair, blew out breath and struggled to poke his diary back into his pocket. He roughly handled his chin, and forced words out of his throat.

'It's down in my diary. A date to remember.'

'Do you look every day?'

'Roughly. Sometimes there's a whole week with nothing there. Of course, I don't add a great deal these days. A few deaths, the odd wedding when I remember. That sort of thing.'

Anna considered, mischievously but to herself, the possibility that she appeared in the diary. She bit her lip, and asked him if he was well.

That provoked a long answer, with his ailments carefully described. She half-listened. It probably did him good to catalogue these complaints. When the list was complete, or he had tired of it, she asked if he was going away for a holiday.

'Where would I want to go to?' he groused.

'You used to tell us now and again about your trips to France and Norway. It made a pleasant change to maths.'

'I was younger, then. I had the wishes of my wife and family to consider.'

His wife had died while he was still teaching. She remembered it. He had taken a day off and the headmaster had mentioned the bereavement in assembly. She, and other girls presumably, had watched him on his return the next day, but he seemed the same man, clearly explaining his algebra or geometry. He'd taken another day's absence for the funeral, and that was that. Mrs Norman had been unknown; she never appeared at prize distribution, or at the school play, or at the annual sports meeting. The Normans had lived out here in Ashby. No-one mentioned the cause of the woman's death. The two sons, she had learnt this later, had at the time finished their university courses, and lived away. Norman would have been fifty or thereabouts, the time when he claimed to be on the top of his form as a teacher. And he'd drive over to school and back to this large gloomy house five days a week in his neat, well-polished Rover. Next year she had gone off to her boarding school, and forgotten him.

They had met, twenty-five years later, at a village fête to which she had gone with her mother and father. She recognised Frank Norman at once, though he had difficulty in placing this well-dressed mother of two children, daughter of the wealthy Meyers. On her explanation he said immediately, 'I only taught you for your "O" Level year. Then you went off to a public school, Denton, wasn't it? I never connected you with the Meyers here.'

'No. They didn't live here then.'

He had invited her to visit him, and months later she had telephoned him and offered to call in. He had accepted her proposal, though reluctantly, to judge by his voice. She had not known what to expect. Neither did her father know Norman. He said he played no part in village social life, seemed eccentric in a harmless, quiet way. Their housekeeper, Mrs Johnson, lived quite close to him, but found him moody, not very approachable. Anna had no idea why she had bothered. Her chat with him at the fête, out in the sunshine, had been very ordinary. They had spoken about their children. Clearly he admired this young woman, was proud that she chose him out to chat to; as people passed the time of day with him, he spoke to them, or inclined his head as one of a superior status.

Anna found it difficult to talk. Frank Norman would answer questions, but always with a slight hesitation, as if he watched for traps. She equated this with his mathematics. He looked out for the right equations to describe life, but they were couched in the special language that he spoke without trouble and she did not. Therefore he was never in a hurry for fear of misunderstanding. Anna admitted to herself that this might all be imagination on her part. Perhaps he was an old man unused now to conducting conversations with younger women.

When she first called on him she had wondered what the condition of his house would be. She expected to find it stuffy, enclosed, dusty, faded, without sunlight, crowded with old-fashioned furniture. On that first bright summer morning she was surprised beyond all telling. The curtains had recently been cleaned; the lace in the upstairs rooms had been washed and

19

re-hung in the last few days; window panes were spotlessly polished. Indoors, in the hall, a slight tang of not unpleasant disinfectant suggested that the terrazzo floor had been mopped during the last hour. Rooms rested, calm behind huge windows, the walls white or in pastel-shades of blue or green, the few pictures uncluttered in thin black frames. The chairs, settees, bookcases, cupboards, sideboards stood well apart and shining. Space ruled. The kitchen shone with sunlight which sparkled on the hanging knives and aluminium saucepans. In her own ironic way she looked for evidence of his trade as a mathematician, but found nothing. The titles she was close enough to read were of English classics, Victorian, in hardback. Dickens, Trollope, Thackeray, Eliot, Lord Lytton, Wilkie Collins. She wondered if these had been bought by him in the first place or by his wife. Norman, she remembered, had made reference to books, seemed to regard them as the zenith of culture, unlike the instructors of her own children who boasted of IT or the imminent genetic revolution. She supposed they were all, Norman and Co. included, hypocrites putting themselves in a good light.

Frank Norman, hands clasped, had now begun to question her.

'Do you ever see any of the boys and girls who were in your maths set?'

'Hardly. I imagine a good number of them must live elsewhere. I did run across Madge Fry the other day. I've forgotten her married name. She seemed well. And prospering.'

'What's the name again?'

'Madge Fry. A tall, pretty girl with fair hair.'

'No.' Norman shook his head. 'I don't recall her. But then, I taught so many. Was she a mathematician?'

'She was in the top set. Like me.'

'Fry. Fry. No. At one time I kept all my mark books, and I went through them a year or two after I retired. That's nearly twenty years ago. I couldn't remember too many of them, then, so I threw the lot in the dustbin.'

'You'd know the names of the very good mathematicians.'

'Yes. Or their faces. And the utterly stupid. And good athletes and swimmers or those who drew attention to themselves.'

'Do you remember your teaching career with pleasure?' she asked.

'I gave value for money.'

'I taught, you know. After I came down from Oxford. Not for long. Four years, and then I got married.'

'Four years? And after that?'

'Children.'

'Some women go back to work after maternity leave. You didn't consider it?'

'Not for a minute. There was no need, financially and I could always find plenty to do.'

'Did your husband object to your teaching?'

'No. Why should he?'

'I thought,' Norman's voice crackled with phlegm, 'a man of finance might think it infra dig for his wife to work for a pittance.'

'He never said so.'

'No. I suppose not. He owns nearly all of this terrace. But I imagine you knew that.'

'I didn't.'

'It must be half a million's worth of property. Even more. And you didn't know. Doesn't he ever talk about what he's doing?'

'Oh, often.'

'But you don't listen?'

'I don't think in terms of specific bits of bricks and mortar. Unless there's some private interest of mine attached to them. I shall remember these houses from this time on.'

Norman nodded, and sat in silence. Suddenly he jerked himself upright for another question.

'Perhaps I shouldn't ask this,' he said. 'If you think it's none of my business, don't answer.' She smiled her encouragement at him. 'Would you say your husband worked hard for his money? Harder, let's say, than a teacher?'

'It's a different sort of work. I'm always told teaching is more stressful these days. Remember it's eighteen years since I went into a classroom. But, yes, I'd say he did. Much longer hours, shorter holidays, more risks. More crucial decisions. And if he's at the head of his firm then he has to make his own mind up for himself.'

'So does a teacher.'

'Oh, I agree. But if a teacher, even a head, makes an error then it doesn't close the school down and so affect half-a-dozen other schools. My husband could make a bad decision and ruin himself.'

'Do you fear that will happen?'

21

'I did at first. Especially when my father, who's the soul of tact, hinted that Colin was chancing his arm more than was safe. But it's never happened, and you get used to it.'

'But it might?'

'Yes, it's possible, I suppose. Look at the Tiger Economy these days. But he has a good many irons in the fire, and covers himself.'

'And insures himself.'

'Yes. Not exactly in the way you insure your house, but, yes.'

They sat looking across at each other, host and guest, as if for the first time they began to understand a new subject. Anna made her excuses, muttered that she must go as she was out lunching with a friend and mustn't be late. They shook hands and in no time she was negotiating his garden steps. His last words had been: 'I am willing to bet that Nance Johnson will be in this afternoon, to see how we got on. What a world.'

The summer wind ruffled her blouse. She hurried into the car parked on her father's long drive and set off, speaking to nobody.

III

Colin Turnbull whistled as he drove along the road from his home to the offices of Turnbull and Bland, the company which handled his property investments. He did not feel particularly happy, was troubled by indigestion and knew that his conference with one of the junior partners would be dull, necessary to clear up legal matters but without further interest. The young woman on the desk at reception greeted him with smiling courtesy, stood to make a miniature obeisance and asked if he'd mind just calling in for a minute on Mr Bland.

'He's here, is he?' he asked. The clock showed nine-fourteen.

'Yes, sir. He knew you were coming in to see Mr Cartwright. He won't keep you long. He needed your advice, he said.'

'Tell him I'm here.'

She had already contacted the Bland's office, and said obsequiously to Colin, 'If you'd care to go up, Mr Turnbull.'

'Thanks, Leonie.'

She showed her pleasure that he remembered her name.

'Off on holiday soon?' he asked.

'France. Camping. This Saturday for a fortnight.'

He nodded, smiling, rather grimly and made for Bland's office, his mouth twisted.

Henry Bland invited him in, walked across the excellent carpet to shake his hand. He looked older than Turnbull by a good ten years, though he had barely reached fifty. His grey hair was thin, but his clothes were admirable, well cut to disguise rotundity. The hand he stuck out was large, powerful and white, the grip almost fierce. Bland looked old-fashioned, in his dark suit and striped shirt, but trustworthy. This, Colin knew, was a not quite accurate impression. Where money was concerned Bland, modest in manner as a bank-manager with an influential client, could be ruthless. For that reason Colin had poached and then promoted him. This office was in safe hands. Bland made short, soft-spoken inquiries about the Turnbull family, which Colin barely bothered to answer.

23

'You wanted to see me?'

'Yes, I did.' Bland seemed, for all his professional manner uncomfortable. This was obviously not a matter concerned with business. He handed over a transparent folder, which Colin flicked open. Inside were details of an estate for sale, Morton Old Rectory. Colin sniffed, read rapidly through the papers. 'I thought of buying it,' Bland announced nervously.

'Aren't you comfortable where you are?' Colin asked sharply. He felt in his pocket for an indigestion tablet, carefully pressed it from its foil, put it to his mouth in slow motion, as if to give Bland time to think up a satisfactory answer.

'Yes, we are. But we've been there for fifteen years.'

'Rosemary unsettled?'

'In a way, yes. But I equally so.'

Bland moved back behind his desk and sat awkwardly. Colin legged the length of the long room to pick up a small, leather-seated chair which he placed with a whirl a yard in front of Bland's desk. The whole short exercise gave the impression of a caged but violent energy, perhaps critically exposed by his partner's intentions.

'Go on,' he said.

Bland drew in a long breath and looked out towards the three large windows. His face displayed no emotion, his lips pleasantly curved. He had recovered.

'I wondered what you would think if I bought this place.'

'I'd be puzzled, I admit.'

'I've had a surveyor looking it over.'

'Who?'

'Mark Firkin.'

'You'd have done better with Edwin Cole. Firkin will be good enough on a town property, but Morton's a bit larger than, and outside the period of, his usual work.'

'The report was exceptionally thorough,' Bland answered pacifically.

Colin sat back, saying nothing.

'Come on now, Henry. Let's have the full story. What's the idea? Now your children are off your hands I'd have thought your present place was too big, if anything. I imagine you can afford to buy the house, easily enough, unless you've been gambling it all away.' Bland was not being straight with him.

'I can. The children have cost me a fair amount, but Morton's

24

not beyond my means. I ask you because your father-in-law did something similar, and you might know some of the not quite obvious snags. In any case Rosemary said I was to chase your advice.'

'Anna and I often talk about Kuno's decision. Into the squirearchy. When he bought Ashby Manor I did wonder if Hilda had pressed him into it. Anna said "No", and thought her mother would be against the move. And I think she was right. Kuno, though he's spent most of his life in England, and looks and speaks and acts and dresses exactly like a true-born Brit of his age and status, doesn't quite believe it. He's German deep down inside himself somewhere, and doesn't exactly like it. That's my story. I don't know whether it's true. I've never found simple explanations very satisfactory.'

'Going in for psychology, are we?' Bland asked, almost rudely Turnbull laughed, judging his partner to have found the explanation, in some way, uncomfortably applicable to himself.

'What's Rosemary's angle?' Colin said.

'She's tired of our present house.'

'You don't think of a holiday home or a villa abroad?'

'We've talked about it. No.'

'Why not?'

'I'm nearly fifty, as you know, and that means, health and all the rest being favourable, I shall expect to do another ten years in this office. Thus I shan't have the time to be flitting abroad.'

'Rosie and the children might.'

'We've talked it over.'

Colin was now reading the house-agent's advertisements, squinting at them as if he found their contents difficult or unpalatable. He kept Bland waiting, and once held up his hand to cut off an interruption his partner had begun.

'Eighteenth century. Some Victorian alterations and additions. Outbuildings. Three acres. It sounds almost the size of Kuno's, but nothing like as much ground. You realise that once you've bought it, you need to maintain it, and heat it, and keep the gardens in good order. That means money, and some of your time.'

'I've looked into that. No trouble.'

'What's the drawback, then? Why do you want advice?'

'In some way I seem to be tempting fate. Hubris.' He began to explain for Colin. 'Arrogant insolence. Courting disaster.'

'You mean you'll sink all your savings and insurances and investments in this, so that if something went wrong here in the office, it wouldn't be long before you couldn't manage the upkeep.'

Bland bit the index finger of his left hand.

'It's nothing like as tight as that, but, and this is what worries me, it feels as if it is. I guess if I retired tomorrow I could buy the house; it would not need a large mortgage, I'd see to that, and maintain it, as well as our present standard of life as a retired man. And yet . . . And yet.'

'Um.'

'Are you growing more uncertain as you get older? I haven't noticed it.'

'Not here. I can't understand myself.'

'Rosemary's determined to move?'

'I wouldn't say so. Not determined. She'd like a change. And living in the country has its attractions.'

Colin leaned back, boss to office-boy.

'You know all about instituting close inquiries. Do that, and if you're satisfied, go ahead. If you find when you get there it's not what either of you wants, sell up and move again. It'll cost you good money, but you can afford it, I hope. Put it all down to experience. You will have paid a price, but then you'll be like everybody else in this world.'

When Colin put Bland's questions to Anna she listened and answered half-heartedly.

'And what advice did you give?' she said.

'I told him to get on with it.'

'That's right. They both seem to me to enjoy not making their minds up. He's not like that at work, is he?'

'I'm fond of Rosemary. But he's a computer. Not quite so quick, perhaps.'

'Don't you like him?'

'I don't have enough to do with him. He wouldn't be my choice as the ideal companion on a desert island.'

There the conversation stopped. It often did these days. They found little enjoyment in prolonging verbal exchanges. Each made a demand, or asked a question, commented briefly then left it, and went back to self-consideration. Colin felt guilt from time to time; he could, given the leisure, after all these years sit chatting to Linda, his sister-in-law. What they said was of little

26

importance, but he took pleasure in their trivia; he would rate it no higher. At one time he and Linda could not be left on their own without almost immediate sexual advances from both parties. Now they offered words to each other, and these seemed sufficient. For all he knew that innocent pastime would soon lose its appeal, and they'd never meet, and he'd take his pleasures in the company of some pretty, compliant secretary. The whole business seemed unsatisfactory. He ought to have more concern for his wife, more common interests, but they had been married for nineteen years, and he had been fornicating or committing adultery most of that period, and, moreover, he was fairly certain in spite of his circumspection that Anna knew exactly what was happening. Had he been cross-examined on his present behaviour, he would have claimed to act with vigilance and tact, to have caused no grief or embarrassment either to his wife or children. He would have liked to know exactly what Anna thought of him and his ways, but neither broached the subject, and no unconsidered misbehaviour on his part raised in public the strength or otherwise of their relationship.

He admired Anna, but could not understand her. He wondered how much she knew of his extra-marital affairs. That she never mentioned them to him seemed to diminish him in his own conceit. She did not rate him highly enough to feel jealous or express that jealousy. He was not sure that this was the case.

After her next visit to her parents Anna said she had questioned her parents. Her mother had been most forthcoming.

'I love it here, now,' Hilda Meyer confessed, 'though I didn't want to come, but I'm glad now that I did. Kuno's very happy, fills every minute of his day up.'

'Even in winter?'

'Yes. He's enough to do, and to spare. One evening a week he has Fred Cole in for an evening's snooker or billiards. Cole's a good player and that means your father has to keep practising to make sure he puts up a decent contest. And he has meetings, and I drag him out to Beechnall at least once a month for a theatre-visit and equivalently to a concert.'

'Does anything happen in the village?'

'Yes. Not very interesting to either of us. We open the grounds for a church harvest-festival fête in autumn, and a summer sale. Means people keep calling round for this purpose or that. Yes, there's always something to occupy us, though your dad gets much more easily tired these days. How old are these friends of yours?'

'Getting on for fifty. I thought you'd know them. The Blands. Henry's a partner in Col's property companies.'

'I know the name,' Hilda said.

'You'd like Rosemary.'

'Do you want to bring her to see me? Is that the idea?'

'It never crossed my mind.'

Her mother clearly did not believe her. These suspicions seemed out of character. Perhaps her mother's life was nothing like as tranquil as she made out.

'Right,' Anna answered. 'I'll bring her round to question you herself.'

Anna reported this to her husband, who said Rosemary would at least be open with Hilda, say plainly what was what.

'But Henry wouldn't?'

'He must always give an appearance of cleverness, most of all to himself.'

'But he asked your advice?'

'If they move, I shall hear soon enough. So he might as well tell me now. But he puts it in the form of a question, so that possibly I feel flattered.'

'He'd made his mind up already before he asked you?'

'Quite likely.'

The interrogation petered out, but half an hour later Colin had suddenly turned as he left the room to mutter, 'Let me know how Rosemary gets on with Hilda, will you?'

While she was visiting Ashby, Anna had run across Frank Norman in the street. The old man spoke almost eloquently about his pleasure in seeing her. She listened, pleased with his good spirits. In the end he asked, 'Were you just coming down to see me?'

She declined to lie, told him the purpose of her appearance in the village, to push a note from her mother through the door of Mrs Thomas-Rhys.

'Have they run out of servants, then?' he asked.

'Oh, dear. Do I detect malice?'

Norman blushed under his tan, and grinned. She, pleased with the success of her thrust, explained why she had been to consult her parents. Briefly she outlined the Blands' predicament.

'How old are the people?' he asked. 'These Blands.'

'Late-forties.'

'And well-to-do?'

'He's a partner of my husband. In the property firm.'

'Well educated?'

'Both went to universities, I think. I've no idea what they studied. He'd do law or economics, I'd guess.'

Norman asked a few more questions about their family commitments, their present home, their leisure activities. The interrogation appeared lively to her, as if the old man had determined to sort this out, but then he kept silence; maybe something of his usual pessimism had settled back.

'Well?' she teased. 'What should they do?'

He shook his head glumly.

'You moved into the country,' she encouraged him. 'It meant you drove in fifteen or sixteen miles every day. Now, why?'

'Edna thought it would be good for the boys.'

'Was it?'

'The local primary school was good. She liked the life. She walked out a few miles every day. I quite enjoyed the drive back. It helped settle me after a day's slog. It was a bit out of the way, or so it seemed then, though the bus service was better than it is now. I did as Edna wanted. She died out here. We scattered her ashes up in Snape's Hill Wood. It suited us. Luck, perhaps. Or Edna had the knack of making things work.'

'And what about the Blands, then?'

'They should rush in and grab it, if they want it as much as all that.'

'And ignore the snags?'

Her face signalled annoyance.

'When I hear of presumably intelligent people like your friends spending their lives worrying about what sort of house they should live in, I feel sad. And baffled. What about the hundreds of unemployed in this country who are lucky if they have somewhere dry and warm and with a roof to sleep under? And they'd be considered lucky by thousands, let's say, in the Horn of Africa who've not eaten a square meal for weeks or months.'

'Yes?' she said.

'Aren't these Blands, if that's their name, misjudging matters?'

Anna waited in the quietness of the village street.

'What are you suggesting, then? That every time we think of going to a concert or a play, we should not do so and send the price of admission to Oxfam or Save the Children?'

'It wouldn't be such a bad thing to consider it, and act on it now and then.'

'We can't change the world?'

'We can change ourselves.'

'So what shall I tell the Blands? Not to move, or, if they do, into something much smaller and less expensive, and send the money saved to a charity?'

'I'm not presuming to give you advice. I don't know these people. They'd probably regard you as mad. Or tell you to go and do likewise. Nor am I anything to boast about, myself. I live in a house big enough for a large family. I buy books and newspapers which I don't always read. I sometimes take myself out for a meal. I put money into banks. I don't give it all away to good causes.' He cleared his throat. 'All I am trying to say, badly, that when I hear of rich people worrying themselves silly about whether they should live in one large, beautiful, suitable house rather than another, I think something's wrong.'

'They are not worrying themselves silly. They're enjoying the opportunity to choose. Just as you decide on beef or pork or vegetarian for your lunch.'

'Sausages,' he said. 'Today's Wednesday. Sausages. I'm a man of habit.'

He'd recovered his good humour.

'I'll have to push off,' Norman said. 'Or it won't even be sausages. Bread and scrape. I must apologise again before I go. As I get older I get more tetchy. I'm always amazed how generous some people are towards good causes. But I latch on to some topic, and before I know where I am I'm laying down the law, right or wrong. That's the trouble with schoolmasters and parsons. They get used to a captive audience.' He laughed. 'Though, from what they tell me, I'm not sure it's so today. Education's child-centred. They don't want an authoritarian figure at the front telling them what they have to learn. They must dredge it up from their own interests and experience. I'll tell you this. If I had waited for some of my classes to come up with mathematical principles, I'd be there waiting still. And my pupils were grammar-school students, the top ten per cent when I started and no higher than twenty when I retired.'

'I don't think I could use log tables now to solve a big multiplication or division problem of the sort you used to set us.'

'I'll tell you this. It wouldn't take you long to regrasp the method and start using it.'

'Oh, thank you very much,' she said.

Old Norman seemed delighted. She looked him over. His shoes were not as highly polished as in his class room days, and his suit appeared more crumpled. But he had shaved that morning. He used to dust the chalk from his hands after a blackboard demonstration with a large silk handkerchief. Now, he walked down the street with her as far as Alexandra Thomas-Rhys's front door. In no way was he short of breath. He embarked on a lecture to the effect that young people had abandoned the great works of classical music in favour of pop music, loud, illiterate performances by people who could barely manage a few notes or chords on their instruments.

'All of them are tarred with the same brush?'

'With very rare exceptions.'

'And why is it bad?'

'It's ignorant. They don't know any rules. They're incapable of tackling anything difficult. They only listen to other people who are as short of knowledge and training and practice and technique as they are. You couldn't play, let's say, a classical violin concerto a month or two after you've seen a fiddle for the first time, however gifted you were. And that's what happens with your pop singers and players.'

'Why is it?' she asked, egging him on.

'Economic pressure. The big record companies saw to it that there was a huge market amongst the uneducated, and they catered for it, exploited it. It's the same with clothes manufacturers. It's made worse by the Sunday papers which are full of reviews and reports on pop music, presumably written by educated people. Trahison des clercs.'

'This wasn't so with classical music then?'

'Well in the first place I guess it was intended for a small, highly selective audience, a church, a court, an aristocratic élite. Ah, that's a word they hate. "Elite."' He laughed hoarsely in the sunshine outside Mrs Thomas-Rhys's eighteenth-century cottage and floriferous front garden. 'You do me good, young lady. Go and put your letter in, and I'll shuffle off. I feel so pleased I might even call in at The Wheatsheaf.'

'Don't say I've driven you to drink.'

He raised his hat. His walk as he left her was as yet nowhere near a shuffle.

31

Anna felt real pleasure at Norman's delight. It cheered him just to grouse in her presence. She wondered if he was typical of teachers of his generation. Even the scientists had some knowledge or care for literature or art or music. Or so he claimed. She wondered about the truth of it. She remembered him one afternoon (and he disliked teaching his top sets at that time of day; he wanted them in the morning while their brains were fresh) pausing to tell them how when he was in the grammar school in the Thirties, there were few jobs for scientists. Industry affected by Depression got rid of research people first. 'Talk about eating the seed corn,' he had said scornfully. 'But the advantage was that we were taught by really bright young men who should have been engaged in their university laboratories. And don't imagine that we were lagging there. They split the atom in Cambridge when I was a boy. Scientific advance of the highest order. Of course, the war changed the mistreatment of scientists to some extent.' Frank Norman had shaken his head at them, while they had listened, the students glad of the interlude before he returned to his simultaneous equations or geometrical progressions or the binomial theory or whatever was the afternoon's chore.

Mrs Thomas Rhys-opened the back door as Anna slipped the letter through. She must have been looking out at the window.

'Come in, Anna.'

'No, I mustn't. I have to get back home, but my mother wanted you to have this note sometime today.'

'Is it important?'

'I doubt it.'

Alexandra Thomas-Rhys ruthlessly ripped the envelope open with a forefinger, and read the note.

'No, it isn't,' she pronounced. 'Instructions. As usual.'

'As usual?'

'Hilda always has some scheme on hand. And she makes sure we know what our part in it is.'

'How exciting.'

'I see,' Alexandra said, 'you were talking to that Mr Norman. I didn't know you knew him.'

'He taught me maths at school.'

'Where was that? I thought you went away to some boarding school.'

'Only in the sixth form. He taught me in Beechnall.'

'Was he any good?'

'Oh, very. He got me a distinction in maths at "O" Level.'

'He's a funniosity now.'

Anna waited, unwilling to provoke criticism.

'Do you know, he looked over the fence and told Mrs Marshall, his neighbour, that the colour and shape of her underclothes were unsuitable for a woman of her age?'

'I don't know her.'

'She's in her seventies. A widow. She seemed upset at the time. "What business is it of his?" she asked me, and then she said, "I shan't dare to hang them out again for fear he's looking."'

'This village is full of hidden interest,' Anna said.

'I've always found that if I should glance over my neighbour's hedge and find something I don't quite like, it's best to say nothing. What would I think if Colonel Cruikshank told me that my mallows clashed with the hydrangeas? It's nothing to do with him.'

'But if he was right?' Anna asked.

'Then I'd know that myself. I wouldn't need him to tell me. Not that he would. And it may be that I'd deliberately engineered the contrast for its effect.'

'You could explain that to him.'

'The difference, and it may seem slight to you, is that Mrs Marshall's underwear is not to be spoken of by men. They were called "unmentionables" at one time. And she'd regard the topic as having sexual connotations. I'm not saying she's prudish. I don't know her well enough. I expect, like all of us, that she has her notions of what's right or wrong in all sorts of ways. Nor do I think she'd feared Mr Norman would suddenly leap the fence and rape her. She saw him as a person of her age who ought to have known what it was proper to talk about or about which to keep silent.'

Mrs Thomas-Rhys spoke almost fiercely, a headmistress admonishing some thoughtless fifth-form rebel.

'Well, then,' Anna said.

'You don't think those things are important, do you?' Alexandra pursued her.

'Not really. Mildly amusing, or unexpected. Is there any answer to my mother?'

'No, I don't think so.'

The expression on her face and the sourness of the voice conveyed Mrs Thomas-Rhys's view that she could barely bring

33

herself to trust Anna with a message. Anna pleasantly wished her goodbye, turned and walked the garden path at speed. She had made an enemy, quite without intention. She would join Old Norman in Alexandra's rogues' gallery. She said as much to her mother when she picked up her car from the manor house.

'She's touchy. One has to be careful. But she's a good sort. And useful.'

'God bless her,' Anna said with sarcasm.

'She bullies her husband.'

'The major?'

A day or two later Hilda telephoned to report on a visit from Rosemary Bland.

'She's nice,' Anna said, at once.

'Yes, I really liked her. We walked round the house together and the gardens and I pointed out all the drawbacks.'

'And what did she say?'

'Well, for one thing, that we had met before. Twice, in fact. She gave chapter and verse. But I couldn't remember.'

'What of it?'

'How could I forget such a pleasant, good-looking, intelligent, well-dressed young woman. It doesn't seem possible. And yet it happened. It made me wonder if I was losing my marbles, if this wasn't the onset of dementia.'

'Unlikely. Does it run in the family?'

'No. But I'm sixty-nine, and I'm always forgetting things. Mainly trivial affairs, I must admit. But Rosemary Bland made a favourable impression on me, really extraordinarily so. And yet our earlier meetings had been erased clean from my head.'

'I can't explain it. You'd other matters, other people on your mind at the time.'

'Have you told Pa?'

'Yes.'

'And what did he say?'

'Dismissed it. "You can't expect to remember every Tom, Dick or Harry who crosses your path." That was his line.'

'Was he angry with you?'

'No. why should he be?'

They stood in slight disarray, at their phones, as if they'd suddenly decided to speak in another language. Anna wished she could see her mother's face. In a very few years that would be possible. All she had at present was the slightly metallic voice by which to judge her mother's frame of mind. She changed the subject sharply and cheerfully.

'And what had Rosemary to say about a move to the country?'

'Precious little, really. She didn't seem to mind one way or the other.'

'So it's Henry, her husband, who's keen?'

'That's what I suggested, but she seemed surprised at that. They had discussed Morton Old Rectory and two other similar houses, but not very seriously. It had almost appeared to her as if Henry was trying her out as a prospective client, so that when such properties came up in his business, he'd have some idea what it was people wanted. Not that that's his line, really, she said.'

'Does he often use her like that?'

'I've no idea,' Hilda Meyer answered. 'She never mentioned it.'

'You didn't ask?'

'No, I didn't. I rang her up and told her that you had spoken about the prospect of living in the country, and invited her over. She made a very favourable impression on me.'

'Yes. I told you she would.'

'What baffles me is why her husband bothered to question Colin about the idea if he wasn't really interested.'

'A second opinion. From a man he knew. A man with his head screwed on the right way, who knew about property.'

'You might be right. She did obviously seem surprised that her husband was questioning his friends about buying the house.'

The pair had, according to Hilda, spent a pleasant hour walking round the house and part of the grounds at Ashby. They got on well. Rosemary was lively, amenable, polite, interested in all sorts of topics except the suitability of Morton Old Rectory as a home. That was a puzzle to both women.

When Anna raised the matter with her husband, Colin wrinkled his brow like an amateur actor, and said,

'He seemed serious enough when he questioned me. And a bit nervous.'

'Does he often?'

'Quizz me? About business matters? We have meetings. He knows what he's doing. I wouldn't have taken him on as a partner otherwise. It wasn't the soundness of the property or the possibility of planning snags that worried him, it was whether he'd be able to put up with life in the country. Unless . . .'

'Do you think he could?' She interrupted him.

35

'Don't see why not. It's not too far out. And if it pleased his wife, well . . .'

'But she knew next to nothing about it according to my mother.'

'Then either one or the other or both are lying.'

'Is he a straightforward sort of man?'

'If it suits him.'

'What does that mean?' she asked.

'In business you lie, and act, and dissemble to suit your purposes. There aren't too many Honest Joes about. People put the best side of their case. I expect them to.'

'Aren't there any honest men left, then?'

'My brother. He'll tell you what's what, what needs doing, and what it will cost. But his sort of trade allows it.'

'And it tells against him? He'll never be rich?'

'Terry won't, no. At least not stinking rich. But he'll always have enough and to spare, because he's a worker. He does a good job. At a reasonable price. And so if people play fair by him and pay up, he'll always be moderately well-off.'

'And you don't approve?'

Colin shrugged, but she could not tell whether the stupidity of her question or the slur on his moral character made it impossible for him to answer her.

A few days later she was sipping coffee in Lewis's, the department store, when Rosemary approached the table. She stopped, smiling expansively.

'May I sit down with you?' She deposited her parcels and placed her cup on the table. She let out a small gasp of relief, and faced Anna. 'I paid a lovely visit to your mother last week. Apparently on your suggestion, she invited me over. Your parents have a superb place out there at Ashby.'

'Yes. It's my father's hobby now. Or one of them.'

'The house?'

'Keeping it in tip-top order, though he wouldn't like the expression. He'd want something more orderly and serious. He's preserving something important, he says, in these days when standards are slipping.'

'Are they?'

'Some are, but that's always been so. We lose interest in some ideas, once considered important, take up new notions, or routines, and so don't worry if the old standards are dissipated or are allowed to disappear altogether.'

36

Rosemary sipped at her coffee, and stared into the distance.

'So my father replaces worn-out decoration with brand-new that looks similar to or better than the old. He chooses paints or wall-papers that are tasteful, but in late-eighteenth or early-nineteenth century style. He reads it all up. If he calls an architect in, he gives him a hell of an examination before he employs him.'

'And is this good?'

'It depends. If you like Georgian styles, you'll be delighted that somebody takes the trouble to preserve an example or two. If you don't, then it doesn't matter.'

'And do many care?'

'About this in particular? No, I shouldn't think so. From time to time Georgian or Regency colours will be popular for domestic use, and copies of repro furniture will be on sale. I don't know how fashion manages to change. Some firm is persuaded to spend some money pushing the sale of some line. The advertising agency is good; the newspapers take it up, the directors and managers of shops like it, are convinced. And if they're lucky then the public is ready to part with its cash for the product. Why they should be so willing is perhaps chance: some film or TV programme has brought the style to their notice. I don't know; I don't even know if anyone else does.'

'And your father?'

'He loves it because it belongs to him. He bought the house, and came to like the look of it. In the end, it was what he wanted. And so he's prepared to spend money on it.'

'And he won't change?'

'I wouldn't think so. He's well into his seventies now. He's sprightly enough to be able to walk round the grounds every day, and run up and down stairs in the house inquiring about things.'

'Does he modernise?'

'Yes. Within reason. He installed central heating before he even moved into the place. And he's made sure it's draught-proof, that sort of thing.'

'Does your mother have any say in all this?'

'I expect so. She'll tell him what she thinks, and I guess he'll pay attention to her views. Had she, for good reasons, come down against buying the house, and he'd thought she really was opposed to the plan, he would have given in. He knows that she's the sort of woman who lives to make her husband comfortable, but she has to have the means. If that house had been too big and needed, let's say, two years' continuous work on it so that there'd have been workmen tramping in and out all the time, that would have been sufficient cause for her to say "No".'

'She sounded very happy there. To me.'

'I believe she is. She's not the sort to make big demands on life. She has an efficient housekeeper, and a man who looks after the gardens. And two girls from the village. She listens to music, goes to concerts, visits friends, organises a few local affairs, does a little entertaining, less and less as they get older. She has got all she wants, and it fits in with her husband's wishes, so all's well.'

'What if your husband suddenly decided to change houses?'

'It would depend where he wanted to put us.'

'So you'd object?'

'Not on principle. For a start I'd want the children, who are seventeen and sixteen, to remain in their present school. They like it. They seem to be doing well. In two or three years both will, we hope, be at university.'

'It would harm their prospects to move them now?'

'To some slight extent. They'd be resilient enough to recover. For instance, Kuno, my father, moved me after "O" Levels to Denton.'

'Why?'

'Good experience, he thought. The academic standard was higher than Beechnall Grammar, where I was. And I'd learn more of the wide world. Meet a different sort of people in a public school.'

'And did you?'

'I suppose so. It did me no great harm. They prepared me for Oxford as Beechnall Grammar wouldn't have had time to. I wasn't homesick, or not for long, and I was amongst the first girls they allowed into their sixth forms. They made a fuss of us, and looked after us properly. And incidentally encouraged us to compete with the boys academically.'

Rosemary smiled her way through her friend's exposition.

'If Colin decided to change houses would he consult you?'

'Yes. I think so. I hope so. Unless there was some absolute advantage that needed no argument. Then he'd move on his own.'

'And hang the consequences?'

'The advantage would outweigh the consequences, and that would be that.'

They ordered more coffee, regrouping their questions.

38

'Colin was convinced by your husband that it was you who wanted to move. And I think he understands what people are saying to him,' Anna began.

'Henry might have put it like that to underline his need for advice. Even when it wasn't true. Men often lie.'

'Do they?'

'Does Colin always speak the truth, then?'

'I shouldn't think so. Not for a minute. We did wonder, that is Colin and I, whether Henry wasn't thinking of making this move as a pleasant surprise for you. A kind of birthday or wedding-anniversary gift. And so he'd need to know whether there were any snags that would put you off. And he'd know that my parents had made such a switch and so would be able to tell Colin all about the drawbacks. But we, perhaps, have let the cat out of the bag. His secret's out. We've done the one thing he didn't want: speak to you about it.'

They chatted thus through the second cup. Neither touched either biscuits or delicate cakes. Virtue seemed to have gone out of the pair. They had spoken too freely about their husbands, or their own ignorance. Each regarded her companion with suspicion. Anna felt that she was to blame for interfering in her friend's private life. They said perfunctory goodbyes after Anna had settled the bill, made bustling steps towards the next chore.

Musak accompanied them to the widely separated doors by which they left the building.

IV

Colin Turnbull sat at his office-desk.

It was ten o'clock, and he had been at work since seven-thirty. Always an early riser, he had showered, dressed and let himself silently out of the house and had driven down to his place of work. He enjoyed the quietness of the place; any cleaning was done at the end of the day. His personal assistant did not arrive until nine o'clock. By that time he'd have a pile of tasks ready to occupy her. He did not miss her in this early period. He could use his computer to check, and knew in the few necessary cases exactly where to lay his hands on relevant information of other kinds. This is what he liked best, planning the day, the week, the month ahead. No-one could do it better than he, he had decided, and as he dashed about amongst electronic information he discovered all sorts of bits and pieces, unimportant indeed, about the firm which others might wish to keep hidden from him. He did not resent these attempts at concealment, if that is what they were, merely noted and remembered them, raising them only when he wanted to embarrass or encourage his underhand subordinates.

This was, he felt, his creative time. New schemes were broached, and then detailed. Later, when he had grasped the essentials, his younger colleagues would be asked to set them in motion, but exactly as he outlined. He had not much faith in their creative edge; they were good, hard workers, had a wide knowledge of their specialities, could, and did occasionally, raise objections to his schemes; sometimes though not often he took note of their doubts, and worked on them. His investments were many, and he knew them well. People and businesses were always short of money, and he was ready to lend it to them, at his price. There were difficulties, dangers even, but he knew when to strike and when to hold back. He preferred this handling, 'fondling' he called it, of money. Property he enjoyed, but there were no astute moves that could double his investments as he sat at his desk. The sorting out of some financial problem of a business or civic

40

corporation brought in small returns financially, by his standards, but he still would act as a consultant in these cases because he learnt something of their methods or intentions and this could prove useful. Besides, he had been trained as an accountant, and did not wish to lose his skills. It was dull, day-labour, but he took pleasure in the exercise. He would be driven mad, he thought, to do this every day of the working week, but now and again he won sober satisfaction from these tasks.

Sometimes, while in his office, he felt hungry and went out to a 'caff' on the other side of the main road. He never ate before he left home, confining himself to a cup of tea. He did not need that, he thought, but now the habit was ingrained. It sprang from a chemistry lesson at school; the master, an old soldier, had said that the Army had always insisted that squaddies on early duty were provided with a mug of tea, known as 'gunfire'. One know-all had not drunk his cup, and collapsed on an important parade before a visiting general. From that time the old schoolmaster said he had begun every day of his life with a cup of tea. Colin had done likewise, whatever the evidence for or against the practice. He was amazed that he had paid so much attention. He could not remember much of the chemistry he had learnt, though he had gained a distinction in the subject, but he had taken in and followed this marginal advice. Old 'Stinks' always lowered his voice at the important parts of his lesson, so that they had to strain to hear. On one occasion he had told them that a man who could not cut the nails on his right hand for himself was not fit to marry, and the thirteen-year-old Colin had struggled with his mother's nail-scissors to prove himself ready for matrimony. Such behaviour hardly seemed believable to him now, but it was the truth.

This morning just before eight he had gone out for his 'breakfast'. There was nobody about in the offices yet. The flexi-time secretaries would not appear much before eight thirty, but outside the streets were already busy. He walked the hundred and fifty yards of the wide side-street, crossed the main road by the underpass, running up and down steps, and into the warm darknesses of the transport café. The tunnel had been crowded; silent men and women pressed forward both ways to work. There were no beggars at this time in the morning, he noticed.

On his return he felt optimistic. He had eaten his two slices of toast and two overdone sausages and drunk a great mug of

41

espresso coffee. The proprietor, serving behind the counter knew who he was for all her Mr Er-ers and had asked him to sit down and personally delivered his tray to his table. This smattering of obsequious politeness pleased him. He supposed that not many of the professional men with offices in this part of the city called in here; these solicitors, physicians, surgeons, accountants arrived at work at nine having breakfasted to their liking at home, and so he was marked out, worthy of preferential treatment. He did not want this, but it flattered him slightly. His sausages, he noted with satisfaction, were crisp and overcooked, exactly as he liked them. As a gesture of his regard he returned his plate and mug to the counter.

'Colin Turnbull.'

He had reached the centre of the underpass, a circus open to the sky, when a voice stopped him. A neat man, hatless in a grey suit faced him.

'You don't recognise me, do you?'

'I'm afraid not.' His reply sounded neutral to himself, not rude.

'We were in the same form at Beechnall Grammar.'

Colin looked hard, but still did not know the man. He shook his head.

'James Glover.'

Colin thought, stared, smiled.

'You used to bowl leg-breaks,' he said finally. He felt a touch of pride at picking out this snippet from his bran-tub memory. He recalled the small boy who flicked up those looping, spinning deliveries. James's brother had played cricket for the County.

'That's right. Mind if I walk along with you?'

'Not at all. I'm going up Regent Street.'

'Is that where you work?'

'Yes.'

They took the two flights of stairs together. Glover used the hand-rail.

'What are you doing with yourself these days?' Colin asked.

'I'm teaching. At a school at Trent Bridge. The Mellors Comprehensive. Do you know it?'

'No.' He had not even heard the name. 'I'm not very well versed in educational matters. Do you catch a bus up here?'

'No,' Glover answered. 'We're still on holiday. I've an appointment at the hospital. I'm in very good time. One thing they drummed into us at the old school. My appointment is at nine-fifteen. But they double-and treble-book.'

42

'Do they?'

Colin did not know this in spite of the frequent references in the media to the deficiencies of the Health Service. They had now reached the portico outside his office.

'This is my destination,' he said, stopping.

Glover examined the highly polished brass plate. C. G. Turnbull and Partners.

'Rather grand,' Glover said, not unpleasantly. 'Is the whole building yours?'

'Yes.' He did not mention that he used only the spacious ground floor. 'Are you ill? You said you were going to the hospital.'

'Yes. I am.' Ill? Going to hospital?

'Not serious, I hope?'

'I might learn this morning. I'm going to hear the results of some recent tests.' Glover bit his lip, passed two fingers across his forehead. 'It's cancer. I do know that.'

'I'm sorry.'

'It's not the end of the world. They can do things for you these days. It's not always the death sentence it was. I'm here this morning to find out exactly what sort mine is.'

'You won't be required at school?' Glover had already told him. He'd not listened properly.

'No, we don't start until next week. The second of September. Colin looked at his watch.

'You'll be very early for your appointment,' he said.

'I like to be in good time. Be there at nine for quarter past.'

'Even so you'll be hanging about the streets for getting on for half an hour.'

'It's a fine morning.'

Glover's shoes shone polished, and his light raincoat and trousers appeared smart. His wide tie was even snazzy in a restrained way. His sallow face wore a pleasant expression, like that of a shopkeeper or policeman about to do someone a slight favour.

'Come and sit in my office for twenty minutes. I can even provide you with a cup of tea or coffee.'

'It's wasting your time.'

'Let me be the judge of that. I don't get worried by people outside until we officially open at nine, and you'll be on your way by that time.'

43

Colin had no idea why he had invited the man in. He had not known him well at school, and had never thought of him, not once, since that time.

'Hang your coat up,' he ordered. 'Make yourself comfortable.' He filled and switched on the kettle in the outer room. Glover, feet together, admiringly looked at the computer on Turnbull's desk.

'You're very up to date,' he said, diffidently pointing a finger. 'Information technology. Cybernetics.' Colin fiddling with the instant coffee and spoon did not reply.

'That comes from the Greek word for a steersman,' he coughed, 'a helmsman.' He waited in vain for an answer.

'Sugar and milk?' Colin said.

'Milk only, please. But black would do just as well.'

Colin came across with a small china cup and saucer.

'I can run to a biscuit.'

'No, thank you.'

Glover sipped at the coffee, and seemed to grow smaller. When he spoke again it was to express his admiration at the magnificence of Turnbull's office.

'We don't have rooms this size in my school,' he said. 'Our common room is about half the area of this.'

'Is it the only one?'

'No. There is another. In our building.'

'There you are, then.' Colin sounded friendly. 'This is quite unnecessarily large, but that's business. At one time we'd have lined the walls with books to impress the clients. Now it's all this . . .' He pointed sardonically to his machines.

'But they must be useful.'

'Oh, yes. Can't do without it. But people are impressed by size and modernity. It's so everywhere. You can't be famous these days unless you appear on television regularly.' His conversation had veered within reason.

'Do you?'

'Rarely. They ask for a two-sentence comment now and then. Mostly on things I know nothing about.'

'Such as?'

'The cost of sporting events. Airline fares. The Hang-sen index.'

'Why do they do it, then?'

'I appeared once on some pretext or other and spoke to their satisfaction. So if some matter of finance arises they call on me for

44

an opinion. I shall appear decently dressed; I shall make a few sensible remarks without hesitation. Nothing outrageous; the sort they could think up for themselves. But I'm different. That's television. I shall not look like their economics or business correspondents. There'll be a variation of books or computers behind and in front of me. The producers have to provide pictures, things for people to look at. If you appear on radio, you're put into a chair, they try your voice, and immediately question you. That's that. They'll pose the same queries on television, but they're often more concerned with the background, or your posture, because most people are going to look rather than hear.'

'The price of fame,' Glover said, pulling a comical face. The comment made no sense to Colin, who went on to question the other man about schools.

'Education seems to have a fair amount of media coverage these days?'

'Yes. But they don't question the other ranks. It's some head-teacher or inspector or union official you'll hear.'

'And that's bad?'

'Not always. But they don't work all day at the chalk-face.'

Turnbull questioned Glover about his family. His wife also taught, but in a school at the other side of the city His two children, girls aged nine and eight, were doing well at primary level. The family had two cars and a small detached house. Their garden was larger than usual, and they grew vegetables. They were thinking of taking on an allotment. Marilyn was keen on organic food. Yes, he did a fair amount of DIY. His latest project was a large heated greenhouse. 'I had hoped to finish it this holiday, but, well, you know how it is. Still, we had an excellent fortnight camping in France.'

'You were well enough to enjoy it?'

'Yes. Not a hundred per cent. But, yes. I could manage. Marilyn's very well organised.'

Glover suddenly stood, handed his cup to Colin, saying that he daren't put it down on any of the polished surfaces. Well trained, this man.

'I must be on my way now. Mustn't be late.'

Colin fetched Glover's coat, and helped him on with it. The visitor was profligate with thanks. Colin walked with him out of the door, along the corridor, towards the street. Three secretaries, bright as foreign birds, entered and scattered to let the two men through. They greeted Colin by his name, but their chatter had died. The two men shook hands in the street. Glover still breathless with thanks, or cancer.

'I hope all's well up there,' Colin said.

'Yes.'

'Let me know how things go.'

'I will, I will.'

The thin figure forged ahead up the hill. Colin one hand behind him on a cold pillar of the portico watched his progress and the shining shoes.

Back in his office, he felt the emptiness of the place. He stood by his desk and considered himself. Quite out of character he had invited Glover in for a few minutes; he did not understand why. The man was harmless enough; at school he used to come up with these useless bits of scholarship. Greek for 'helmsman'. He'd be a good teacher. And father, growing spinach and sprouts in his garden to make his daughters strong and beautiful. You would never see him in a Rolls; not even a BMW. He'd choose something sensible and cheap. He and Marilyn would count the ha'pence and discuss the advantages of one mass-produced car over another. He was the sort who made the world turn steadily.

Glover had been faced with death.

Would he be able to handle it better than his coevals? He'd be about Colin's age, forty-six or forty-seven. His children were comparatively young. He'd rushed at nothing. Marilyn knew her mind, could guide him. Then he felt rotten; the illness did not go away, had been diagnosed as cancer. Surely the disease couldn't be all that serious, or they would have sent for him immediately, immediately after those last tests. Perhaps they had. Perhaps the man feared the worst.

Colin sat down, placed his hands flat before him on the desk.

What would he have done? If doctors had served a death-sentence on him, so that he would not know how his children shaped in adult life, how Anna coped without him, how his empire would hold together under his junior partners. At forty-seven. Seventy-seven, fair enough. You'd have had a good whack by then. Even so, you wouldn't want to die, unless you struggled with your life, overwhelmed by pain, nausea, weakness.

Colin himself had no sense of defeat. His head seemed clear, his schemes sorted out, decisions taken and remembered. But he had

46

no cancer. It was the other fellow. He recalled the small, highly-polished shoes twinkling up hospital hill.

A tap on the door and Tracey Haywood his secretary entered. She carried a wire tray containing the mail.

'Good morning, sir.' She sounded inordinately cheerful. 'The mail.' She placed the basket on her desk. 'Shall we deal with it now, or is there something else you'd sooner do first?'

'Is there anything important?' he asked.

'Two faxes from Japan and a long report, well, three sides, from Hong Kong.'

'In English?' he asked, cheering up.

'I could understand them, so they must be.' She had matched his joke with her own.

'Bring 'em over. Let's do the drudgery first.'

Satisfied, she brought the tray across, then her chair. She perched, note book at the ready, legs crossed, bare in sheer tights to the top of the thigh. Her thick hair had been knotted to a bun at the crown of her head giving an air of balance and efficiency. The brown eyes looked up, ready for his service. Her blouse was spotless.

'Clarke, Wyburn, Oldham,' he said. 'Usual fax. Polite "No".' He put it into the empty out-tray. 'Fearn, Beechnall. Thank you. Can you hurry up?' He picked up the next. Miss Haywood would produce the right letters for signature at the end of the day. Or almost immediately send off the faxes where appropriate which would, in grammatically correct English, exactly convey his wishes. She was a treasure, unafraid to ask if she did not understand, but in ninety-odd per cent of cases able to translate his laconic phrases into language both appropriate and even eloquent. Of course he had trained her, but she was a quick learner. Personal assistant to the managing director. Exactly. He felt certain that he could go away without notice for four or five days and his office be run to perfection. She would make no large decisions, that was not her place, though she would be capable of taking them with real judgement. To her, however, it would be just a job, but to him a matter of life and death, a fight on the precipice's edge. He combined, as she did not, applied reason with ferocious, competitive ambition.

When they had finished, she raised another point or two, and when they were clear she waited. Often he'd mention some private matter with her and they'd spend five minutes on it. This kept

47

them in contact, he considered. She'd know how he felt, and this intimacy ensured that the firm was kept not only together but on its toes. He'd no scientific evidence for his conclusion, but they had fallen or wormed their way into the habit in the last year. Some made mistresses of their PAs, but Colin, a man with a roving eye, congratulated himself in keeping clear of such behaviour with Tracey. She was attractive, and given an extra drink or an unexpected opportunity he might well have succumbed, but so far not. They were friends, allies as well as employer and employee. She lived in a flat in the Park, only ten minutes' walk away, and had recently kicked out a live-in partner, and was now, in her own words, 'on the prowl' for the next.

'Will that be all?' she asked.

'For the present,' he answered.

'I liked the quiet old days,' she said. She knew he wanted his five minutes' chat. 'Once first post was over, that was it for the day. There'd be a small second delivery, and one or two local things by hand, but that would be that.'

'You're not old enough to remember such sedate times,' he said. She was twenty-five.

'If something important comes in at five-to-five, now I have to do something about it. Ring your office to see if you're still about. And if it really calls for immediate scrutiny, I'd ring your home.'

'It might take some time finding me even on my mobile.'

'That's what you pay me for.'

He looked at his watch. Five-minutes-to-ten. He wondered if James Glover had been admitted to the consultant's sanctum and heard the worst.

'If you had a message . . .' he began, and then broke off. 'Did you see the man who was in my office first thing?'

'No. I came in early. I thought there was nobody about. One of the girls told me you'd had a man in. I have my spies alert.'

'He might at this moment be getting his message that he's only got a month or two to live.'

'At the General?'

'Where else?'

'Might be the Mafia?' she laughed. She'd keep it light.

'He'd had tests, and was going up for results. He knew he had cancer.'

'What was he doing in here?' She bluntly asked, without hesitation, what she wanted to know.

'I met him. I knew him. He was very early for his appointment. I asked him in and gave him a cup of coffee.'

'Oh.' The blank monosyllable showed her surprise. She did not expect acts of philanthropy from him this early in the morning. Or at any time.

'What would you do?' he asked, 'If you were told you'd only three months to live.'

She did not answer immediately, but sat still, eyelids lowered as if she prayed.

'I don't know. Burst into tears. I can't imagine it. It doesn't happen to people my age.'

'It doesn't happen so very often to people of my age, even, but Glover, the man, was in my class at school and for all I know has been sentenced to death.'

Neither spoke, nor looked at the other. After a substantial silence she said,

'I guess that I'd be asking, "Why me?"'

'Exactly.' Tracey had lighted on his thought. 'He's a teacher, married, has daughters eight and nine.'

'They'll remember him then when he's gone.'

He jerked his head in surprise at her statement. 'Yes. I wonder if he's properly insured, if the house will become hers. His wife is also a teacher.'

'Another one-parent family.'

'He was quite a clever boy at school. A mine of out-of-the-way information. I learnt a great deal from him. He read books by the yard.'

'Were his parents educated?'

'Shopkeepers, I think.'

Tracey breathed deeply, loudly in. 'Do you think they've told him yet?'

'You never know with hospitals. They don't seem to keep good time.'

'It must be unpleasant to be a doctor and have to break the news,' she said.

'They're used to it. We don't worry ourselves to death if we hear someone we know has been declared bankrupt. We might even gloat a bit, say it's their own fault. There's plenty of it these days.'

'That's different.'

'Yes. You're right. Still, we'll have to get on. It does us no good to drive ourselves mad over James Glover.'

Tracey tapped her note-book with polished nails.

'If you'd just heard your death-sentence,' she asked, 'would you want to complete these,' the nails tapped again, 'transactions?'

That's what he liked about this woman. She didn't let things go easily.

'I should be emotionally disturbed,' he answered, keeping his voice low, 'but it might well be that I'd want to carry on with my work as usual. It might take my mind off it.'

'I'd be too upset.'

'You're more like a human being than I am.' He grinned at her.

'You invited that man in,' she said. She gathered her papers together in the tray, nodded pleasantly and walked off. The beautiful legs gave no sign of mental discomposure. She would be settled at her desk before he had recovered.

He mentioned the matter to his wife. He phoned that he'd be home early and she said dinner for him and the children would be on the table at six. The young people, Thomas and Alice, perhaps because it was unusual to eat with their father, talked amicably. They seemed cynically interested in reports of a pop concert in Sheffield that they had attended on the previous Saturday. He had been away and was only vaguely aware of their weekend activity, though they had asked his permission. They had returned in the early hours, and had expressed satisfaction to their mother on Sunday morning. Now it appeared that two young men had been stabbed to death, and the police were connecting the deaths with the sale of drugs.

'Did you see anything of all this?' Colin asked.

'No. There were thousands of people there, all crushed together. You wouldn't have noticed anything if it had happened only twenty yards away.' Thomas, now seventeen, spoke with the hauteur of an adult to a naïvely questioning child.

'Were there drugs on sale?' Anna asked.

'You don't need to go to a pop concert for that, you can get them anywhere.'

'Where, for instance?' Colin asked, voice as sweet as he could make it.

'Our school yard.'

'From boys in the school or from outsiders?'

'Both.'

Thomas frowned, looked worried. His father could be awkward if he so wished.

50

'Do the school authorities know about it?' Colin asked.

'I expect so.'

'Do they do anything about it?'

'Yes. They expelled two second-formers last term.'

'Thirteen year-olds?' Anna.

'Yes. They were selling the stuff.'

'What was it?'

'Cannabis.'

'Did you know them?'

'Not really. They were nerds, really, or so they tell me. Trying to make themselves look big, or popular.'

'Who bought the drugs?'

'Fifth formers, I believe. The head gave a long spiel in assembly. It's rumoured, and I don't know how true it is, that some boy let on to his parents and they 'phoned the headmaster. It happens fairly often in places like ours. Not only with drugs.'

'And the head sacks them?'

'He'll look into it. Investigates in his fashion. Summons the parents. They say their say. And that's that. Out. No option.'

'Is that sensible?' Anna asked.

'I suppose so. There's not much else he can do. He then sends a letter to every parent telling them to be on the watch.'

'Have we had one?' Colin asked.

'Yes. I told you about it,' Anna answered.

'And do you have drugs in your place?' Colin demanded of Alice.

'I've never seen any,' Alice replied, neutrally. Her eyes grew large. She was beautiful.

'The headmistress hasn't sent us a letter yet,' Anna said sarcastically.

'I expect there are,' Alice thoughtfully answered. 'You sometimes hear talk. But I don't think it's serious.'

After the meal the parents sat at the table.

'They're pretty lucid, our children,' Anna began, toying with black coffee.

'I should think so, the amount we cough up for their education.'

'Do they sound balanced to you?'

'I can understand what they say, if that's what you mean. But I imagine they'd talk much the same if they'd tried drugs. I don't mean if they were totally addicted.'

51

'Did you when you were young?'

'That was in the swinging sixties. Yes, I occasionally smoked pot, but I didn't find much pleasure in it. The people I was friendly with had plenty to occupy themselves besides drugs. Even tobacco. We were all too busy making our way in life. And we hadn't money to throw about.'

'You played the guitar at school in a group,' she said.

'Not for long. I wasn't good enough at it. When I think about it now the only thing we could do well was make a hell of a lot of noise. Only one of us had anything like talent, at words and music.'

'And what's he doing now?'

'I'm not sure. Last time I heard he was some sort of scientist in the civil service.'

'Porton Down?' She laughed at herself.

'I don't think so. London somewhere. He was very good at everything. Witty. Even with the music he wrote, if you know what I mean. But I don't suppose he even owns a guitar now.'

'Could he have made a living in the pop world?'

'If talent counted, yes. But I've never understood quite how some got on, and some didn't. I imagine those who'd no other strings to their bows and just kept hammering away might, one or two of them, made a name. Most of us switched to something else.'

'You mean university, or a career in accountancy or journalism, or medicine?'

'Yes.'

'Did university help you in yours?'

'Not really. It gave me time to look round.' Colin could see his wife was waiting for an answer, but instead of expanding on his remarks, he began to tell her, with something of Thomas's judicial but modest manner, about his meeting that morning with James Glover. Anna listened with interest. It was not often these days that her husband spoke to her at such length. Like Tracey Haywood she was expected to interpret and expand his curt sentences for herself. When he had finished, she did not immediately comment, but left him to silence so that he would realise that he had acted strangely, out of character. He glowered, not at her, but at the azaleas, pink and rose-like, on the far window-sill. His face seemed drained of life, of intelligence. No, that was wrong. No liveliness played about his expression. He sat

52

handsome, and rock-solid, a different man.

She tapped the table, calling the meeting to order. It was a habit she had picked up from her father.

'You think he'll die, do you?' she asked.

'I don't know. That's what he feared.'

'And what did you say to him?'

'Nothing. There's nothing I could. What would you have said?'

'I'd have been too shocked to say anything coherent.'

He nodded, strongly.

'I mentioned it to Tracey Haywood when she came in with the letters.'

'And what had she to say for herself?'

'She said if it had happened to her she would have asked, "Why me?" That's about right.'

'She didn't come up with any answer to her question?'

'How could she?'

'I suppose religious people would,' Anna said, ruminatively, 'have instructed her to trust in God, and that Divine Providence would see that all was well in the end. "I will trust Him though he slay."'

'You've got to believe in God first.'

'I realise that, and to you and me the evidence seems on balance to be against the existence of a benevolent God. Earthquakes, floods, natural disasters. I suppose they don't logically mean that a caring deity doesn't exist. His defenders would say that all would be set right in due course. We're too quick. We want it demonstrated straight away.'

They looked at each other in surprise after Anna's little gloss. He felt proud of her, and then remembered Thomas's distant judgement of his headmaster. Colin had never profited from his wife's education. She read and thought as he did not. He chased about, successfully indeed, making money. It filled his time, was utterly satisfactory. Anna considered philosophy and religion as he did not. She did not attend church any more than he, but the bits and pieces she had acquired early in her life had clung to her, as his had not. They had had acts of religious worship at school, and lessons in Divinity as they'd called it at grammar school, but he'd not remembered much. The chemistry master's anecdotes had had more influence on him than the words of Jesus or the denunciations of the prophets. Anna's training had been in literature, and that set a considerable gap between them.

53

'I've enjoyed talking to you like this,' he said.

'Thank you.'

She smiled, and leaned back, pleased herself.

'We don't talk enough,' he said.

'I'm always available.'

'We get on well, don't we?'

'Don't you know?' A sarcastic tang sharpened her voice.

'We go out together often, but when we're out our conversation is to other people not between ourselves. There seems something slightly awry about that.'

'We're not the young couple who married nineteen years ago.'

'No, but we're still together.' He spoke with a kind of wooden triumph.

'Perhaps that's because we aren't always talking to each other. We'd soon be quarrelling or getting on each other's nerves. People who live together make a modus vivendi for themselves. Marriage isn't very like the idealistic stereotypes we read of in romantic fiction.'

'I see.' He spoke with a jaunty grumpiness.

They talked across a second cup of coffee trying to prolong the new relationship. Soon Colin was himself again, and shot away to his computers.

V

Anna, casually shopping in Beechnall, bumped into Nancy Johnson, her parents' housekeeper, and invited her to coffee in the department store where they had met.

'It's lovely to sit down,' Mrs Johnson said. She looked old, dry, with the skin of her cheeks wrinkled. 'I don't know why I come into town.'

'Can you get everything you want in Ashby?'

'My food I buy at Tesco. Their petrol's cheaper than elsewhere, and they're only six miles away from Ashby. I go once a fortnight. It justifies keeping a car. Clothes I buy off the hanger.'

'But where?'

'Here. Or on little outings. I don't need to appear fashionable, so I cling on to my old things, and add little bits and pieces. It keeps my interest in life alive.'

'I'm surprised you say that.'

'Well, perhaps I'm not as full of initiatives as I ought to be. My main concern is keeping your parents' place in good order.'

'Is that difficult?'

'No. Things like plumbing or major decorating your father likes to be told about so that they can be attended to at once.'

'You make the arrangements with the builders or plumbers, do you?'

'On the whole, yes. Your father will always look over what they've done.'

'And does my mother have no say?'

Mrs Johnson jerked her head back, as if she suspected some catch in the question. Anna must know her mother better than she did, so the query was either supererogatory or cunningly inquisitive.

'You know your mother. She's really interested in the pictures or statuary or wallpapers. If she thinks the latter need changing she says so, and I am consulted. Your mother makes the final choice.'

55

'Not my father?'

'No, he trusts her. There are only certain things that she'll concern herself with. Yesterday's dust is not high on the list.'

'Wouldn't she notice it?'

'I'm sure she would, if I didn't get rid of it. But I do.' She smiled, with rat-trap mouth.

Anna slightly changed the subject as she poured Mrs Johnson a second cup.

'Is there plenty to occupy you in the village?'

'By "you" do you mean "me" or "people"?'

'Answer both,' Anna said, like an examiner. 'Well.' Mrs Johnson spoke hesitantly. Clearly Anna's brief instruction struck her as rude and unexpected. 'I look after your father's house, and my own. Both need time. I like to keep up my reading. I attend a concert now and again. In town. In the early summer two of my old colleagues usually visit me, they live together, and we have a run out to Chatsworth or Haddon or Newstead or Calke Abbey, that sort of thing.'

'Does your son come up?'

'No. Never.' Snapped. Taboo subject. 'But the garden takes time. I've always plenty to occupy myself.'

'Even in winter?'

'Even more so. I'm used to the long evenings, and I've plenty to read and listen to. She sat complacently. 'There are things in the village. School activities, anything from Nativity plays to car-boot sales. The church has its events with this vicar. There's a new-year concert.'

'Folk-dancing?' Anna did not quite understand why she wished to goad Mrs Johnson.

'Not that I've heard of. Line-dancing's more likely. Most people are commuters, professional men and women. The wives will have meetings, so I hear, though I've never been, if they don't work, though many of them do.'

'So it's friendly?'

'I suppose so. I talk to my neighbours. Mrs Trent even gave me a bowl of tomatoes yesterday. We're not in and out of one another's houses. That suits me.'

'And Mr Norman? Frank Norman?'

'Oh, yes. You know him, don't you? He taught you at one time, I think you said. Yes. He's something of an eccentric. Very odd. Will make a fuss of you one day and the next walk straight past you as if he's never seen you before in his life.'

'Does he play any part in village life?'

'Not that I've heard of.'

'He's lived there for a good length of time?'

'Yes. He's been a widower for years. Well before we moved here.' She looked up eagerly as if wishing to prolong the conversation. 'I was a teacher.'

'I think I knew that. What was your subject?'

'History, with a bit of Latin. And, when they were short, maths.'

'Did you enjoy it?'

'It's what I'd been brought up to expect. It's thirty years ago. I imagine schools were quite different then.'

'What sort of school was it?'

'A grammar school in Colchester. Girls only. The discipline was strict, and the standards respectably high. I enjoyed my work. I often think I was foolish to get married.' A red spot glowed on Mrs Johnson's face as she made the confession.

'You left when you married.'

'Not immediately. Not until I was pregnant.'

She offered no further information. Anna asked one or two questions. No, she had not thought of teaching when she came up here. Clearly Nancy had by now, in her own opinion, given away more than enough about herself.

'And is there anything exciting planned for the village?'

'Not that I know.'

'My mother said something about some sort of harvest feast at the house in October.'

'Yes. The harvest supper. The date is fixed, but I've heard nothing more. Your parents, as you know, won't be back until September.'

'Will it mean a lot of extra work for you?'

'Not really. There's plenty of unofficial help offered. And I know where to accept. Or to reject.'

'Is it just a meal?'

'No. There's entertainment.'

'By the villagers themselves?'

'No. Recruited locally. Well fairly. Last year it was a comedian and what I call a concert party. It wasn't altogether a success. Rather low-brow. Bad taste. After all, the event is in aid of the church rebuilding funds.'

'Some people didn't like it?'

'That's so. I among them.'

'My mother didn't say anything to me.'

'There would be no call to do so. It was not an important matter to her. I don't suppose your mother took offence. But one or two old-fashioned people of influence didn't like it, and said as much to the vicar, and to me.'

'And he?'

'Clergymen have to be diplomatic. I understand the subject was raised at parish council level, and with the small committee who organise the supper. This year, I hear, we shall be entertained by a small group of opera singers.'

'Professionals?'

'Semi. Or so I'm led to believe.'

Anna half amused at Nancy Johnson's distancing herself from the proceedings by her use of 'believe' and 'understand', said, 'We've never been invited. Father always asks us over for the summer fête.'

'No. It is not, you realise, what one could call a gourmet meal.'

Nancy Johnson made excuses now, claiming she had much to do while she was in town, and profusely thanking Anna for the coffee. As she was about to leave she suddenly turned and said,

'I hope I haven't said anything out of place.'

'Not at all.'

Mrs Johnson twisted her face into a caricature of a smile and marched off. Anna, still at the table, mildly wondered at the woman's discomfiture. Perhaps she felt outside these matters of village importance, and resented it. The people of influence, those old fogeys, regarded her as a kind of high-grade servant of the Meyers, not as a graduate in history, one to be consulted rarely and then only on marginal matters. She obviously had not been present at the parish council. Anna had no idea.

The next time she visited Ashby Manor House she made inquiries about Nancy Johnson of her mother who had just returned from her European holiday.

'Mrs Johnson, ah,' Hilda Meyer said, 'ah?' She loved mysteries. 'I've never quite made her out. If you want my opinion, she feels that life has treated her badly. Her husband was no good to her, and her son just about as useless. Not that I ever met either. She's very useful to us. Very efficient. She also makes excellent suggestions.'

'Which you accept?'

'On the whole. She once tried arguing with your father, but very soon learnt what an obstinate old mule he is. Since then she tells us what wants doing, or what she would do in our place, and I encourage this.'

'But not Daddy?'

'Well. He's an unusual man. When we're in Germany or Austria and he's chatting away to the locals, and finding us opera seats, or dining tables, or river-boat trips I sometimes think that he's where he should be.'

'What does that mean?'

'He'd be happy as a well-to-do, retired German bourgeois.'

'He was educated mainly in England, wasn't he? He's lived here since he was a boy. He looks and sounds exactly what he is, an Englishman.'

'You're probably right. Perhaps because I don't speak German fluently, though I did it at school, and he seems so much at home in the language, it makes me feel he's in some way a stranger who's suddenly changed from the everyday husband I know to some foreigner, much at his ease in what to me is a thoroughly different society.'

'You've been married to him for forty-six years.'

'That's so.'

'And has he always been this alien character?'

'That's too strong a word. No. It wasn't too bad when he was at work, and you were small. We did go to Germany then, to meet with some old aunt and cousins, but our main summer holidays were in England or France, at the seaside. He went over there on his own once or twice a year for a week or two . . . On business. Or so he said.'

'I remember the presents he brought back. Lovely they were. I still wear one of the necklaces. And now he's reverting, is he?'

'We were there for eight weeks this summer. It's quite a long time.'

'Can you speak German now, then?'

'Yes, to some extent, and understand it, but your father's like a native.'

'Do they think so?'

'Yes. They take him for a German. So they said. Perhaps from some other region.'

'And so you've decided he's not happy here?'

'Nothing of the kind.' Hilda's voice signalled alarm.

'He's not likely to whip you over to Hamburg or Munich or Dresden for good?'

'Unlikely, unlikely.' Her mother almost danced. 'To revert to our Mrs Johnson. At one time I thought she was setting her cap at your Mr Norman. She talked about him, dragged his name into every conversation. That lasted for perhaps a month. Then no more mentions.'

'Were they seen together?'

'I didn't see them.'

At this moment Kuno Meyer came into the room, in smart tweeds, his brown shoes a-gleam.

'Hello, Anna,' he said. 'I saw your car.'

'She's been here more than half an hour. You didn't come in very soon.' Hilda spoke without rancour, setting a question she expected he was capable of answering competently.

'Ah, I let you have your time for womanly secrets together.'

'Gossip,' said Anna.

'About what?' he asked.

'The village and the villagers.'

'Oh.' That had no interest for him.

'How's the garden?' she asked.

'Oh, it's the end of season now. Pretty full of flowers, but we're beginning to think about winter.'

'You miss the best of it with such long holidays, away all July and August,' she scoffed.

'That's what I tell him,' Hilda supported her.

'No, at this latitude and climate the garden is at its best in late May, early June. That's what Ferdy and I aim for.'

'Who enjoys it while you're away?'

'The Almighty,' Hilda said.

'Ferdy. Nancy Johnson. The village on Summer fête day. But it's unusual for us to be away the whole two months.'

'Are the villagers allowed into the house while you're away?'

'Certain rooms,' Hilda answered. 'Nancy knows exactly what's what. She's fierce.'

'She wouldn't think of letting them wander about. She'd have the job of clearing up afterwards.' Both parents laughed, as if they enjoyed the idea of Mrs Johnson the dragon schoolma'am or policewoman. 'How's Colin?'

'Fine. Busy as always.'

'He's not worrying about all these stock-market rumours, and financial crises we hear about?' Hilda asked. Her husband looked at her with surprise, as if she had been a precocious child talking out of turn but with real intelligence.

'He's not mentioned it,' Anna answered. 'Should he be?'

Neither parent answered, but her father placed a hand carefully and unusually on her shoulder. He then quietly left the room, gently raising one finger in careful, half-comical farewell to his daughter.

Anna raised the question with her husband, reporting her mother's question. Colin looked at her with quiet amusement, as if she'd demanded an answer to something utterly unimportant to him: what make of boot polish he used, perhaps.

'Hilda wanted to know, did she? So she must be worried. What did Kuno say?'

'Nothing. He said nothing.'

'Wise man.'

'What does that mean?' Anna felt exasperation. Her husband had dodged the question.

'He wouldn't want to upset your mother unduly.'

'There is something, then, in what she says?'

'There's always something in what anyone says, even if it's all wrong.'

'So all this talk on radio and TV is untrue.'

'You know as well as I do, Anna, that it's not. But let's put it like this. I'm like a man who just had a very good dinner and who walks down into a restaurant where people usually wait on him with all sorts of delicious food. I find they are no longer there. Now am I upset? I may feel slightly hurt that nobody offers me these pleasures. But I'm replete. I have eaten all I need, all I can cope with. That's how it is.'

'But you could have taken the food and put it in the freezer for a time when you are hungry.'

'Let's not take the analogy too far, but I don't see that as a possibility. Money doesn't fall into my hands as readily as it did, let's say, two years ago. But we're not short. You won't find yourself living in a terraced house on bread and scrape with fish and chips once a month as a big treat.'

'And Kuno?'

'He'll be nicely settled, don't you worry. A good long-term investor.'

61

Anna reported her mother's observations on Kuno's time in Germany and Austria.

'Interesting,' Colin said.

'I'm not saying,' Anna pressed, 'that he's reverting to his Teutonic background, but he seems more at home in Vienna than in Ashby.'

'That's Hilda. He'd be talking away in German, and making jokes she couldn't follow, and she'd feel left out. Kuno's a very talented man socially. He'd talk his way into any sort of society without any trouble as I couldn't. It was an advantage sometimes in our work. Soft soap succeeds occasionally where hard advice fails to come up with the goods. And presumably he can do it as well in German.'

'So my mother's no need to worry?'

'I don't suppose so. And certainly not financially. Your grand-father French left her a great deal of money and property.'

'And this hasn't disappeared?'

'Nor is it likely to.'

Just before he left the room, he turned back and wagged a fist at his wife.

'Money, the stock-market sort, is a matter of confidence, really. The same resources are there, but people don't trust them, and begin playing about with their money, and you get, in the worst scenario, a run on the banks. Business is the same. Things we make are no longer required, or are superseded by something better and cheaper. If all your money is invested in unwanted commodities, then you'll be ruined.'

'And do you know what'll be proved useless next year?'

'Not really. Doesn't matter much.'

'Because all your eggs aren't in one basket?'

'Exactly.'

He waved to her, not with one finger like her father, but with the same sort of jocular confidence, then stood looking back at her as if he hoped that he had quite restored her equilibrium. She stared down, not at him. What sort of man was this husband of hers? Who did his bidding and where? Keats' lines sounded in her head, and she spoke them out loud.

> 'For them the Ceylon diver held this breath,
> And went all naked to the hungry shark;
> For them his ears gush'd blood; for them in death

The seal on the cold ice with piteous bark
Lay full of darts . . .'

'Is that me?' he asked.

'The two brokers in 'Isabella'. Rich entrepreneurs, business men.'

'Obviously before the days of unions or industrial legislation,' he laughed.

'It's mediaeval. From Boccaccio. Though I guess Keats's own ideas of employers and mistreated work people and slaves are being given an airing here.'

'It's very good,' he said. 'What's that first line?'

'"For them the Ceylon diver held his breath"', she repeated. 'He certainly lays it on. ". . . many a weary hand did swelt/In torched mines and noisy factories." And they were proud of themselves.'

'Were they? I'm not a proud man.'

This time he waved with a flat hand, openly, all smiles.

'You be careful,' she warned.

He slipped from the room. The place seemed empty without him. While he was in with her there was an edge of expectancy; one did not know which chair he'd choose or leave, which length of carpet he'd stride across, what he'd touch or stare at. All now were passively still, inanimate objects. Life had disappeared; a cloud crossed the sun.

VI

On the next morning as Anna was writing letters after breakfast she received a 'phone call from Linda Turnbull, Colin's brother's wife. Colin had been away at work for at least an hour and a half.

'This is Linda.'

'Hello. How are you?'

'Is Colin at home? Oh. Yes. I thought he might be at work. I've some bad news.' She paused again, in no hurry to deliver her message. 'It's Terence. He's in hospital.'

'What's wrong?' Anna contrived to make the short query sympathetic.

'He's had a stroke.' She stopped there.

'When was this?'

'He got up early this morning. He usually does. He'll bring me a cup of tea, and get his own breakfast, and be out of the house before I'm even up.'

'Like Colin.'

Anna's intervention seemed momentarily to throttle her sister-in-law, but Linda hardened, strengthened her voice.

'I suddenly heard such a crash, and I grabbed my dressing gown. It sounded as if he'd knocked the tray of cups over. The row was frightening. And he was such a careful man, so neat with his hands. He was never clumsy. I rushed downstairs. He was sprawled in the middle of the kitchen floor, smashed crockery all over the room. He must have been just about to make my pot of tea and bring it upstairs. I tried to turn him over and managed it to a small extent. He was breathing and his eyes were open but he couldn't speak. I don't know if he was trying to. I rang 999, made him as comfortable as I could, and ran back upstairs to dress so I could go with him to the hospital.'

'Did they take long to arrive?'

'No. They didn't . . . Well, it seemed long enough. I was dressed and downstairs. They came round the back. They had the stretcher out and Terry on it in no time. They were very good. I

64

asked them, 'Shall I come with him in the ambulance?' and they said, "If you came in your own car, you'd get back more easily." So I did. I followed them. They were very good. They told me where to park. And all the time I went behind them I kept worrying about two things. There wasn't much traffic about; it was early. First was: "What if anything happens to him in the ambulance? I ought to be there." And the other was: "Did I lock the front door?"'

'How is he?'

'They'd examined him, and put him into a bed. And some nurse said, "He's in good hands now. They'll keep seeing him for examination and treatment. There's nothing much you can do. Just sit with him for a few minutes so he feels at home, and then go back and see to yourself." "But if he dies," I said. "He won't. You just hold his hand for now."'

'How long had you been down there at the hospital, then?'

'A good hour or more. Perhaps longer. They dealt with him straight away.'

'Have you had any breakfast?'

'No. I've not had time. I rang Henry in London. He's taking a day off from his office and coming up as soon as he can get away. I tried to get Colin at two of his offices, but he's not there.'

'I've no idea where he is, but I'll get him on his mobile. As soon as I have I'll come round to your place. You have a drink and something to eat, and think of the things you need to collect for his stay in the hospital. I'll take you up there in my car.'

She reached Colin by 'phone. He was apparently on his way to Stamford. He said he would be back later in the afternoon, but that he'd do a U-turn straight off if it was necessary.

'No,' Anna said, 'they've found him a bed and are working on him. I don't think he's in any great danger. You'll be able to visit him this evening.'

'And Linda?'

'As soon as I've finished talking to you I shall drive across there. I've a free day.'

'Don't bother preparing a meal tonight.'

'Are you sure? I don't want two sickly brothers.' She hoped her pleasantry reassured him about Terry. She imagined her husband in his Jaguar speeding over flat East Midlands roads, 'phone held to his ear, no reduction of speed, no sign on his face of shock. She'd no idea why he was making for Stamford, whether it was to

65

a long arranged assignation or whether he'd suddenly decided this morning to sort out some newly discovered difficulty, or a problem that had in his opinion been allowed to run on too long by his subordinates. She wondered if he had taken his jacket off, hung it in the back, to drive in comfort in a car already air-conditioned. Colin mastered his environment, even as his brother lay helpless, perhaps paralysed, for all she knew with his working life at a bitter end.

Anna smartened herself, changing one expensive trouser suit for another. She locked the house, having switched on the answerphone, and made swiftly to Linda's in Templeton Avenue. As she drove her uncertainty grew. She had never quite understood her sister-in-law. Linda seemed always to be trying to impress, with her Grecian temple in the back garden, and her rows of CDs, never played in Anna's hearing, her two computers, her manuals of information technology and her forthright way of speaking her mind. She seemed, for no reason Anna could see, to be slightly ashamed of her husband, as if the personal appearances he made to repair or install televisions or computers demeaned her. They were not short of money, the Terence Turnbulls, though nothing like as rich as Colin, and Anna had suspected that Linda resented this. Anna was never sure, only uncomfortable.

She suspected, and this was the basis of the coolness between the two at their very rare meetings, that Linda and Colin had been lovers. Not fifteen months ago, Anna had come across, in a drawer of her husband's, a cache of letters from Linda to her brother-in-law scribbled in passionate terms. Linda had not held back her hand. Sexual intimacies were luridly exposed and dwelt on; lust scorched. Anna had found herself shocked. The well-dressed, quietly spoken, self-possessed young woman wrote down her adulterous desires with unbridled zest, as if under the influence of drugs, or as if crudely employed to turn out cheap-jack pornography.

Anna had read the letters through carefully twice on the day she had found them and had packed them away, only to turn them out again on subsequent days and scrutinise them with hot eyes, stumbling on unnoticed touches of sexual appetite, or innuendo. Each time she meticulously replaced the sheets in order, then the envelopes. Colin had made no great attempt to conceal these. True they had been thrust, not chronologically, into a large buff envelope, made to hold A4 sheets, but this had not been sealed, had been heedlessly thrust in half-way down a pile of underwear. Colin knew that she would be in and out of the drawer packing away articles after they'd been laundered. Perhaps he enjoyed the risk that she'd discover these letters, or was so confident of his position in the marriage that he felt he could dice with it.

She had not faced her husband with the discovery. She noticed that the letters were dated over five years, from a period just before her own marriage to something like fifteen years ago. There'd be perhaps twenty letters, none very long, three or four sides at most; on average, she thought, four a year. After her initial and violent shock, she wondered whether Colin had made a selection of Linda's missives and destroyed the rest: '*The Best of Adulterous Love*, by Linda Turnbull, selected by Colin Turnbull.' Such bitter gibes did nothing to comfort her. She thought now and then she could occasionally deduce from the letters something that Colin had previously written or said, but these passages were relatively rare. Most were dashed down with the anguish of a prisoner or exile longing for the day when the loved ones would reunite. Perhaps the two had been prevented from meeting. Colin was often away, and she in her trouble had taken to her pen. All the letters were handwritten, and all addressed in type, marked Private and Confidential, to his office. The only exceptions were those, three only, written before his marriage. Terence, Linda's husband, rated very few mentions, almost all unfavourable. 'All I could think about was you, and there was Terry moaning on and on about some woman who didn't know what she wanted, and kept ringing up to change her mind. If he had seen us together last Friday he'd have had something to complain about,' or in another letter two years later: 'When I compare the two of you, I'd think you were sprung from different families, species even, you like a naked, overpowering god and he a shambling, snuffling washout. Oh, Colin my love, my Col, I want you round me, on me, up me, in me, splitting me.'

Anna was puzzled that she had not come across these letters before. She had often enough been in this drawer, and had been through the clothes looking for garments to be thrown away and replaced. She could only conclude that Colin had recently hidden these missives there, having removed them, for whatever reason, from some more secure hiding-place, his safe, for instance. Perhaps this was only a temporary arrangement while his real hiding-place was refurbished or renewed. She had looked at the neatish strokes of the pen, and compared them, in breathless tears, with the cries of love, the longing, the pulses of desire, the wild details of coition, the illegitimate and splayed relaxation of gratified lust. Even now as she thought of these letters while she drove, Anna blushed. And these had been written while she, Anna, had been enjoying revelling in the fullness of her husband's love. It did not seem possible.

Linda let her in at the front door. She, soberly well dressed, seemed in control of herself.

'Any more news?' Anna asked.

'No, nothing.'

Linda described again the stroke, the reception at the hospital, Terry's condition as it had appeared to her. She asked if Colin had been reached, and seemed pleased that he'd call in to see his brother that evening. Henry, her son, would also be over.

'Did they give you any idea of future prospects?' Anna inquired.

'It was too early, the nurse said.'

'I see. Have you prepared the things he'll need?'

'I have.' Linda seemed to resent the implied slur on her efficiency.

They drove to the hospital in silence. Traffic clogged the roads and when they arrived they found it almost impossible to park even at the far end of the grounds. Only the intervention of a passing sweeper, impressed by Anna's car, showed them where to leave the vehicle.

'And you won't have to pay there,' the man said smirking. 'Do you find that a satisfactory car?'

'Yes. Big for parking.'

'Roomy. Comfortable. And fast.'

He patted the car-door and left them, not refusing a tip but brushing hard at the ground with his broom. The women set off for the main entrance. As they walked, negotiating at one point a curved concrete staircase, Anna said.

'These places terrify me.'

'Why's that? Have you had bad experiences in hospitals?'

'No. I've never been a patient. I brought Alice down when she broke her leg, and the staff were all very efficient.'

'A sister and brother both died in this hospital,' Linda said.

'Yes. I knew that.'

68

'And I had a spell in here not long after Terry and I were first married. That would be over twenty years ago.' She paused for mental arithmetic. 'Twenty-five years.'

'Were you in long?'

'Three weeks. On and off.'

They walked now at speed, approaching the foyer. The huge forecourt was busily cluttered with cars, buses, people moving. Inside they consulted the notice-boards, made for the lift.

'On my own, I never use a lift,' Anna said. 'I prefer to walk.'

'It's not a phobia?'

'Not as far as I know.'

They acted like duellists, testing each other's skills. Their voices sounded subdued, not friendly, without laughter. In the ward a young nurse gave them a favourable report, led them towards the patient.

'Hello, Terence,' she called. 'Here are two ladies to see you.'

He did not move, even when the nurse straightened the bed-clothes. His eyes were open and he looked from one to the other.

Linda bent to kiss her husband's forehead, stood back to allow Anna to do likewise.

'Can he hear us?' Linda asked.

'Yes. You can hear what we say, can't you, Terence?' the nurse spoke as to a child.

The main impression on Anna was of Terence's helplessness. He lay unmoving except for his eyes. Once or twice when they spoke he made some attempt to answer but from the still lips the sounds were more like a groan than articulate speech. The two sat at one side of the bed, Linda holding desperately on to her husband's right hand.

'He has movement here,' she whispered to Anna.

The man's haunted eyes sought her out as if he understood every word.

After a time, Linda searched through Terence's locker, replacing flannels, clothes, soap. She must have packed the first bar before the ambulance picked him up, but now she removed it and laid a new, as yet unwrapped tablet of Camay on the shelves. She handled the packet ostentatiously, crackling the shining cover, as if making it certain to any observers that nothing but her best was good enough for her husband. When she had completed these chores, she walked swiftly round the bed, resumed her seat, took her husband's hand almost militarily and stiffened her body.

69

Not once did she look at Anna. They exchanged no words, though from time to time she bent to speak to her husband, to ask how he felt or if there was anything he wanted. The eyes opened as she spoke and once or twice saliva bubbled on his lips as he attempted to answer.

Anna slipped away to arrange the flowers she had brought in the vase a nurse provided. She took her time giving Linda the opportunity, if it presented itself, of speaking to or touching her husband without being closely observed. She congratulated herself mildly to herself on the tact of this, knowing quite well that playing about with a bunch of chrysanthemums, a pair of scissors, a vase of cold water in a strange, cramped kitchen was more interesting to her than sitting at her brother-in-law's bedside.

When she returned she placed the flowers on the top of Terence's locker, saying,

'There.'

'Look at the lovely flowers Anna has brought,' Linda whispered. Certainly Anna had made a workmanlike job of the arrangement.

There was no response from the patient, and soon afterwards the ward-sister, a smiling, energetic woman, said they'd be serving lunches any minute and that if the two visitors wished to return to their own meal this would be the right time.

'It's early days yet, but the consultant was optimistic when he saw your husband this morning. They'll probably have another look at him this afternoon, and then perhaps you could come in again this evening.'

'I'll do that,' Linda said.

'He needs rest, and some stimulation if you see what I mean, but just this afternoon he'll have plenty on his plate. If you come in after six this evening. I think he's as well as he can be.'

The sister straightened the edges of the sheets.

'Your wife will come back to see you again tonight,' she said in a bright voice. The visitors bent to kiss Terry, then hurried from the ward. The sister frowned, as if only half relieved.

'Come over to my place, and I'll find something to eat,' Anna invited.

'No. You come to mine. Then we'll be there to answer the 'phone.'

'That's sensible.'

'I'll find us something from the fridge, and if you can come I'll be glad of the company.'

For the first time Linda had expressed gratitude, and Anna kissed her cheek. She did not like her sister-in-law, but felt that the woman showed up well in her wifely duties. She'd see to it that her husband was as carefully looked after as was possible.

During the next days Terence showed a marked improvement. The stroke had not been as serious as they feared at first. The paralysis began to recede, and Terence could talk intelligibly from the second or third day. Colin offered to look into the running of the shops, but Terence thought the managers were capable men, and could keep the concerns busy and profitable at least for a month or two while he had the chance to recover.

'Shall I go to see them?' Colin asked.

'I don't think it's necessary, do you?'

'I'll just carry a message from you.'

'You will?' Terence grinned, something like his old self. 'You'll frighten the life out of the poor sods.'

'And that won't do?'

'I bawl them out, but you'll terrify them. They know your reputation, and think you'll have 'em out on the street with a redundancy payment in dolly-mixtures at the drop of a hat.'

'Um. Yes.'

When Terence returned home he walked stiffly with a stick, and sat outside in the mildness of early autumn. Leaves still crowded the trees; sunshine warmed and shirt-sleeve order satisfied. He spent a half-day each week in each of his shops, enjoyed himself as he dismissed thoughts of retirement. Linda found him less trouble than she expected. He could occupy himself in silence, argued very little, did not take umbrage at the suggested schemes of either his work-people or his brother.

'I told you they'd do well. You chose them, and they have been with you long enough.'

'By "doing well" I suppose you mean "not making a loss", and that's right enough. My only complaint is that they can't always do those extras that make my sort of business really successful.'

'Such as?'

'They're conscientious, and they've learnt a good deal about the present market. They'll tell customers just what the equipment will do for them, and make sure it's all there when it's delivered. You'd be surprised how often that's not the case in our line. And

71

they'll see it's properly installed and in good working order. Where they are not quite up to scratch is when something goes wrong.'

'Why should it? If the set's well-made and properly put in?'

'The customer. There are some bloody fools about in this world, I can tell you. They try some bit of fancy work of their own and are surprised when it does damage. Then they send for me, and I worm out of them what hanky-panky they've been getting up to. Then I read 'em a lecture on what they can do and not do, charge 'em a reasonable price to set it all right. They're pleased, because some of the installations have cost them a lot of money, and my price won't break them, I see to that, and they're not altogether shown up as fools. That's the sort of business I like. It's only a fairly small fraction of the whole, but it gets me a good name. "Turnbull's will see you right." You'd be surprised how many people who've not bought their equipment from us come squealing to me to set it right. And next time they'll buy from us. Word gets round. Word of mouth. It's good for trade.'

'And your managers can't or won't do it?'

'That's so. And properly. Only one of them could manage what I do technically. But he's the sort who'd work all day on a twenty-pound job if it was interesting enough.'

'You wouldn't.'

'I would not. Half the reason for success is that you spend your time profitably, know when to go out, and when to stay back. I have to balance interest, to me, with profit.'

Linda listened to this, and knew that her husband was well on the way to recovery. As soon as he could drive, he'd be back full-time. She warned him against too early a start. 'You're not losing money,' she urged, 'and the stress is much less.'

'I tell you,' he said, almost roughly, 'when it gets more stressful staying at home than going to work, I'll be off.'

'The doctor said you were to be careful. You've had your warning.'

'Ah, doctors. They don't know everything.'

Terence continued to improve, but a change began to afflict him. Though he could now drive, he still did no more than three or four half-days. His speech was slightly affected, but so little that only those who had known his old voice well could recognise a difference. His left hand was as deft as formerly, and Colin who had called in at the shop one afternoon watched his brother as he swiftly and carefully repaired a music centre.

'I'm only doing it because I enjoy the job. It's simple, but long-winded and I know I can get it right. Financially I shall lose money on it if I charge them for time.'

'The amateur,' Colin mocked.

It became clear to Linda that her husband's attitude to his work had changed. This was borne on her only slowly. In the early days of his illness, thoughts of taking over the business again was the goal, the ambition. Now she began, reluctantly because it contradicted her beliefs and his pronouncements, to realise that he was quite content with his half-idle retirement, that when he pottered about in his garden, closing it down for winter, he was happy. When the garden offered little in the severe months, December, January, February, she'd no idea how he'd occupy himself. She discussed this with Anna, whom she met much more these days. They were driving over to Ashby, when Linda suddenly blurted out.

'Do you know, I don't think Terry wants to go back to work.'

'And is that good or bad?'

'Well, I'm not sure.'

'Is he properly fit? To go back full-time?'

'He's not quite the man he was. I think that's true. But he's quite capable of doing a full week. But before the stroke the business was the be-all and end-all of his life. He hadn't much else to talk about. He could be really quite interesting when he did tell me about it, how stupid or opinionated some quite clever people could be. He was always an argumentative sort and didn't suffer fools gladly. He didn't mind, either, who you were. If you wanted to do something he considered silly, or too expensive, or inefficient he would say so plain John Blunt to your face.'

'But now?' Anna eased her BMW without show along each country lane. She spoke quietly, her voice clear inside the large car.

'He was up and away before I was awake, and regularly wasn't back until seven or eight o'clock. Now he strolls out at nine as if he's all the time in the world, and he'll be home before four.'

'I see.'

'I don't like to worry him. God knows the stroke was bad enough. When I used to ask him now and again before it happened about retirement, I always got the same brush off. Now, he's part-time, and there's no doubt about it.'

73

'Do you ever go for trips out anywhere?'

'No.'

'Why not?'

'I've got enough on my plate as it is, without making him go to places he has no interest in. My computer studies take up most of my time.'

'But if he retires . . . ?'

'If he retires, he'll have to learn to occupy himself.'

Anna reported this to her husband. He pulled a quizzical face.

'What do you think?' she asked.

'He's sixty. A good many people think of retirement at that age.'

'But Linda says he was dead-set against retirement, even after the stroke. When he first came home from hospital all he talked about was getting fit so he could start again.'

'Is that so?' Colin wrinkled his forehead, scratched his chin. 'He's lost his confidence, perhaps.'

'Suddenly?'

'Well, I don't know how quickly. But just think of the effect of that stroke. He was a strong man physically and mentally. And then one morning when he'd got up normally and was about ready for work, he's flattened, has lost the movement on one side of his body and can't talk properly. That's enough to make anyone think twice. As far as I can see there had been no warnings, not even on that day. Perhaps there had been, and he disregarded or didn't recognise them and Terry's not the sort of man to sit down and send for the doctor because he feels a bit dizzy or has an ache or pain somewhere.'

'But Linda says even after the stroke, when he came home . . .'

'I know, I know. I heard what you both said. But once he was something like himself again, and I'm not altogether sure that he is, he realised that he was nothing like well and he'd better be careful. You just imagine. Fit one day, the next flat out, limbs useless. It's enough to take anybody's confidence away. It would alter your view of life completely.'

'Will he grow out of it if he continues to improve?'

'I don't know. He's something of a mystery is our Terence. He'll do his exercises, and visit the physiotherapist and all the rest, but he's perhaps come to the conclusion that he'll never be the same man, and once he's decided that, then he won't see anything, wife, family, job, pleasure, leisure in the same way as he did.'

She looked over at Colin who stood waiting for her comment.

'That's pretty pessimistic,' she said.

'It's how I understand it.' He raised a finger. 'A stroke's a fairly serious warning, even if you recover physically. Mentally you'll be crippled.'

'Suppose he had financial commitments that he couldn't manage without going back to work?'

'Terry would go back, but whether he'd be able to bring it all off I don't know.'

'You doubt it?'

'I've said I don't know.' Temper edged his voice, and he swung immediately from the room. Anna had smiled to herself. Her husband who had seemed in these last years to be nearer the stereotype of a successful business tycoon had revealed himself, if not openly, as vulnerable. It did not exactly surprise her. They had grown apart, only conjoined by a tenuous string of social engagements, meals at home or out, formal dinners or conferences, rare visits, which Colin did not enjoy, to the theatre or concert-hall. Confidences were rarely exchanged, even about their children, who in any case would have left home in three years' time. Question him about financial matters and he'd answer at once, confidently. He was generous with her as far as money was concerned, and if she asked about something she'd heard on Radio 4 he was clarity itself in his explanations. But they were two different persons, personae, personalities from those wild lovers of twenty years back. Anna thought that must always be so with all married couples, but in her case it seemed to verge on the extreme. They were two handsome, wealthy middle-aged people who had the same name and address, but who made their own separate way through life. If he died, she would miss him, but not beyond bearing. Yet she admired him.

Now as she drove Linda gently towards Ashby, she asked, suiting her voice to the autumnal morning,

'What will you do if Terry gives work up?'

'He's the one I worry about, not myself.'

'Have you some good holidays in the pipeline?'

'He wouldn't be interested, and I'm occupied up to the eyes with my garden and teaching my computer classes, but not he. I suggested that he took up with radio, short wave stuff. He knows enough about it. But do you know what he says. 'Suppose I get in touch with folks in Greenland or Australia, what shall I say to them?' I tell him that if ordinary conversation about holidays or weather won't do, then he can chat about the latest technical innovations. And do you know what he answers? It maddens me. "I know already what they'll say."'

'What does that show?'

'That he's no interest there. The satellites make phone calls dead easy. The internet hands you all sorts of new information if you want it. What's the advantage of getting in touch with some enthusiast in Japan? In the past one needed up-to-date, state-of-the-art sets to do it. That's what appealed to the likes of Terry.'

'But not talking to someone you've never met from an alien culture?'

'Not him. He talks to people here, in his job, but he doesn't say anything human to them.'

'Human?'

'Not about their wives and children. Nor their politics. A pound to a penny nobody talks about football or tennis to him. They mean nothing. He's interested in his work, and in the ways people can help him do it. And making money. That's why I'm worried.' Suddenly Linda's voice changed, leapt, became lively. 'This is a lovely approach road, these trees.' They were cruising down the now wider lane into Ashby. One final corner was occupied by a copse which petered out into hedges with occasional oak trees before the first houses appeared. 'There must be a stream here?' Linda asked.

'Right by the road in a moment, then it veers off. It runs through my father's grounds.'

'Has it got a name?'

'Not that I know of. Must have; people call it "the brook".'

They turned into the long drive of the manor house. The place seemed deserted. They stood, shadowed under the portico, for a short time staring over the neatness of the gardens, before Anna rang the bell. Nancy Johnson appeared, led them into the hall, used the internal 'phone to contact Mrs Meyer. Only then, did Anna introduce her friend. Mrs Johnson shook hands, said that she had felt winter in the air as she had walked up this morning. By this time Hilda Meyer was descending the stairs, tentatively, left hand on the rail, as if she found the descent difficult or dangerous. The three below stopped talking, glancing upwards from time to time. Hilda finally made the hall-floor.

'Nancy,' she said, 'I shall have to have my study at ground level.'

'There's nowhere really suitable,' Mrs Johnson answered. 'There are only these poky little cloakrooms.'

'That might put an end to all my clutter.'

They spoke their lines like actresses, confident because they had often delivered them successfully before. Hilda advanced on Linda, kissed her on one cheek, as they shook hands.

'I haven't seen you for long enough. How's your husband? I'm told how much better he is.'

She concentrated entirely on Linda's answer before kissing Anna almost absent-mindedly.

'Your father's out,' she said.

'A pity. Linda would like to look at his computer. Where's he disappeared to, then?'

'Some committee meeting. Bowls or the Christmas party.' She turned to Linda. 'We haven't got a big enough village hall, only a sort of hut. It shelters the tennis players when it rains. For anything bigger they borrow our ballroom.' She pointed to the ornate door for Linda's information. 'Where are you having your coffee this morning, Nancy?'

'In the kitchen.'

'That won't do. Not for visitors. We'll use the small drawing room. The sun won't bother us there. Not this morning.'

Mrs Johnson withdrew at a good speed. Mrs Meyer led the younger women into a spacious, panelled room. Above the marble fire place hung an oil-painting of Anna as a twenty-year-old standing against a background of blue sky and apple-blossom.

'I've never seen that before,' Linda said.

'It's very beautiful.' Mrs Meyer spoke faintly, reverently to a far wall, away from her visitors. 'We had it painted when Anna was at Oxford.'

'School of John Singer Sargent,' Anna said.

'A man who lived in Southwell at the time. Edward Ernest Wells.'

'Is he still about?'

'I don't know. He'd be pretty old now. He and his wife went to live abroad. In Malta, I think. I've not heard anything of them recently.'

'Did the portrait take long?'

'Three or four sittings. He did sketches and photographs at the

77

first. His wife took the photographs. He sat with his book on his knee.'

'She didn't come back,' Anna added, 'I'm pleased to say. She was a typical photographer. Look this way. Bend your neck. Smile with your eyes. All the rest. He just looked and sketched, and came back later for two more days. He didn't make many demands.'

'Did he talk to you?' Lorna asked.

'Yes. We hadn't much in common. He asked me about Oxford. He was going to paint the Master of Balliol that summer. And he said a little bit now and again about his methods. He borrowed the dress for a month later on. He hung it on a model figure.'

'A shop-window dummy?'

'I suppose so. I never saw it.'

They stood now in a line in front of the portrait.

'What do you think?' Mrs Meyer asked. 'Anna always made fun of it.'

'He's hit off an expression of Anna's exactly,' Linda said, still scrutinizing, moving her own head to match the posture portrayed. 'It's excellent. It really is. Nobody's ever mentioned it to me before.'

'Anna would never allow us to hang it in public in the house,' her mother answered.

'He showed it in an exhibition in London,' Anna objected.

'It won a prize. The Society of Portrait Painters.'

'The Royal Society,' Anna mocked.

'Now she's married and away we do as we like. Daddy always calls this 'Anna's Room' because of the picture. He's very fond of it.'

'Yes,' Anna said, 'and he always points out that the big advantage of the picture over the model is that it doesn't answer back.'

'Anna, Anna.' Mrs Meyer laughed, approving of her daughter.

Linda, much at ease, talked freely about painting. She had been quite recently to exhibitions in London. Without deception she praised the setting of Anna's picture explaining how the portrait was exactly the right size and intensity with the perfect frame to lead the eye onwards from the rest of the room, from the large windows, the three watercolour landscapes, the warm furniture and carpets, beautiful as all were, to the figure in white, the thoughtful girl and the apple blossom.

78

Anna had to admit to herself that she was impressed not only by Linda's knowledge but by the confidence of her expression of ideas. Here was the suburban housewife, with the pretentious Greek pavilion in the back garden and her computer-office, transferred to a Georgian room and allowed to speak her mind. She did not fail; the subject matter matched and inspired her imagination. Linda should have been a designer, or an architect, a curator of a museum, an organiser of exhibitions. Mrs Meyer sat back smiling, the complacent owner of these lauded riches.

'Would you alter the furniture at all?' Hilda Meyer suddenly asked. The question surprised both younger women. Linda was not at a loss.

'It depends on the purpose of the room. And the heating, for instance, and the artificial lighting. If you have, let's say, two elderly people, or three, chatting to each other on a winter's night then the furniture, or such as is to be used, will be drawn closer together and nearer the fire. That's obvious.'

'But you'd place the pieces in such a way that their aesthetic effect was pleasing?' Anna asked.

'Yes. I would. But my primary object would be the comfort and convenience of my three old people. Otherwise, if the room is not to be used then I'd place the tables and chairs so that they'd make an immediate impression on someone entering through that door which is rather unusually placed. It's a matter of taste, of course. And light. Someone observing on a bright summer morning will take away a different impression from that of, say, a dark winter afternoon or artificial light.'

'Does it matter?' Anna asked.

'Yes and no.' Linda laughed pretension away. 'In the end we come to some compromise arrangement that suits most eventualities.'

'Suppose,' Hilda Meyer said, 'I asked you now. Would you move anything.'

Challenged, Linda stood, then moved about the room, face serious but untroubled. Her eyes raked walls, the ceiling the carpet. At that moment Mrs Johnson entered with her tray.

'Your coffee,' she announced.

'You've only brought three,' Hilda Meyer said. 'Where's yours?'

'You've guests. You don't want me.' She spread the cups and saucers and began to pour. 'I'm sorry I've been so long bringing it in.'

'That's all right. I'm sure there's a good reason, and besides we've been having a lesson in aesthetic appreciation from Mrs Turnbull.' Hilda nodded towards Linda.

Mrs Johnson drew herself up.

'They've found a body in the village.'

She allowed them a moment to gasp their shock, or ply her with immediate questions, but they disappointed her. The young women evinced mild interest by their facial expression, while the hostess, now graciously standing, handed round the biscuit-plate. No-one spoke.

With a shrug Nancy Johnson started again.

'It's Mrs Marshall,' she informed them.

'Erica Marshall?' Hilda asked, without confidence.

'Erica Marshall.' Mrs Johnson swung round to face Anna. 'She lives next door but one to your friend, Frank Norman.'

'Was it an accident? Or a heart attack? She can't be as old as all that.' Hilda now acted sociably, more excitedly, seeking information for her guests.

'Sixty-seven.' Nancy now made them wait. 'They say she was killed. Murdered.'

'Who are they?' Hilda asked, rather disdainfully.

'I had my information from Dorothy Lyle. She came up the drive to tell me, and knocked on the kitchen window. Quite out of order. She said, "I thought you and Mrs Meyer ought to hear. You both knew her well."'

'I'd hardly say "well",' Hilda murmured, but immediately changed her tone, and relaxing ordered Nancy to fetch in her own coffee before adding the fine detail. Mrs Johnson went out, having made her point, with shoulders back.

'Who is she?' Anna asked her mother.

'A widow. Her husband was some sort of engineer connected with one of the utility boards, electricity or gas. Smart little man. He retired a couple of years ago, and died.'

'And Mrs Marshall?'

'She joins everything. Always ready to give a hand. So they say.'

'Any family?'

'Two sons. Both away. Visit occasionally. Good jobs.'

'No enemies?'

Mrs Meyer shook her head dolefully.

'To think it took place in this village,' she said. 'And the poor woman was lying there while we sat here discussing where we should put our furniture.'

Nancy Johnson reappeared with her full cup of coffee. She rapidly occupied the free chair nearest to the door, and sipped as if she knew her place, was not prepared to interrupt the conversation of her betters.

'Come on,' Anna said, 'Nancy. Tell us all.'

'I know next to nothing. Another police car just went by as I was in the kitchen now getting my coffee. All I know is what I learnt from Dorothy Lyle. Second hand.' Having cleared the credibility or otherwise of her story, she continued. 'It's the milkman's day for being paid. He knocked at her door. No answer. That was unusual, because she's always up and about.'

'You get milk delivered in the village here, do you?' Linda asked out of the blue. Mrs Johnson's frown and body language showed that that question was not in order.

'We do. We're not the back of beyond. He knocked again. No answer. So he looked through the letter box. There she was, lying in the hall. He tried the door, but it was locked, so he ran round then to the neighbours, the Moores, and got them to ring 999. When the ambulance and police arrived, they found the back door unlocked. The milkman and Mr Moore hadn't tried there. There are no through-entries to the back. The only way is at Mr Norman's end.'

'And?' Anna.

'She was dead.'

'What time was this?'

'Just before eight. Mrs Lyle said she had been killed by an intruder. She must have interrupted him.'

'Last night?' Hilda.

'Or early this morning.'

'How does this Mrs Lyle know so much about it?' Anna asked.

'She has a cousin who lived in the house between the Marshalls and the Normans.' Mrs Johnson sniffed the air in superiority. 'The police when they question you pass on a certain amount of information.'

'I suppose the police surgeon and photographers have been?' Linda queried.

'I suppose so.' Mrs Johnson made the most of her knowledge or lack of it. 'They've taken the body away.'

'Did your Mrs Lyle's cousin hear anything?'

'That's odd. She did and she didn't. She heard some sort of commotion in the night. It must have been loud enough to wake her, but she can't pinpoint the time.'

'Screams? Or sounds of a blow?'

'I don't know.'

'Not enough to get her up?' Anna persisted.

'No. You'd be surprised at the noises one hears in a place like this in the small hours of the morning. Young people, men mostly, driving back late on Saturday and Sunday from the night-clubs in Beechnall. They're shouting and banging car doors and yodelling and emptying their bladders. Everything at the tops of their voices. One lot took the Leigh-Pearsons' front gate off, a heavy five-barred contraption, and laid it on the other side of the road. And it's no use complaining. Major Leigh-Pearson said the police as good as laughed in his face. He complained to the Chief Constable, but nothing improves.'

'And is this every weekend?' Linda asked.

'Of course not. But more often than we like.'

They settled again to their coffee, spoke casually of weather, health, the grinding of coffee beans. The talk was sporadic, forced, as if the murder had dissolved the social niceties. Each of the women tried to introduce a topic, but silence ensued after a costive sentence or two. Anna watched the others in their difficulties and wondered. After all nobody seemed to know the murdered Erica Marshall at all intimately. Anna made another effort. She directed her question at her mother, rather than Nancy.

'Is this the first murder you've had in the village?'

Hilda almost leapt from her chair.

'As far as I know. At least while we've been here. They found a corpse three or four years ago, up on Freestone Terrace, where this one took place, right outside Mrs Marshall's door.' No one asked the expected question. 'He was a stranger and had drunk a great deal. It was a cold night. They say he'd probably had had a heart attack and he fell in a wet ditch and died of hypothermia. I guess he was a tramp.'

'He was too well dressed for that,' Nancy contradicted.

'I don't remember. What was he?'

'He came from Yorkshire. Ilkley, I think.'

'But what was he doing here?' Linda this time.

'He'd be one of these car-people. He hadn't been in the local pubs, so it appeared. He must have got out for a call of nature and wandered off.'

'Didn't anyone look for him.'

'This village is pitch-dark in the middle of the night. And if they were drunk, they'd not stand much chance of finding him once he'd staggered off the main road and up toward the terrace. And nobody heard anybody calling out.'

'Who found him?'

'Mr Norman. Frank Norman.'

'He wasn't murdered.'

'No.' Both Hilda Meyer and Nancy Johnson answered together. Their word formed a sort of subdued chord. Both looked at the other. 'Natural causes,' Mrs Johnson answered the conclusion.

'And it didn't come out who he was?' Anna asked.

'Oh, yes. It was in the papers. Name and address. But we didn't know him.'

'What's the name of that woman who clips cuttings out of the newspapers if they make any reference to the village?' Hilda asked.

'Elsie Orange,' Nancy, at once. They all giggled at the name. Anna glanced at her watch, and at Linda, said they must go. The meeting broke up just as contact between the women had been established.

VII

Anna kept close contact with Linda.

At the beginning of Terry's illness Colin had called in on his sister-in-law, though he only twice visited his brother in hospital, but once Terence was back at home, Colin seemed to expect a bulletin from Anna most evenings. She frequently 'phoned or occasionally drove over to Templeton Avenue.

'Linda's a pretty efficient sort of woman,' Colin warned, 'but we mustn't allow her to think we've left her all on her own.'

'She might not want us to interfere. She's occupied nowadays.'

'Then she can say so.'

'Has she no contact with her own family?' Anna asked.

'I don't know. Her parents are still alive. I think they live somewhere on the East Coast. I'm not sure.'

Anna could not make out Linda's attitude to her. The woman appeared grateful for the frequent 'phone calls, even said she looked forward to them, but seemed stiffer, slightly more aggressive or resentful whenever they met. She would come over on Anna's insistence, but declined proffered help.

'I'm quite all right,' she insisted. 'We're managing. I'll tell you if we want anything.'

One morning in early November Anna called in on her sister-in-law by prior arrangement. The day was exceptionally mild and the sun bright, so that as they took their usual walk round the garden at a leisurely pace, Anna sat herself down in the Grecian temple, though that seemed not to suit Linda.

'Don't go in there. It's far too cold.'

Linda stood on the steps, one hand on a pillar, as if posing for a photograph. Anna scuttled up and out, then faced her sister-in-law.

'I'm worried about Terence,' Linda said. The set face and use of the full name suggested seriousness. 'He's getting better physically, so quickly in fact that I'm not sure the stroke was as serious as we thought. He can drive now, and he eats and sleeps as well as ever he did.'

84

'What's the trouble?' Anna asked.

'His work. He's lost all interest in it. He goes off, not very early, though that's sensible, three or four days a week, but, that's where it stops.'

'Isn't it what you wanted?'

'Yes. But he's not the same man. That bothers me. His work meant everything. He was dedicated. Now he trots out to it, or stops in, as if one was as good as the other.'

'Why don't you put it to him?'

'Do you think I haven't? And all he answers is that he's taking it steady according to his doctor's instructions.'

'And why aren't you satisfied with that?'

'It doesn't seem like him. That's not the Terry Turnbull I married. There's something changed for the worse.'

'Isn't that the result of a serious illness? He's lost confidence. He's not sure that he won't bring on another stroke or worse by throwing himself into his work as he used to.'

'Do you think Colin would look into the books sometime?'

'Is there something wrong there?'

'I've no idea. I'd just like to find out.'

'I'll ask him. He's very busy now, but I'll put it to him.'

Anna reported the conversation to her husband who listened with an expression of amusement.

'It's her: Linda. She doesn't like change. Rather as Terry doesn't. But he's been knocked back by his stroke. As far as the business is concerned my guess is that they're doing well enough. It's not a great time for selling things, but his staff seem pretty efficient to me. He won't be losing money.'

'Will you look at their accounts?'

'I can't just barge in and demand to see the books. But you can tell Linda that if she can get Terry to agree, I'll do it. It might be another test for them. If he says "No" and gets stroppy, well . . .'

'Well, what?'

'It might show he's still interested. Or the other way about. Tell her to ask him, and if he says "Yes", I'll do it.'

'You don't usually do his audits?'

'No. I don't do much myself by way of accountancy these days. It's done by others. Under Fred Stokes's eye.'

The upshot of this was that when Colin looked into the accounts of his brothers' shops he reported favourably. He drew attention to certain anomalies, all fairly small but worth investigating.

Linda thanked both Colin and Anna, by letter and in person.

'Has it done any good?' Colin asked her.

'He was quite interested in what you said, almost as if he expected something to be wrong. He said they were all a bit concerned by this audit, and you frightened one or two.'

'I threw my weight about, and had a very sharp young chap from Meyer, Turnbull and Stokes with me. He wouldn't miss much. It wasn't a big job. Accounts were in good order to say they'd had the audit suddenly sprung on them.'

Terry, it appeared, continued as he had, with three or four days a week at work. He had now started to go out to instal or repair equipment. The manager at the main shop said he was just as efficient and as quick with his hands as before his illness.

'That's satisfactory, then,' Colin said. 'We'd better leave it there.'

Anna could see, after a week or two, that Linda was by no means reassured. When she questioned her sister-in-law Linda threw her arms about and claimed that the fault, if faults there were, lay with her.

'Perhaps it's the time of life,' she groused. 'I'm within three years of fifty.'

'Do you never think of taking a full-time job?' Anna asked.

'Doing what? Terry doesn't want me in the shop. If he did, I should have to learn it all from scratch. And as to teaching, well, I don't like the sound of what I hear. And that's if they'd take me on after this long gap. I do a bit at night school with computers.'

'Colin's always inquiring after you. What am I to tell him?'

'That I can cope.'

'But can you?'

'Oh, dear. Quite an interrogation.'

'I'm sorry. But Colin seems pretty determined to find out how you're shaping. And I'm the one he asks.'

'Why is he so interested?'

Was Linda thus prying to find out if Anna knew about her affair with Colin?

'Since he did that audit he wants to know how things are progressing.'

'They're different men,' Linda said. 'Terry's worked hard all his life, and yet he's nothing like as successful as Colin. He regrets now that he never went to the university. There was a big difference in ages, thirteen years, and I guess that when Terry was at school his parents hadn't the money to consider higher education for him. They'd made sacrifices enough sending him to the grammar school. When Colin's turn came things were easier. Not least because Terry was bringing in some income.'

'Is that so?'

'So I gather from things he's said.'

'You knew Colin before Terry, didn't you?'

'We were in the same class in the junior school. We didn't live too far away from his parents.'

'And what was he like?'

'As a small boy? Bright. Very sharp. I think some of the teachers feared him.'

'Was he a nuisance, then?'

'Not in that sense. He'd be full of good suggestions. And often be proved right when they were wrong.'

'And were you childhood sweethearts?'

'No, not as far as I recall.'

'There was an interval, then.'

'Yes, my parents moved away. In any case Colin went to the boys' grammar school. I trained as a teacher in Lincoln, and then accepted a post back here. And almost immediately I met Terry.'

'Did you know him before?'

'I knew who he was, but he was a lot older than I was, and seemed a grown-up man to me.'

'And how did you meet?'

'At a theatrical group. He was doing some voluntary electrical work at nights when I was there rehearsing.'

'I never knew any of this before.'

'Well, that's not surprising. We've hardly talked to each other. You and I hadn't much in common. You didn't make your appearance in Colin's life till later, after Henry was born. We've met at family gatherings, and though there was once talk of a holiday together, somebody knocked that on the head. And we didn't seem to run across each other. I think,' Linda proceeded cautiously, 'there was some bad blood at one point between Terry and Colin.'

'I didn't know that, either.'

'No. I don't know what the cause was, but it blew over. Especially after you and Colin were married. That's if I remember properly.' Linda shook her head. 'I quite like talking to you now. You sound like a human being. That's rude, isn't it?'

87

'I know what you mean.'

'Colin takes some holding down, doesn't he? That's a full-time job.'

'Not really. He's his own man. If he's doing something he considers important, that'll take precedence over everything else.'

'And you don't mind?'

'I've got used to it. I do what I want to do. On the rare occasions when we clash, I am angry, like anybody else, but I've learnt that my best policy's to keep my mouth shut.'

'Does he realise you're annoyed?'

'I guess so, but he's so intent on what he's about that he doesn't care. Haven't you found him like that?'

Linda frowned as if she found difficulty in answering.

'I don't know him well enough.' She murmured to herself. 'It was only recently when Terry wanted to borrow money from him that we made anything like real contact. You knew about that?'

'Borrowing money? No. Was there some financial trouble?'

'Trouble. Not at all. Terry wanted to expand the business, and that meant he'd have to lay his hands straight off on the necessary cash. He could have borrowed it easily enough, from the usual sources. He'd the collateral. But he thought he'd try the family first. Colin can be very generous when he feels like it. And perhaps Terry thought Col might join in, in some way, insist on shares or whatever. That would have made Terry much more comfortable to have a rich man as part of his company. Colin never mentioned this to you?'

'No, not a word.'

Linda shook her head.

'What seems like life or death to one man is not even worth a quick mention to another.'

'This wasn't life or death, was it?' Anna inquired.

'No. But it was a fairly radical project, and it would worry Terry.'

'That wasn't the cause of his stroke?'

'No, not really. Contributory, perhaps, in a minor way. Col lent him the money straight off. No ifs or buts. And I don't imagine the thought of paying back caused him any great stress. He said to me that he'd easily pay off the whole and be in profit inside two years. Not that I understand money. From what Terry says sometimes it pays you to remain in debt. I was brought up to believe you didn't buy anything unless you had the money to put down for it'

'Including a mortgage on your house?' Anna queried.

'That was the one exception.'

They had walked three times round the garden, and returned to the kitchen.

'It's warmer in here,' Linda said. 'Can I make you more coffee?'

Anna refused, said she must go, that she and Colin were off to a dinner in London that evening. 'Neither of us likes such functions, really, but I think Colin was flattered to be invited. He's friendly with the master of this gild. They spelt it without a "u".'

Linda asked a further question or two, but Anna's replies were vague. They parted, pleased with each other.

Anna had hardly been home for ten minutes when Nancy Johnson telephoned from Ashby.

'I'm sorry to bother you, but I'm rather worried about Frank Norman,' she began.

'What's wrong?'

'It's this robbery, this murder.'

'Was he quite friendly with the lady?'

'Not as far as I know. He keeps himself to himself, as they say. But it's affected his nerves. So badly in fact that he's visited the doctor's surgery about it.' Nancy pulled a sour face. 'Now I got to know about this because the doctor rang your mother to ask if there was anybody who'd keep an eye on him.' Again the same tart expression. 'That shows the doctor must have taken it seriously.'

'And?'

'Your mother mentioned me. I said that you knew him quite well, and that I'd get in touch with you once I'd been to see for myself.'

'I talked to my mother this morning' Anna said. 'But she made no mention of him.'

'Your mother's a trifle forgetful. Anyway, the upshot of all this was that I went in to see him. I made some excuse. I took him a couple of pots of thick cut marmalade I'd made. I know he likes that, and I said I'd never get through the amount I'd made.'

'And how did he seem?'

'Well, much as ever. At least, at first. Grumpy, mumbling to himself. I brought the subject round in time to this Marshall business. He looked suspicious at first, but he said a few things. In fact he was quite eloquent before he'd finished.'

'About what?'

'The state of the world, and Ashby. In his view the police weren't taking this as seriously as they might.'

'Has he any theories, then?'

'No. Not as far as I could make out. But the police haven't arrested anybody, and he thinks it's about time they had.'

'And you want me to go in to hear all this.'

'I do. And so does your mother. Our doctor, George Graham, is a very laid-back young man. And doesn't take very easily to interference from lay people. He has no time for counsellors. But he was worried enough to 'phone your mother.'

'I'll go.'

'Thank you. It'll set your mother's mind at rest.' Nancy added a word or two about village affairs before she rang off.

Anna wisely rang Norman.

'I'll call in tomorrow to see you,' she announced.

'Why?'

'That's rude. I've not visited you for some time, so I think it might not be amiss if I called in to check up on you.'

'To inspect, assess and report, as they used to say.'

'Well, you're having neighbours murdered, I hear.'

'Mrs Marshall. Yes. Didn't know her very well. She wore yellow knickers, quite unsuitable for a woman of her age.'

'How do you know that?'

'I've seen them on the clothes line.'

'She might have been helping someone out with their washing,' Anna objected.

'And she might not. They made regular appearances.'

'She might well have been doing this friend's washing week after week. And besides, I'm shocked to think you old gentlemen in the villages go round scrutinising ladies' underwear on clothes-lines.'

'What else is there to do?' he asked, but he immediately sounded more cheerful.

When next morning she called, his house was bright in autumn sunshine, every corner neat. She could see no dust, and in the front-room they occupied the three books he'd been reading were squared up on a gleaming table. Next to them lay the day's paper neatly refolded at the crossword puzzle. To judge, upside down, he'd made fair progress with it this last hour.

They argued whether they needed coffee; she convinced him they did not. He took to his arm-chair disgruntled, squinting at her.

'Now what can I do for you?' he asked.

'First of all, tell me how you are.'

'Old. I don't like it. My knees creak. I can't remember things. One of the advantages of being a schoolmaster was that I had a structured life, with a set order each day. I knew exactly what I'd be doing at ten-fifteen on Thursday morning. Now I've all day to myself, and nothing to do.'

'The garden?'

'I have a man in. I manage a bit for myself. We're beginning to clear up for the winter. But that depends on the weather. I try to have a rota for the main household jobs.'

'You get help with that?'

'Yes. And the village gossip. But I have to clear up before my home-help appears.'

'Is she good?'

'Not bad. Enthusiastic, energetic, but not very thorough.'

They laughed together. Norman clapped his palms down on his chair-arms.

'And what does she say about the murder?' Anna asked.

'Plenty, but nothing worth hearing, because she knows nothing. After all the initial excitement, the police give us no more information. They don't know anything. Nobody's been arrested, never mind charged.'

'Was it some burglar?'

'That's the common theory. She heard him, got out of bed, went downstairs, interrupted him.

'You've some alternative theory?'

'No. That seems to fit in with the known facts.'

'Are there any burglars in the village? Living here, I mean?'

'Not that I know. We have our quota of petty crime, break-ins, vandalism. We even had a raid on the post office in broad daylight a few months back.'

'And did they catch the criminals?'

'Not to the best of my knowledge. The police are too far flung. The thieves are half-way out of the county before the patrol car arrives.'

'So you're afraid?' she asked.

'Of what?'

'You feel vulnerable, unprotected?'

Frank Norman rubbed his chin.

'Villages are like towns now in that we find an element of criminal behaviour. People get drunk, or take drugs, and do the uncivilised things that are the results of this. The first week I came to this house fifty-odd years ago there was a robbery at the end of the terrace. We never found out who was responsible. Small-time crooks nowadays are after spare cash or small objects that they can sell off in the pubs or car-boot sales. A town offers more opportunities. A couple of suburban streets will have as many houses as this village.'

'So you don't feel ill-at-ease here?'

'I feel ill-at-ease, as you put it, because of my age, infirmities, incapacities, lack of opportunity.'

'But not because you might be murdered.'

He laughed until his laughter exploded into a bout of phlegmy coughing.

'No I don't go to bed at night afraid for my life. Nor do I take a loaded shot gun with me. That's the stuff of books and films. I was reading a review of a book, a novel, about a man who lived in the country. He milked his cows; he had once to call in the vet; he had to struggle on with the 'flu; his wife had a hysterectomy; he worried about the present state of farming; his only son won a place in the town grammar school, ten miles away. The reviewer praised his accuracy, spoke favourably of his prose, called it low-temperature poetry, but asked in the end what was it all for. He found it dull.'

'And you didn't?'

'I did not. The man knew what he was talking about, varied the action from page-to-page and chapter-to-chapter, raised ideas I hadn't considered myself so that I felt at the end of the book (I'd borrowed it from the library; I'd put its title down at the back of my diary and made them get it for me; it took them long enough), that I knew this man, this small tenant-farmer.'

'And?'

'The reviewer wanted something more. Murder, and bestiality, paedophiles, paederasts, better word, transvestites, AIDS, outlandish diseases, decapitations. I'm only guessing, of course. I have a suspicion that if the writer had set the same dull stuff in the Dordogne and Tuscany or Rhodesia, Zimbabwe, if that's what they call it now, it would have been more acceptable, whereas I felt privileged to share or empathise with the not very out of the ordinary life of the sort of man I'll see next time I walk out of the village. Of course, it was well-written, and that would be as far from our local farmers' capabilities as doing murder or committing bigamy, but it was, with its ups and downs, its little miseries and griefs and pleasures, much like our, my younger life.'

'Well, you know what that's like. You don't need to read it from a book.'

'If it was well described, set into a shape that makes me feel it more poignantly. You know, the ancient builders knew practically about the square on the hypotenuse of a right-angled triangle being equal to the sum of the squares on the other two sides. They used it every day of the week in their work. But Pythagoras proved logically that it would always be the case. And some of us not only are pleased to know that in geometry of this sort it will be so without exception, but we take real pleasure in Pythagoras's use of logic. It's satisfying; no, it's beautiful.'

'QED,' she said, sarcastically.

'But, you, Mrs Turnbull, you want the unusual case, not the humdrum everyday. I know, I know the analogy is not strict. But you came to see me because that poor woman got herself killed, and you might pick up some gory details, didn't you? Admit it now.'

'I came here to see whether the murder, gory or otherwise, had done you any harm.'

'Oh, thank you.'

'Don't you believe me?' She laughed with the question, softening it.

'As I get older my understanding of human motivation grows less. You feel sorry for me, mouldering away here all on my own, but suppose you found me up here terrified and at my wit's end, what could you do?'

'Daddy would speak to the Chief Constable or the Lord Lieutenant. Colin knows two people, both articulate and youngish, on the police committee. There'd be questions asked in the right places.'

'It would be too late if my nerve had gone.'

'Daddy would chase your doctor. Or Mummy. She'd make things hum. And besides all these inquiries and this bullying would help to make sure that nothing similar happened in future.'

'And you approve of influence of this sort.'

'It's not fair, but that's the world. If you have influential friends you'd be a fool not to use them.'

'I shall be quite safe in future, then?' Frank Norman smiled grimly.

'Safer.' She comically stressed the second syllable.

'You've no means to hand to keep death at bay?'

'Not this morning, no. No, sir.'

'You do me a great power of good. Mrs Marshall's murder made me think that here I was, on my own, at the mercy of criminal elements or diseases or even of my own mind. But in you come, bright as a button, and I realise once again that the sun's shining this morning and that I can enjoy it.'

'Let's walk round the garden, then, because I can't stay for much longer.'

Norman took off his carpet-slippers and struggled to push his feet into a pair of polished shoes standing ready by his chair. His exertions to tie the laces troubled her, but she did not offer to help. At last, scarlet-faced and panting, he sat up, declaring himself ready. In the hall he dragged on a baggy, leather-elbowed, old schoolmaster's sports coat. When he taught her he wore only three-piece suits.

Deep in the garden he pointed out recent acquisitions. Though still breathless, he talked.

'When you get old,' he said, 'you seem on the edge of things. When I was younger I didn't mind that, and, in fact, thought it was what I wanted. I could do just as I liked. Now I'm so far away from what's happening I feel shocked.'

'In what way?'

'The newspapers talk about men, whom I consider young and vigorous, as though they are too old to carry this appointment or that responsibility. And events that I remember clearly are spoken, written about as though they're ancient history. It's troubling.'

'Why?'

'It's not the thought of its ending before too long, provided the process is comfortable, it's the feeling that I no longer belong here. I'm nearly incapable. The phrase I'd use most of myself is "a bit". That's all I can manage. In every department of life.'

'We are pessimistic this morning.'

'No. This is my cheerful mood. If I felt down I'd sit there glowering and saying not a word. You've done me good. I shall be humming to myself, and try to puzzle out why a pretty, rich, busy, young woman wastes her time on me.'

They walked on. She had spent longer with the old man than she had expected. She saw little difference in him; less incisive, slower of movement and speech he still seemed the same figure of quiet authority she had always known. He would be disturbed by his neighbour's death as would any normal person, whatever the age, but he'd sit it out, learn to live with trouble, recover his equilibrium by staring disaster straight in the face. She reported as much to her mother and to Nancy Johnson.

VIII

'Terry's decided to retire,' Colin Turnbull announced over dinner.

'How do you know?' Anna asked, slightly annoyed that her husband had kept the information back until they were well advanced on their main course. He held his wine up to the light.

'He told me so himself.'

Outside, rain rattled on the windows. The late November night blew boisterous. Colin had settled happily to his meal.

'Oh, come on. Let's hear some detail.'

'Well, nothing is definitely decided yet, but he's had a good offer.'

'To buy him out?'

'Exactly. Lincoln Electronics. They're a large firm, and expanding.'

'From Lincoln, Lincolnshire?'

'They may have been originally. I thought they were American, so perhaps it's President Lincoln. I don't know. I only spoke to Terry this afternoon, and we hadn't long. He wasn't altogether sure of their original base, but they seemed in a hurry to take over. He was dealing with somebody in London. But you know him; he's not very forthcoming until it's cut and dried.'

'Has he asked you to look into the offer?'

'Yes. If I had time. He asked me. Everyone said it was a good deal. For him.'

'Who's everybody?'

'His solicitor, his accountant. The one or two shareholders. But what he wonders is whether he'll have enough to live on.'

'And will he?'

'I'd think so. And they have, moreover, to sweeten his pill offered him a kind of consultancy. He's a whizz, no doubt, when it comes to this sort of thing, or the practicalities of it, and he'll, if he wishes, be able to supervise installations and some of the larger alterations that they'll want to make. Besides, Linda earns quite well now on her computers.'

'Why don't this Lincoln firm just set up their own shops? Advertise? Make a splash all over the papers or the TV?'

'Presumably they think his goodwill is worth buying. I'm no sort of expert in their field, but presumably they'll know what they're about. They're a big concern, and can easily afford to swallow up Terry and his like, but sometimes they think it's advantageous for a start to keep up local connections.'

'Are you a shareholder?'

'To a very small extent. We shall make a penny or two if he sells. Enough to decorate your Ascot hat next summer.'

'You're taking me,then?'

He nodded, grinning.

'And he seems keen?'

'I wouldn't say that. He hopes he's sensible and knows that he's lucky to have had such an offer at this time. But he realises that his real work will be over and done with.'

'He's sixty. Most people are only too ready to retire at that age, and enjoy a few years of leisure while they're in good health.'

'I'm not so sure. Even in these days, when everybody is supposed to be stressed out of their minds by economic crises or political shifts, you'd be surprised how many people still want to hang on to their work. It's always been important to them; it's given them their status, their place in society and it's a constant test of their present fitness and intelligence. They suspect their powers are diminishing, but if they can keep up at their work with the younger men, then they're reassured.'

'Does this apply to jobs at factory-benches, or driving buses, or typing and tapping away at computers?'

'I don't know. But I wouldn't be surprised. I'm speaking of people I know.'

They ate together now for a thoughtful period of silence. Anna prepared her next question, weighing its implications. She asked it quietly, without hurry.

'Do you ever think of retiring?'

'I'm forty-seven. With plenty of energy left.'

Again the silence fell. Colin waved the vegetable-dish in invitation in her direction before he helped himself.

'The answer is "No". Why?' he sounded suspicious.

'I just wondered.'

'Come on. You must have reasons for asking.'

'To pass the time. To make you talk.' Anna would not be bullied.

Colin raised his serviette to his lips as if he needed to clean them for this conversation.

'I just about belong,' he said, 'to a generation who reached the top of its professions at my age, late-forties, early-fifties. Then these people, oldies, wrinklies did their creative work, at that age, altered the firm or the department, often radically. Whether it would have been better if they'd got to positions of power earlier is arguable. But on the whole that was the situation, and this tempered expectations all round. You didn't become senior partner until you were nearly fifty and you waited, impatiently for all I know, for that and all it meant. I've been lucky myself, and reached my objectives early, but that hasn't dimmed my ambition any more than it did those of our ancient forerunners with their bowler hats and silver moustaches. They made changes, considerable in some cases when their time came. My hat is still in the ring.'

'But it's not a bowler?'

'You should thank God it's not.' Again he paused as if to regain seriousness after their feeble witticisms. She noticed how handsome he was. He breathed deeply in. 'How do you think Linda will take Terry's retirement?'

'It's what she's alleged to want, but I guess it will depend on the form his retirement takes. If he's at home under her feet all day, she'll not take kindly to that. And will they want to change houses? Settle by the seaside? Henry's in London now making his way in the world. I think it was you who told me that Terry was disappointed that the boy hadn't followed him into the business. Linda principally pressed for him to go to university.'

'Is he doing well?' Colin demanded, carefully laying knife and fork on his empty plate. 'He's an architect, isn't he?'

'He's twenty-two or -three. Has a degree in architecture and is reparing for the RIBA examinations. He is working in an office in London. A quiet boy, happy as a king grubbing about in his books. He's thinking of doing a Master's degree in due course. He's very like his father in many ways, or so Linda claims.'

'Have you seen anything of her?'

'Not this week.'

'Do I detect a note of irony?'

Anna felt pleased by these exchanges in that only months before they were unusual. Colin now almost made speeches. He hadn't exactly fished notes out of his pocket, but there had been more than a vestige of rehearsal. He had known she'd ask questions, and had prepared, however perfunctorily, to answer her. As he grew older he became more of a human being, aware of his errors, his dependency on others. When he was younger he'd run through fire, ignoring the world, certain of his objectives. That was why, she imagined he'd done so well so early. Even her father had been impressed. Kuno Meyer was no fool, but he had seen in his son-in-law a cleverness, a boldness, a power of both thought and action that put Colin out of the range of his contemporaries. He had once surprised his daughter by applying the term 'genius' to Colin. When she had jibbed at the word, he defended his usage. 'Outstanding' is nowhere near it. 'And for all your ifs and buts, young woman, one can be a genius at handling money as at music or cosmology.' Her father had looked down his nose at her, mock-seriously, two jokers together.

A day or two later her father telephoned her, another surprise. When she visited Ashby it was not always certain that she'd see Kuno for more than a few minutes as he'd be out in his garden or wood, working, 'not fit to come and trample mud all over the dining-room carpet.' He loved her, and admired her, of that she was sure, but he made no public show of these feelings.

'It's your Mr Norman,' he said, after the usual inquiries after health.

'Oh?'

'Your mother's been on to me. He's had a fall, at home, nothing very serious. The doctors have patched him up, but he's said to be very depressed.'

'Who says so?'

'Your mother and Nancy Johnson. I don't often see him. He's not the sort who throws his weight about in the village. He doesn't attend meetings as a rule, so I only meet him by chance, in the street. And as I'm usually in a car this means we don't exchange much beyond a quick wave. But on the rare occasions we have stopped for a chat, he's always impressed me favourably. He lives on his own and has done so for some years now. Since his wife's death, I believe. He's friendly enough with neighbours, but doesn't in any way depend on them. He's in good health for his age. He can occupy himself with his garden and his books and his competitions. Whenever I ask his advice about village affairs he seems to know what's happening and offers reasonable opinions.'

'That is: You agree with him?'

'No more; no less. He has all his marbles, and keeps himself alert.'

There followed silence. Anna had become used to the pauses both with her father, and, more frequently, with her husband. Neither would risk a half-thought-out argument on her. She was prepared to wait.

'But now he's very down. Nancy Johnson thinks it may be a result of the death of this Mrs Marshall. The police, I heard this morning, have pulled somebody in for questioning. In Swansea. He's a distant relative. So it looks as if it wasn't a casual burglar, but somebody who had called, was perhaps expected.'

'I've seen none of this in the papers.'

'No. I ran across the local Inspector. The Welsh police will be sending him up here for questioning.'

'So there's no need for him to be afraid of casual criminal attacks?'

'I don't know that he is. Here's a woman, younger than he is, apparently in good health. Next time he hears of her, she's dead. This triggers off his depression. It's not what I would have expected of him. I thought he'd take it in his stride.'

'"This is a long preamble of a tale"', she said. 'For you.'

'Who said that?'

'Chaucer. Or his Friar. After the wife of Bath's Prologue.'

'Chaucer, eh? Is that one of your quotations? Yes. Very good.'

'What do you want me to do?'

'I don't exactly know. Your mother says you occasionally call in to see him, have recently done so. But I'm not even sure that he's at home. I have the impression that he was so low that he couldn't look after himself, even with the aid of district nurses and so on. Is that possible these days? From what I hear or read in *The Times* wards are crowded. They'd put him into a nursing-home, wouldn't they? The trouble with me, Anna, now I'm old, is that I don't properly listen to what people try to convey to me.'

'So?'

'So.' He did not see a way out of his difficulty.

'I tell you what. When I call in on Sunday I'll nip across. But before that just ask Nancy Johnson to make inquiries, so that I don't put my foot in it.'

'That will suit her down to the ground. Both of them.'

Kuno cackled and rang off. Slightly worried, she 'phoned, then

100

called round on Linda, who was busy in her kitchen stencilling patterns on small wooden boxes.

'Christmas presents,' she smiled. 'All I've time for these days.'

'For whom?'

'I've a friend who visits old ladies in a nursing home. And they're fond of these. They keep their things in them.'

'What things?'

'Handkerchiefs, letters, bits and bobs, knick-knacks. I put in each one a little silk cachet of lavender and a lace-edged hanky.'

'You make both?'

'Yes. I need to be careful. Each box must have its own particular design, because the old dears fight like cats over ownership. You talk about civil war.'

'Do you make the boxes?'

'No. I think I could, but Terry gets some old chap he knows to do them. He's very good. Just look.' She lifted down a finished object. 'Dove-tail joints. Smooth. I think I'm spoiling them with my stencils. They'd be better stained and polished; in fact, we tried them like that one year, but they weren't popular. "Dull." "Can't tell one from the other." That's the sort of comment I got. They need something bright, eye-catching. That's the story.'

'Do you go along for the presentation?'

'If I can find time.'

'How many do you make?'

'A dozen or so, usually. It varies. We need only four this year.' Linda shook her head. 'We only present these to the new girls.'

'And the old residents?'

'Two hankies and lavender.'

'But if you do a dozen?'

'Actually I ordered only eight. Two last year. I save what I have left over. I like to be on the safe side. Old Tom Shaw who makes them isn't getting any younger.'

'How many in the cupboard now, then?'

'Twelve. I counted them. I needn't have done any extra, but I want to keep my hand in. I'm getting very like the old dears. Everything by habit. And making boxes in November to December is my line. They prefer the bright colours. Is that because their eyes are failing? And the presentation is a kind of initiation ceremony. They feel that they're not properly accepted, senior members of the society. It's odd how we need these rites to let us know exactly where we stand.'

'Has anybody stayed so long in the home that she needed another box?'

'It's happened only once. One of the oldest had put her box by the open window and then a cleaning woman knocked it out. How she did it, God knows. It would have taken quite a complicated movement, but did it she did and by chance just as the provisions lorry backed into the yard. Its wheel, a big double thing, went over it and splintered it. There was uproar. The old dear, Sarah Smith, played Hanover. She screamed and cried and stood up out of her chair, something she hadn't done on her own for months.'

'Were you there for this performance?'

'No.'

'Matron and at least three of the inmates told me about it. One of them said it was like an opera. Went on for days. I said I'd bring a new one in at once; I had these spare ones in the cupboard. But do you know that didn't suit. Ma Smith complained that it wasn't such a good pattern as the old one. "Less tasteful," she grumbled. And some of the rest said it wasn't right to give her a new one straight away. Though it was not her fault in the first place, she should wait until Christmas time. It's a good job she didn't try, because she died in the November. All this took place in August. That's why the wretched window was open. And some of them groused because I'd put in a new sachet and a handkerchief. It wasn't fair. She'd had more than her rightful due. When I said it made up for the hassle, a compensation for her pain at the loss, one of them, I thought she was a friend of the Smith's, said, "If that's all she has to bear, then she should be thankful and put up with it."'

They laughed together.

'What a drama,' Anna said. 'But perhaps it won't be long before we're as bad as they are.'

'Well. You be careful. Do you know what Terry said?'

'Tell me.'

'He said, "Now I'm about to retire I reckon I've qualified for one of your celebrated Christmas boxes."'

'Did you ask him what he'd do with the lace handkerchief?'

They talked about Terry's retirement. Linda declared herself as apprehensive as her husband. She spoke at length, boringly repeating her banalities. In the end Anna suggested that they drove out to Ashby to call on Frank Norman. Linda, three years older than Anna, had also been taught by Norman.

'He didn't seem the sort of man to go off his head. Not when he taught me. Not that he'll remember me. I wasn't one of his star-pupils at mathematics.'

The run out to Ashby was pleasant, alight with reddish, early-winter sun. They drew into the side at the top of a hill and looked down towards a large copse.

'I often stop here,' Anna explained. 'I even get out, the view is so good.'

Linda nodded, then pointed, portentously towards the wood.

'That's where I lost my virginity,' she said.

Anna had not expected this, did not know what tone she should adopt in her reply.

'Worse places,' she said, lugubriously.

Now it was Linda's turn to show surprise.

'I shan't forget it,' she answered mulishly.

'No.'

This snippet of conversation seemed to Anna to be typical of their exchanges. Neither knew nor quite liked the other, so that they were constantly on guard. Now and then one or the other let slip some confidence, mainly Linda, though her companion was never sure whether these secrets were revealed as bait.

'Shall we leave this hallowed ground?' Anna said, switching on the engine. The rest of the journey to Ashby was completed comfortably enough, with occasional flat sentences about the road, a recent fatal accident there, an anecdote from Anna about Frank Norman's one awkward attempt at humour.

'Did you laugh?' Linda asked.

'I did my best.'

'Creep.'

They parked on the road below Norman's house, marched up smartly, rang his door-bell three times.

'Not at home,' Linda said, finally.

'There's a way round the back, I think.' Anna rang for the last time, at ludicrous length, before they went gingerly by the side of the house, as if they were trespassing. Anna rattled the knocker. The two women stood with their backs to the house.

'These gardens begin to look dreary,' Linda ventured.

'But neat. At least this one is. And there's a rose in bloom.'

'Poor thing. You see them out at Christmas these days or New Year. Roses are summer-flowers.'

Anna banged another tattoo on the knocker.

'That should wake the dead,' she muttered, showing her teeth. It roused the next door neighbour, who peered out suspiciously.

'Who is it you want?' she inquired. Anna answered her.

'He's not at home. He's in hospital or something of the sort. His son has been over. I thought it was perhaps him you wanted.'

'Which son is that?'

'The one who lives in London.'

'They both do.'

'Uh.'

'You don't know Mr Norman's present whereabouts?'

'No, I don't.'

'Have you any idea who'd know? Would Mrs Johnson, do you think?'

'She might. If she's at home. It's possible she's at the manor house. Mr and Mrs Meyer are away.'

'I know. I'm their daughter.'

It could not be said that this information did not impress the woman, for her face grew grimmer. She thinned her lips as if she struggled with her doubts.

'I didn't recognise you.' Grudgingly.

'Have you heard how Mr Norman is?' Anna asked.

'No. He's one like me, keeps himself to himself. I didn't know he was poorly.'

'I see.' Anna took a card from her bag. 'Here's my name and address. Perhaps if you hear anything you'd be kind enough to ring me.'

The woman screwed her eyes to read the card.

'I haven't got my glasses on,' she countered. She held herself upright by the door post, as if the demand was too great for her. 'And I haven't got a 'phone.'

'Thank you very much,' Anna answered. 'Your name is?'

'Bott. Mrs Bott.'

'Thank you. Goodbye.'

The visitors turned away. As they rounded the corner of the terrace they glimpsed Mrs Bott still at her back-door, left forearm upwards on the door post. On the front side of the houses they paused again. Linda seemed interested in the buildings.

'They look more like part of a suburban street. I wonder who perched them up on the hill there. What are they? Late Victorian? Edwardian?'

'There's a date on them. 1903, I think. They're good houses, well-built, with large rooms.'

'They're not estate houses, then?'

'Not for farm labourers, no. I guess that some speculative builder put them up for middle-class workers in Beechnall.'

'How would they get to town? There were no cars.'

'No, but the railway station's only just over a mile away. They'd walk that, or perhaps cycle if they were young. A mile morning and night was nothing to people then.'

'But if the weather was bad?'

'They dressed for it. Raincoats, umbrellas, galoshes.'

'And there were sufficient trains?'

'I guess so. More than now.'

'You don't hear much of the trains from up here?'

'No. The line's low down in the river-valley.'

'Did Mr Norman use the train?'

'Probably when he first came to live out here. That would be after the Second War, but it wasn't long before he invested in a car. Nowadays the roads are so crowded he'd probably be better advised to use the train. He could park all day on the station field if he couldn't be bothered to walk.'

They arrived at Nancy Johnson's cottage, and twice rapped the lion-headed knocker without result.

'Our unlucky day,' Anna said. 'Let's try the manor house.'

'This is a gorgeous little place,' Linda said, as she closed the front garden gate.

'I bet it's damp,' Anna gloomed. 'You'd need to have the central heating on all the year round to keep it aired and dry.'

They parked behind the manor house, tried the bell there.

'Third time lucky,' Linda said cheerfully. She was enjoying her frustrating trip.

'Don't depend on it,' Anna answered. 'I should have brought my keys.'

'Isn't it on your key-ring?'

'Oh, no. Not for this place. It's a whole bunch which daddy insisted I had. He also insisted I didn't label them in case I lost them and they fell into the wrong hands.'

Nancy Johnson opened the door, expressed her pleasure at seeing Anna, was introduced to Linda. Anna had halted just inside the hall.

'We were chasing Frank Norman,' she said. 'We'd heard he was quite ill. There was no-one in. The neighbour, a Mrs Bott, knew nothing but referred us to you. We drove down to your place, then back here.'

'Oh, Bott. Beatie Bott. She'd tell you nothing, even if she knew something, which is doubtful. The woman on the other side would have been better.'

'What's wrong with him?'

'He's depressed. He had a kind of 'flu, and followed that with a sort of seizure. The doctor got in touch with his eldest son; he came up. And they put him into hospital. Now I think he's in a nursing home.'

'For good?'

'That I don't know. I guess not. They gave him a thorough examination because of this stroke or seizure or whatever, and then they transferred him to a nursing home.'

'Have you been to see him?'

'No. I don't know that I'd be welcome.'

'So you don't know how he is?'

'Not really.' Nancy Johnson shrugged and offered them a cup of coffee. Anna looked to Linda who accepted. They were ushered into a small sitting room, and left to look at nineteenth century hunting-prints. Mrs Johnson accompanied the coffee-drinking with an account of the lives and eccentricities of village worthies; she clearly made an effort for the visitors. As they were about to leave, she asked Anna.

'Have you heard from your parents?'

'No. I don't even know where they are. They did tell me, but I've forgotten. Why?'

'Your father wasn't very well. He was a bit loth to go. They're staying with some friends in Malvern. Your mother seemed keen.'

'What was wrong with Daddy?'

'He'd aches and pains and felt listless, he said. Your mother said it was just an excuse.'

'What did you think?'

'I asked him if he'd a temperature, but he didn't seem to know. He can be maddening, sometimes. It's not my place to order him to use a thermometer. It might have been 'flu or even just a cold. Or just feeling down in the mouth. I couldn't tell.'

'Is he often off colour like this?'

'Yes and no. He's getting old. He's seventy-seven. He can't do many of the things he could easily manage ten years ago. And I don't suppose that knowledge comes pleasurably to him. Like Frank Norman.'

'Oh?'

'He's nearly eighty. But they've both been independent men, and don't like it when they feel their strength deserting them.'

Anna took the Malvern address, wondering if Nancy Johnson exaggerated for entertainment value. Gold streaked the sky over Linda's deflowerment copse as they drove back.

IX

Two weeks before Christmas Anna found herself at a loose end. Her husband was in New York, 'enjoying himself, making not a penny' in his own words.

'Won't you learn anything to your advantage?' she had asked. She admired the man.

'I doubt it.'

'Why bother then?'

'I'm preparing for retirement, filling in my time.' She had bought and wrapped presents, ordered the Christmas tree, checked the trimmings, bells and baubles so that she and the children could decorate the house once they had broken up from school. Neither Thomas nor Alice, seventeen and sixteen now, had shown much enthusiasm, but had agreed on a date for the hanging ceremony.

'I don't know why we bother,' Thomas had said.

'Your father likes them.' Both children pulled comical, thunderstruck faces, Tom striking his forehead with a flat palm.

Hilda Meyer telephoned to ask her daughter to attend a party for the school held in the manor house. She gave one day's notice.

'You won't have to do anything,' Hilda pressed her, 'except to appear graciously charming. It's easy for you.'

'Can't you manage that on your own?'

'Your father would like you to be here. To learn the ropes, so that when we die or move elsewhere and you take over the house, you'll know what you're in for.'

'It's Colin you should be after. He's the one who decides where we're going to live.'

'This place is a gem.'

'I know. You've seen to that.'

Her mother purred with pleasure. Anna suddenly felt deeply satisfied with herself.

'How is Daddy?'

'Much as ever. He shows his age sometimes, but he seems to be looking forward to this party. He likes Christmas, and the children are going to repeat their nativity play and sing carols. It'll please him no end if you're here. You know that.'

The weather was fine so that the children could be marched in a crocodile along the village street. The first arrivals were wiping every scrap of dirt from their shoes before the headmistress allowed them in. The players, it appeared, had already been admitted to dress themselves. A piano had been dragged into the foyer. Those outside under the portico worked hard on their shoes, but were subdued, half apprehensive. Obviously they had been warned.

Kuno Meyer immediately crossed the floor to greet his daughter. Hilda and Mrs Johnson walked purposefully, but without ostentation. The headmistress, a rather stout young woman with a strong local accent, eyed her troops and subordinates with suspicion. They were on public exhibition. Kuno introduced her to Anna, who shook hands and said she was looking forward to the morning's performance. The head's lips were drawn thin under her momentarily smiling eyes as if she prepared herself for some social catastrophe. Kuno hurried his daughter off to a side room, asking Mrs Johnson to give them a knock when the preparations had been properly completed. He smiled all the time, glad to be out of it, founder of the feast, but with no responsibility, apart from a small financial outlay, for its success. He sat his daughter down in what was obviously his present working office. Red lights glowed. Machines were ready for action. Anna wondered if his secretary worked behind the second closed door, or if she had been dragooned by Hilda into helping outside.

'How are you, then?' she asked. Anna continued to question him closely about his health, not deterred by euphemisms and evasions. In the end he admitted he had been feeling off colour but said it was to be expected at his age, seventy-seven. A private hospital had recently been giving him a careful physical check, and had made a list of suggestions to him and to his GP.

'Are you paying attention to them?' she asked.

'Oh, yes. Your mother sees to that. She's a devil once she gets the bit between her teeth. She inquires about my tablets. I have to tick them off on her list. She's changed our diet to some extent. She's doing her best to keep me alive.'

'And is it having any effect?'

'I suppose so. I can get about, and that's good at my age. I've still got my wits about me, and my legs. Many are a damn' sight worse off. Old age isn't funny.'

'Talking of old men, how's Frank Norman?'

'I don't know. We've been away, and from what Nancy Johnson says one of his sons descended on him and packed him off to hospital and then to a nursing home.'

'For good?'

'That I don't know. It all happened at speed. And the son said nothing to anyone. He's a bit like the old man. You rarely got anything out of him. Norman, the father, once told me how featureless the desert was in North Africa. Just now and then he'd out with something interesting that came bursting up from inside him like a little volcano, quite unexpectedly.'

'Important things?'

'Not at all. It was as if he'd decided to be sociable, and came out with some item that he thought might catch his listener's interest.'

'Such as?'

'At one time while he was in the army he was in a sergeants' mess and every Sunday night the bar used to clear and these senior n.c.o.s. used to crowd into the main room to listen to Vera Lynn singing. It amazed him, he said. Many of these men were intelligent in their way, technical experts, wireless, tanks and so on. But there they'd sit while she sang "We'll meet again" and "There'll be blue birds over." They didn't comment, or at least not to him, but sat silently, drinks in front of them, taking it all in. That was their idea of serious enjoyment.'

'Didn't Noël Coward say something about the power of popular songs?'

'Did he? Don't know. But Norman said he'd never forget. The intensity or rather the relaxed concentration. All sorts of different men, in character, but united. He said he'd never forget it.'

'What did he think about these songs?'

'I think he didn't mind them. He was a young man, away from home and loved ones, likely to be posted to some distant dangerous place. He said he wondered if Mozart or Beethoven could have such an effect on a moderately random audience. He told me this, and then shut up. He'd never forget it. I expected him to say more, but, no, he just relapsed into his usual reticence. Odd man. I don't know what he was like in school. Would he be more interested in quadratic equations than in making himself popular? Have you any news?'

110

'The Blands who were interested in buying a country house have decided against it.'

Clearly this meant nothing to Kuno, who shook his head. Mrs Johnson tapped on the door, opened it to announce the play was about to start. She led them to seats of honour alongside a dozen other village notables. Introductions were made; these people seemed genuinely glad to see Anna; the choir, shepherds, wise men, angels and Holy Family were all kept waiting until the important people had demonstrated their social graces. Attention restored amongst the well-to-do, the choir and the children seated in rows struck up 'O Come, All Ye Faithful'. The singing appeared some way short of tuneful, but swelled with energy. The young woman playing the piano hammered hell out of the keyboard and hymn. Joseph and the inn keeper argued unconvincingly before the latter left shrugging and two of the larger children held a curtain in front of the parents to be. Shepherds gathered on the unfamiliar stage, all carrying toy sheep, all complaining about the cold, melodramatically shuddering as they adjusted their blanket-robes and tea-towel head-gear. The choir favoured the listeners with 'While shepherds watched'. Angels appeared, and a blonde child with a loud voice imperiously bade them to fear not. The shepherds recovered from their cowardly postures and sat upright, taking all in, and set off, sheep still in their arms, even unto Bethlehem.

The screen-holders sidled off. Mary and Joseph moved towards centre stage where two of the angels provided them with a manger. Mary rocked the baby in her arms. A third member of the heavenly host crossed the stage carrying a large star on a wand covered with silver paper. She now stood on a box behind the seated parents, star prominent, benignly smiling. The wise men, one black, appeared in finery, gold-crowned to present their gifts in three beribboned boxes. The choir set about a calypso-type carol, unknown to Anna, as the actors held their postures according to temperament on the platform. The notabilities led applause, and the children, unrehearsed for curtain calls, stood helplessly about the stage. The headmistress descended on her charges and shooed them to their tiring-room.

The second half proved as brief as the first, and consisted of two reciters of verse, a chorus of speakers, and three carols from the choir, some of whom had now been provided with tambourines. At the end the loud-voiced angel, now in school

111

uniform, thanked the Meyers for their hospitality, and said not one of them would ever forget this morning. She made a curtsey in the direction of Hilda Meyer, and then hung about as if waiting for inspiration.

Hilda stood, not moving place, and thanked them all. Now, she said, it was time to eat, and hoped they would enjoy the food as much as she had enjoyed the play and the singing and the poems. She waved the notables to a side door where Nancy Johnson with a dignified hand signalled them towards their edibles.

The headmistress, in a ferocious voice, ordered her pupils to stay still, standing or sitting, exactly where they were. They obeyed. Anna was shown to her seat in the small drawing room. The vicar and his wife acknowledged her presence. Her father did his best to be sociable. After a decent interval the headmistress was shown into the room, offered coffee, congratulations and cakes. She looked uncomfortable, perhaps because of the society she had been thrust into, or more likely because she felt without her presence her children would create mayhem. This fear may have been fulfilled, for a teacher knocked at the door, glanced over towards her superior, whispered to her at speed. The headmistress deserted her half-eaten cream horn, her almost untouched coffee.

'I wouldn't want her job,' Hilda said. She'd just come up level with Anna.

'She's younger than you are.'

'I think,' Hilda answered, 'of all the work that's gone into the training of those children. It must take hours of drill.'

'Yes.'

'And the sewing and so forth that the parents do. And still they make mistakes.'

'It's not the RSC. That's the beauty of it. The children lack sophistication. Some of them speak their lines like robots.'

'Do you remember when you were in a nativity play?'

'I do. At Miss White's school. I was terrified.'

'You didn't look it. Cool as a cucumber.' Hilda coughed. 'How do you think daddy seems?'

'He says he's not been very well, but he didn't look too upset.'

'I'm worried. He's not himself. I won't say he's given up on everything, but it seems like it sometimes.'

Anna pressed her mother, but learnt little more. She wondered if it was Hilda who read her own depression into Kuno's

112

condition. Or if her father, and it would have been typical, had sworn his wife to secrecy over some serious illness the visits to hospital had laid bare. She could imagine his voice. 'Now don't go worrying Anna with this. She's plenty to do without driving herself silly on my account. I mean it.' And his eyes would be small in their wrinkled pouches, and steely. He could be formidable. Hilda would obey in the initial stages of his disease, but afterwards she'd have no compunction about confiding in Anna.

That evening Colin telephoned from New York.

Yes, he was having an interesting time, and had learnt a thing or two. No, it wasn't eating, drinking and making merry. He'd met some man from the firm that was taking over Terry's business and with him some computer expert from Silicon Valley.

'Are they connected?'

'Yes. But the computer man's more a researcher. He's about forty, a quiet lad, an anorak, but the ideas that spill out of him they're amazing. Nobody'll have anything to do in about twenty years' time.'

'Not walking by the sea? Painting pictures? Falling in love?'

'Not quite, but they'll all be radically changed by the amount machines can do for us. You won't need to go to the seaside. It'll be done at home for you.'

'Virtual reality?'

'I suppose so.'

He talked excitedly. He'd been impressed. It would be a change for him to sit among the dunces at the bottom of the class. She laughed at his new enthusiasms.

'And what about Terry's business?' Anna asked.

'Well, Richard Borowski, the man from the Lincoln Corporation, knew nothing about that particular take-over. He works in America, and is concerned with the larger aspects,' Colin coughed at his own phraseology, 'of business strategy', but he said, when I described the offer and so forth that they must have been pretty favourably impressed with the way Terry was running it. Usually they just steam-roller small firms, and alter them, or wipe them out of existence to suit their own ends. You can pass this on to Terry or Linda if you so wish.'

'Are you having a good time?' she asked.

'Not really. I'm learning some useful things. And meeting some high-fliers, but do you know what I miss is coming home in the evening, and sitting down to a good meal, and a glass of whisky and the newspaper.'

'You're surely getting all those, to the n-th degree.'

'Not at home. That's the point. Home. Five years ago I enjoyed these jaunts, looked forward to them, learnt from them. Now I'm as bad as Terry. A home bird.'

'It wouldn't be so if you had nothing else but home and family. The fact that you can go abroad, or take the chance of investing your money profitably, that's what makes your few nights as a domestic animal bearable.'

'There's no pleasing you, is there?'

She described the nativity play and concert. He laughed with evident enjoyment at her pleasure.

'Doesn't it make you wish you were back teaching?'

'No, it does not. Even all those years ago I wasn't satisfied. Training clever children to jump through academic hoops.'

'I have a fantasy,' he said, mimicking Martin Luther King. 'I'd like to be an employer on a large scale, not like Ford so much, not international but local. With a large factory. And at Christmas we have a great knees-up, all of them there with their wives. And a children's party with presents for all.'

'And you the founder of the feast?'

'With my sporty waistcoat and Dundreary whiskers. That's it. I'd have been hopeless. But it's the comparatively large size of the philanthropy that appeals.'

'In Dickens's *Christmas Carol* Mr Fezziwig's party to his apprentices and a few friends is made to be marvellous. But I suppose that's Dickens.'

It would be only just after lunch in America she thought, daylight still, and possibly snow-swept. He was on his way out at three, he said, to some television studio to discuss a series on transatlantic business exchanges in the future.

'And what line will you take?'

'I shall laugh at them, and their obsession with speed. They'll fare better to do it all at half-pace. And when I'm not on that line, I shall be god-like, watching in mild surmise and waiting for the catastrophes.'

She realised that he was having a high old time, and asked if he'd be back for Christmas Eve.

'I shall be with you next week.'

'Right. I'll warm the TV up. And iron the newspapers.'

He inquired what presents she and the children would like from New York. She began to make suggestions. He did not want them. He'd obviously already made the purchases.

They rang off, both delighted. She told her children that their father had rung. They showed little interest.

'Will he be back in time for Christmas?' Alice asked.

'So he says.'

'Unless something more interesting turns up,' Tom said.

'That's hardly fair,' Anna defended her husband. The children smiled like parents with a gifted infant. She did not argue long with them.

Christmas came with the weather still mild. The younger Turnbulls did not break up from school until four days before the day. Tom explained the lateness with his usual cynicism.

'They're driving us hard so that we can hold on to our positions in the National League tables.' Both schools had appeared in the first ten on the previous summer's results at "A" Level and GCSE.'

'Isn't that to your advantage?' Anna asked.

'Oh, yes. I wouldn't play anywhere outside the premiership.'

Colin returned from New York. His presents to the children were new computers, recommended by the IT expert. The children sat overwhelmed, because both could guess what their father had paid out for them. Both spent much spare time practising hard, expanding skills. Alice, to Anna's surprise, showed a keenness and knowledge to match her brother's. Both were interested enough to discuss the improvements with their father and even to explain the elementary routines to their mother. When on Boxing Day Terence and Linda came over for lunch they displayed the new machines with enthusiasm. The uncle had not seen these before, though he'd read about them recently in some magazine. He wondered how Colin had managed to get these delivered in England. There'd be some chicanery involved somewhere. Colin listened to his reluctantly admiring brother. 'I can get Linda one,' he said.

'It could be out of date in a year or two,' Terence said, unwilling to yield or be impressed.

'I don't think so. They'll hold this one on the market for a few years. They know the state of the game. All sorts of improvements are made all the time. Often for just minor projects in, let's say, university research departments.' He deliberately pronounced the

115

word in the American style, 'ree-search'. 'But there's enough of a monopoly to keep rivals at bay. You'd be surprised what some bright young herbert will find that this set-up, only very slightly modified, can do. I tell you what, Terry, now you're retired you can come over with me next time I go to see Dick Borowski. Trouble is, Linda, he won't want to come back.'

'You surprise me,' she said, ungraciously. 'Could I come?'

'Would you like to emigrate to America?' Anna asked.

'At my age, no. I wouldn't mind a long holiday there.' Terry, surprising them all.

'I don't think Colin would mind.'

'No,' Colin answered. 'Not if I could see advantage in it.'

On Boxing Day the Colin Turnbulls went over to Ashby Manor for lunch. The meal was beautifully cooked and served, with Nancy Johnson and two village girls in attendance, but the atmosphere grew gloomier by the minute. Kuno, it appeared, had been ill most of the night, with nausea and diarrhoea, but had insisted on dressing and sitting at the head of the table, though his wife carved the turkey. The pallor of his face alarmed Anna; his skin gleamed transparent. He ate almost nothing, and rarely spoke. Colin brilliantly described his contacts with American business men, even making his own children laugh. After the meal Anna questioned her mother, and asked if the doctor had been sent for.

'He won't hear of it. But if he's no better I'm sending for him tomorrow.'

'Has he only just started?'

'He's been poorly for a week or more. But you know him. "Don't make such a fuss, Hilda. I've caught some bug, or eaten something I shouldn't." But you should have seen him in the night, shaking and trembling with the cold when he had to get out of bed. He looked so weak, as if he hadn't the strength to stand up. It frightened him, but he won't say so. I wanted him to stay in bed, but not he. "I'm not going to miss Christmas or my grandchildren for some bit of a virus or bacterium. I've taken something for it, and don't feel any better for being ticked off by you." Will you speak to him? He might listen to you.'

'I'll do my best.'

She manoeuvred her father into an armchair and questioned him.

'It's nothing. Some tummy-bug. Unpleasant. I could well do without it.'

'You should have stayed in bed.'

'And missed Christmas. I'll get over it. There's no need for a song and dance.'

Kuno looked at her solemn face. He wetted his lips.

'I know you, and your mother, worry about me. But I'm getting on. I expect illnesses and set-backs and bad days. That's what people don't seem to understand. But I'm not going to give in every time I feel not quite up to the mark. I'd spend half my time in bed. And your mother's not as young as she used to be. I'm not having her waiting on me hand and foot day and night.' He waved a bony hand to signal change of subject. 'How's your friend, Norman?'

'I've not heard a thing. I thought perhaps you had.'

'No. He's vanished off the face of the earth. Nancy Johnson's made inquiries all round the place. It's a mystery. We heard he's in a nursing home somewhere. But why the son didn't leave an address I don't know.'

'In a hurry, perhaps.'

Kuno closed his eyes. His thin cheeks assumed the broken shape of a death-mask. She caught her breath.

'You look after yourself, young man,' she said.

'Yes, miss.'

A thin smile loosened his lips. He'd spoken like that to her when she was a child. She could not see his blue eyes, but they'd twinkle momentarily. He was Daddy of the eight-year-old Anna for a moment. She took his thin, disfigured hand and held it.

The visitors left in the darkness soon after five. Kuno promised he'd go straight up to bed. Thomas and Alice were due at a party by eight-thirty. Hilda had one or two 'phonecalls to make, and after that she and Nancy Johnson would sit together, she said, perhaps even partake of a festive drink to cheer the evening.

'Dry sherry. I don't like it much, so I shan't have more than the glass.'

'And Nancy?'

'Whisky and water.'

'Do you ever get tiddly?'

'Never.'

Hilda shook a lugubrious head.

Anna rang her mother each morning to inquire after her father. Kuno was reported to be improving, and once came cheerfully to the 'phone.

117

On New Year's Day Anna, who had spent the night at a cele-
bration, and felt fragile still, called her mother in the evening. All
appeared well at the manor house.

'No, we didn't stay up much after midnight. Nancy went home,
and once she'd 'phoned that she was safely back, she came in her
car, your father went straight to bed and I had a wallow in the
bath.'

'Nancy spends a lot of her time with you,' Anna said.

'Yes, she does. She's really useful to us. And Daddy enjoys her
company. Do you know, I think that if anything happened to me
he might marry her?'

'Jesus.'

'What did you say?'

'Jesus.' Anna repeated the sacred name more loudly.

'Oh. You don't fancy her as a step-mother then? He could
choose worse. She's younger than we are, and has a good deal
more energy. She's better educated than I am. And she knows his
little ways by now, and loves this house.'

'And why would you think of dying?'

'Shuffling off this mortal coil? What does "coil" mean?'

'Turmoil, hubbub, trouble, I suppose. It's from *Hamlet*.'

'Oh, to be properly educated.'

'You've not answered my question.'

'No, I haven't. I've no reason. I'm well. I went for a check-up
last week. At Plane Trees, the private hospital. They gave me a
good report. Blood-pressure, cholesterol, heart, liver, kidneys,
lungs, the lot. They said I was excellent for my age. They gave me
diet sheets, and suggested a slight change in my tablets.
Otherwise, perfect.'

'Why did you go? Were you feeling ill?'

'This is a nasty time of year, such short days, so dark. It seemed
sensible to find out if I'd any physical defects. Besides I need to be
fit for your Father.'

'Did Daddy go?'

'Not he. He'd been recently examined and he visits the surgery
here from time to time. He likes the young doctor. It's up to him,
he says. He'll send him to the consultants when it's necessary.'

Hilda sighed, without sorrow, almost cheerfully.

'By the way,' she began again slowly. 'I've some bad news for
you. It's Mr Norman. Frank Norman who used to teach you at
the grammar school. He died.'

'When?'

'Just before Christmas. Quite suddenly. In a nursing home in Farnborough, was it?'

'How did you find this out?'

'Nancy saw his neighbour, Mrs Bott. It appears that the son left the address with Beatrice Bott, but she didn't bother to pass it on. Then she went away somewhere, to a relative's, over Christmas, and when she returned there was a message to say that Mr Norman had died, rather suddenly. She made no effort to pass the news round.'

'Why not?'

'She's a funniosity is our Bott. Most people like to hand on some snippet of information that's unknown to everybody else. But not she. It wasn't until Nancy really pumped her that she came out with it.'

'Was she at loggerheads with Mr Norman?'

'Not that I know. She didn't see it was any business of hers. She'd hold on to a key, or take a simple message, but that was about it. She's older than she looks, they say, though nobody knows for certain, older than Daddy, if they're right. And at her age it doesn't seem important. She's always been odd.'

'He's been buried?'

'I presume so. Or cremated. But the Bott creature didn't know. If she had, Nancy would have wormed it out of her.'

'And the son? He's made no attempt to clear the house yet?'

'Not as far as I know. Of course, the holiday delays things. And the son has to go abroad.'

'What does he do?'

'Heaven knows. I thought he was connected with music. Not as a performer, but an administrator or agent. Perhaps I've made all that up. Anyhow he left a message which Mrs Bott did not pass on. That sort of thing is the beauty of village life. We're a very mixed commodity. We're near enough to the city to attract commuters, and we've attracted one or two oddities. In this case two of 'em lived next door to each other. It was fortuitous.'

'I didn't find Mr Norman too odd. He just kept his head below the parapet, for whatever reason. I guess once his wife had died and his family were out of the way he'd enough to occupy himself with.'

'That's unusual. Most people need company.'

'And when I went to see him he was hospitable and in no way eccentric.'

'I don't think you quite understand the effect of you beautiful young women on old men, however grumpy or self absorbed.'

'Is that so with Daddy?'

'He's exactly like all the rest.'

'Beautiful women attract him?'

'Yes. I'm not suggesting that he does anything more than be pleasant to them. He's too old and feeble for anything else.'

'Is he all right? Physically?'

'Well, he can't complain. He does. He hates the winter weather. The cold and the fogs and what he calls the everlasting rain.'

'Why don't you go to somewhere sunny?'

'Your father loves going to Europe. Not for hot sunshine, but for German language and culture. Wagner and Goethe.'

'Does he ever speak German in England?'

'Not to my knowledge.'

Anna had written to Frank Norman's son offering condolences on the father's death. She'd pressed Mrs Bott for the address, reluctantly given, and had been surprised to receive, almost by return, an invitation to call in at Norman's house on a certain date when the son, Robert, would be there in process of clearing the house. There was little time, the day was at the beginning of the next week, but she rang his London home and left her acceptance on his answer-phone, intrigued why he had given the invitation.

It had rained heavily in the night, and fields by the river were flooded, in the curious blue light of this January morning as Anna parked in front of Norman's house. Her ring on the door bell was immediately answered by a small, pretty, bright-eyed, woman who shook hands and ushered the visitor with neat alacrity into the drawing room.

'I'm Felicity Norman, Robert's wife. We're spending a few days here in the house before we get it cleared and put it up for sale. He thought it a good idea to ask you across because you're very favourably mentioned in his father's diary.'

'I called in a time or two to see him. He used to teach me mathematics in the grammar school.'

'I didn't know that. In the sixth form?'

'Oh, no. For "O" Level.'

'I see. He seemed quite fond of you. Your visits are recorded in his diaries. Not just a name, but a description, one or two things you said. I'm not telling you he was Samuel Pepys, but he didn't just put down names and times. It surprised us, really. Literary people not mathematicians write about their daily doings. Bob, my husband, would no more think of keeping a journal than flying in the air.' Mrs Norman swung her pretty legs, in bright red trousers, and stood up from her chair. 'He's a stockbroker. He'll be down any minute now. I don't know what he's playing at.'

'And you read his father's diary?'

'We did. Bob's taken a week off. It won't take that time to look at his father's furniture. We have an expert coming in tomorrow to work his way round. But it's typical that Bob must do it first. He's like that. He must make his own mind up, and then call in some antiques man. Besides, he'll see it as a kind of holiday.'

'He lived here, didn't he, when he was a boy?'

'Yes. But he was away at university, at the LSE, and immediately he'd finished there he found himself a job, and has hardly been back since. They weren't unfriendly. Both self-contained. Didn't want to bother the other. Bob's mother had died soon after he'd started work and his father began to go his own way thereafter.'

'Hadn't you been here before?'

'Oh, yes. Called in, on the way somewhere else. Or back. Bob's father came down to Reigate for the wedding, and was sociable in his old-fashioned way. Made a very good impression on my parents. And we 'phoned if we had news or we, or he, wanted something. I had the notion that that was how the old man preferred it. But perhaps it was guilty conscience on my part. And Francis, Bob's brother, is much the same. That's not quite so understandable, as he has three children. If I were a grandmother I'd want to see my grandchildren. We're childless. Do you have a family?'

'A boy and a girl, seventeen and sixteen, both at school.'

'You don't look old enough. Are they doing well?'

'It would appear so.'

'That's good. Francis's father did right by his grandchildren in his will. And that's why, or partly, why we asked you to call. There's a small bequest for you. Bob will tell you when he duly appears. God knows what he's doing upstairs.'

'Indulging in nostalgia.'

'Not he. He hasn't an ounce of sentiment in him.'

Felicity Norman grinned as if pleased with her judgement. Anna wondered why this lively, sexy woman should have married so dry a stick. The door opened and Robert appeared. His appearance surprised Anna. Taller by several inches than his father, he was slim, and though without a jacket stylishly dressed in tweed trousers and a roughish, expensive loose-knit pullover. His hair was grey, thinning, but brushed up over his pate to preserve the appearance of curls to match those in the nape of his neck. Large eyes, darkly blue, mildly regarded her. He was extremely handsome, with the pale face of a poet, unlined and symmetrical.

'Mrs Turnbull?' He held out a well-manicured hand. 'I expect Felly's explained why we asked you to come.'

'I appear in your father's diary.'

'Squire Mire's daughter. That's how the old hooligan spells it, m-i-r-e.' Robert looked up, affronted by Anna's unsmiling reception of the word-play. 'We're glad to see you. You must have made a considerable impression. He recorded one or two subjects of conversation. The teaching of mathematics to girls. Well, we could expect that. English lyric poetry. That's well off his track, I'd have thought. Second marriages. And he said how beautifully dressed you were. I'm not surprised, if I may say so. Shall I put the kettle on, Felly, to make Mrs Turnbull a cup of coffee?'

'No, thank you,' Anna answered. 'But don't let me stop you.'

'Are you sure?' Felicity said, moving out.

The pause fell awkwardly since Anna made no attempt to re-open conversation. Robert did his best.

'My father was not much of a social being, but he enjoyed your visits. He kept a diary, and you received more coverage than most. Usually he put down a name, together with the main topic of conversation, and sometimes a comment. "I can't understand the man. Seems incapable of sticking to his subject." In your case he even went so far on one occasion as describing your clothes as well as what you talked about. And once he wrote: "I feel better for my talk to Squire Mire's daughter. She's beautiful, and modest." It sounds to me quite like some other man, not old grum and gruff.' Robert sat back. 'And quite recently he added your name to his will. You are to inherit a watercolour. It's a view of a copse and a road in snow, by John Worth. It's early, done when Worth was a student. He lived in Beechnall, you know. My mother bought it for a few pounds all those years ago.'

'Was she interested in pictures?'

'Not particularly. She acquired some for the walls. And she

must have gone to this exhibition where she bought it. The only recorded instance.' Robert sniffed deeply, then laughed. 'She took an immediate fancy to this, and kept it in her bedroom. My father appended a note to it, which you'll see. I guess that he was surprised. The note suggests that Worth would be sixteen or seventeen only when he painted this. And my father put a title to his note: Edna picks a Winner. I think he wrote this some time after her death, or even very recently after he decided to bequeath it to you. It's undated, and his paper's unfaded.'

Felicity came in with the coffee.

'I feel awful,' she said, 'supplying ourselves and giving you nothing.'

'Let Mrs Turnbull choose for herself,' Robert said.

'You're like your father. In love with her already.' Robert wagged a finger. Anna, caught out and uncomfortable, sat unmoving. Robert went swiftly, without a word of excuse, from the room, and returned with a brown-paper parcel.

This he laid on the table and unwrapped.

'Perhaps you'd like to see it now,' he said, agreeably.

Anna rose, stood by his side, her mind only half on the picture. Felicity positioned herself on the other side of the table, stage-managing the production.

'Do you like it?' Bob asked. He never seemed to raise his voice.

The watercolour was small, twelve by seven inches, but in a wide, ivory mount with a plain oak frame. Bare trees leaned from both sides slightly across a road, snow-covered with a few darker, deep cart-ruts. Branches, and verges, and a ragged length of hedge had caught a layer of snow, and the inverted, flattened triangle of sky in its variety of greys seemed to threaten more. The light dropped dull, leaden even, but always interesting. The trees were outlined in detail as if the painter could not bear to miss out the slightest twig. How he had managed to suggest such tortuosity she could not decide. There was no house, nor vehicle, nor man to hint at human connection. Silence brooded, spread from the picture to the viewers. One imagined the cold. Though the conception and execution had about them a neat simplicity, they were like some algebraic equation expressing in a few signs some enormous even cosmic complication.

'He was a marvellous draughtsman even as a boy,' Bob muttered.

Felicity walked round the table and joined the two.

'It's quite beautiful,' she said.

'Then I can't take it from you,' Anna answered.

'It's yours,' Bob said. 'By law. And more to the point by our father's wish. He went to the trouble to add a codicil, so it must have been important to him.'

'I don't know.'

'You do now.' Felicity slipped a hand round Anna's waist and drew her in. Robert, humming, refolded the brown paper round the picture, sealed it with selotape already used, bowed, and handed it out to Anna.

'Madam,' he said. 'Madam.'

'I don't know how to thank you.'

'You don't have to. We're pleased that you brought such pleasure at the end of his life to our father.'

A tear forced itself from Anna's left eye. She felt it, but could not account for it, as her sensibility seemed deficient, distorted, absent. She dabbed at her cheek.

The others watched approvingly. They talked for a few minutes, about painting, the village, Father Norman's interests, their holiday plans. They invited her over for coffee again, or lunch.

'We're here all week. We want to do the sorting out properly My brother and his wife will be down tomorrow. Would your husband like to join us? Just let us know.'

'I'll ask him. I'm not sure what Colin will be doing.'

'All husbands are the same,' Felicity said. 'Engaged every day on supremely important pieces of business that cannot be altered by one second this way or that. And most arranged at the last minute.'

'We must earn our keep,' Robert assured her solemnly. The two women stood together against men, or against this one silently affable man who refused to fight them.

Anna left, carrying her picture which she placed on the back seat. She called in at the manor house; the gardener waved and shouted that her parents had gone out to lunch.

'Is Nancy not here?'

'Yes. We couldn't keep her away.'

He waved without embarrassment to Mrs Johnson who had appeared on the patio and must have heard his every word. She ignored the man, but welcomed Anna effusively.

'I won't come in,' Anna answered. 'I just thought I'd call in to see how Daddy was shaping.'

'He's not too badly off physically, but in these last weeks round Christmas three of his friends have died.'

'Close friends? I haven't heard anything.'

'Friends at school. They all live away. But their deaths all came together.'

'And it affected him?'

'He doesn't say much, or make much show of it. But your mother thinks he broods. That's why she arranges these distractions for him. I don't know whether it does him any good. He'd as lief stay in as go out. But your mother tries. She works hard at keeping him occupied and well and interested.'

Anna gave a brief account of her visit to the younger Normans.

'I didn't know they were coming,' Mrs Johnson said.

'They're staying the whole week. Clearing up.'

'Yes. Somebody would have to do it. And there would be no need to give me notice of their intentions.' Her tone spoke otherwise.

'They gave me a picture. Mr Norman apparently left it to me in his will.'

'Why would he do that?'

'Not for my mathematical ability, that's for certain.' She answered rudeness with triviality.

'Is it any good? The picture, I mean?'

'It's a watercolour by John Worth of trees in snow.'

'I've never heard of him.'

'No. He was local. Somewhere in Beechnall. He's very well known now. This picture was done when he was a boy, and Mrs Norman bought it at an exhibition of amateur artists.'

'I didn't know her. Did you?'

'No. She, if I remember rightly, died while he was still teaching me. The headmaster mentioned it in assembly, which was very unusual because teachers' private lives were private in those days.'

'I know. It was so when I taught. And it was better that way. The children looked on us as figures divorced from ordinary life. That fitted perfectly with the ethos, and so the discipline, of schools. Did she know anything about art?'

'They said not. Apart from the usual "I know what I like." But she snapped this thing by a local schoolboy.'

'Did her husband like it?'

'I don't know. They said little. Perhaps they didn't know. He singled it out as the picture he bequeathed to me. You can make of that what you will.'

125

'Would you show it to me?' Nancy asked.

'Now?'

'If it's no trouble.'

They walked back towards the car watched by the gardener. Anna took the parcel from the back-seat and laid it on the roof. She carefully lifted the selotape and opened the brown-paper wrapping. Nancy Johnson peered for a time, then lifted the painting from its cover and held it, purposefully, in front of her, scowling as she scrutinised.

'What do you think?' Anna asked, modestly.

'Very good.'

'You would have bought it, then?'

'That would have depended on the price. I've never at any stage of my life had money to throw about.'

'But? If the price seemed reasonable.'

'Yes. It's only a small picture, and the hanging of small paintings is difficult. Your mother and I often discuss it. In a place like this,' she waved one hand towards the manor house, the other occupied holding the picture with professional confidence, 'the rooms are large, and a small picture gets lost somehow.'

'What's the answer?'

'To hang it in a group. But that itself brings its problems. It has to match in some way the other pictures, and by doing that it loses some of its originality.'

'I have the vague impression that Mr Norman hung this upstairs somewhere. Perhaps it reminded him of his wife. The son didn't seem to know.'

'What was he like, the son?'

'Robert. Very quiet, polite, while his wife was lively. He was also very handsome. He looked like a romantic poet. Lord Byron.'

Mrs Johnson raised her eyebrows at that before handing back the picture and watching Anna rewrap it and put it away.

'Very acceptable. Indeed.' She sounded grim. 'Will your husband like it?'

'Let's hope so.'

126

X

Colin seemed not averse to visiting the Normans so that arrangements were quickly made. They'd driven over for coffee in Colin's Daimler, rarely used now except for long, exacting journeys.

'This is our last full day here,' Robert told them. 'A removal van arrives first thing tomorrow to pick up the things we want. They won't deliver in London until Monday morning when Felicity will take them in. We've a spare room which we cleared of everything but curtains and carpets. They'll be put in there until we make final decisions. They'll also deliver the stuff that Francis has chosen to his place.'

'You don't mind that chore?' Colin asked Felicity.

'No. There are one or two good things that we'll put among our furniture. That will mean a certain amount of rearrangement. And the smaller objects I'll sort out at my leisure later in the year. I love organizing.'

'And people?' he asked.

'I'm not so sure about that.' She had dressed to make an impression. Colin stared at the neat, brightly coloured, swift woman with judicious admiration. 'On your advice,' Felicity nodded to Anna, 'I asked Mrs Johnson in to get rid of father's clothes and so on. She'll deliver them to Oxfam in Beechnall. She seemed very efficient when she came in for a preliminary inspection. Very useful sort. Full of information. I was as pleased as anything.'

'My parents rely on her a great deal.'

'She knows a great deal about local affairs. And she's very obliging. She said she would be here if the furniture needed second calls next week.'

The four walked round the whole house. One or two rooms were already empty. No pictures hung on the walls. The place seemed slightly shabby, with the walls marked and faintly discoloured by furniture or paintings. The paintwork was almost uniformly excellent.

'My father often decorated rooms,' Robert said, 'even when they didn't need it. That was typical. Make certain. Of course his eyesight became poorer towards the end, but that didn't stop his work with the paint-brush. He always chose the same colours, magnolia, off-white.'

'You'll remember this house when you were a boy?' Anna said.

'Of course. It's not changed all that much.'

'And is it a wrench when you're looking at these empty rooms?'

'No.'

'Not even when you think that you're seeing them for the last time?'

'No.' He smiled, winningly. 'I've not that sort of mind. I can remember that, let's say, I did things in a certain room years ago, smoked my first cigarette, wrote my first love letter and so on, and though I can see that such memories could be powerfully invoked by some people it's not the case with me. I'm missing there. It's the same with books or paintings or music. I enjoy them, I'm sure I do, but I enjoy iced currant buns.'

'There's Proust's madeleine,' she objected.

'I beg your pardon?'

'Forget it. It's a kind of cake or biscuit that suddenly brought back a flood of memories.'

'You think I'm unusual?' he asked.

'I'm not prepared to dogmatise. I've no real evidence. Perhaps the fact that I had a literary education made this sort of feeling or thinking assume an importance for me which it hasn't for other people, who concern themselves with houses and comfortable living or money-making. Or both.'

'And I guess,' Robert answered slily, 'you're asking yourself how we robots get on with falling in love or, even, sexual intercourse.'

'Currant-bun category,' she murmured.

'Only more so.'

At the same time both stared across the room towards the window where Colin and Felicity stood silhouetted. They had slightly turned their heads as if to talk, though at the moment both were silent. They seemed suited, at ease, taking pleasure in the company of the other, yet neither made a gesture or a movement of intimacy. Their stance spoke innocence, as if they discussed football scores or the price of bread. Anna smiled; how well the two suited, both handsome, winsome, smooth-talking, free-standing.

'Hello, the talkers are silenced,' Colin said. He turned.

'What are you looking at?' Anna inquired.

'Your car,' Felicity answered, 'and its high gloss.' She raised a hand to command attention. It looks so good, and . . . It's solid, and beautiful. And your husband has been telling me about such a tragedy . . . that . . .' He waited for her. 'I seem to have the need to latch on to what's well made, and paid for, and dependable.'

'What tragedy's that?' Robert asked.

'Marie Simpson,' Colin said. 'In the offices of Meyer, Goodband. She was a secretary. Two teen-aged children.' He seemed buttoned up, unwilling to commit himself.

'Yes?' Robert pressed. Presumably the other three knew the detail.

'Her husband disappeared. Just walked out on her. A year ago. According to her there had been no great quarrel or even hassle in the home. And, or at least this was the story, no adultery by either party. He packed his bags and left. There was no explanation.'

'Did he work for you?' Felicity asked. 'Mr Simpson?'

'No. He was a company secretary at Baguley's, a large brewery. Again from what we heard, his work was perfectly satisfactory.'

'Were there rumours of a take-over or a closing down of the place?' Robert asked.

'No.'

'Ah, but did he think that might happen?' Anna, sharply.

'We, I don't know what he thought, but as far as his wife and friends and relatives and colleagues were concerned they'd never heard him mention such worries.'

'That's not to say . . .' Anna began.

'No.' Colin pulled a wry face. 'They both used to go out at much the same time in the morning. He delivered the children to school; it was his turn. And then he apparently came back home, packed his clothes and disappeared. Marie got hold of the police, later, and they found he'd not been to work on the day, a Monday. He had moreover, arranged a fortnight's leave. That had obviously been planned. He'd dropped hints about the Med, Malta, Gozo.'

'And money?' Robert.

'He had one small building society account in his own name. Not much. A thousand or so. Their other savings were in both names and were untouched.'

'Did he take his car?'

'Yes. Once the hue and cry was at its height, that was found. In Liverpool. He'd sold it. And the trail went cold, there. You got the usual sightings. One in Devon, two in Scotland, but that was that. She had no word from him, nor did his parents. Nothing. And that lasted for six months.'

They listened, each carefully, but all three in different positions, intent on not losing a word. The narrator stood, relaxed, not hurrying himself.

'Then three weeks or so ago there was a development.' Colin kept them waiting. 'In Stockport he was seen by a cousin, who knew all about the story. He must have been strange, this cousin, because he didn't go up and challenge the man. He tracked him home or to his digs and then rang Marie. She informed the police, and they made inquiries. They were rather reluctant or tactful, but they got in touch with the man. They have to be careful. You're quite entitled to leave your wife if you so wish. But the Child Security Agency, or whatever they call them, will be chasing you if you haven't been contributing to the children's maintenance. Anyhow they made contact, and Marie, it seems, after she'd written a time or two to him actually spoke to him on the 'phone. According to her, the exchange was not unreasonable. He said life at home, and at the brewery, had all proved too much. He'd now got himself a job, in the offices of some engineering firm. He wasn't earning nearly as much as he had been at Baguley's, but as soon as he'd sorted himself out, he'd contribute as much as he could afford to the boys. One thing he's adamant about was that he wasn't coming home. Under any circumstances.'

'And?' Felicity's rising musical inflexion on the one syllable.

'Next day his landlady found him dead in his room. He'd swallowed paracetemol by the ton. He'd left a short note to the effect that he just could not return to his family. He had thought he was settling down in this new job and new town, but now he'd been routed out, that was his expression, he saw it was useless to go on, and this was the one way left to him.'

'Was that all?' Felicity asked.

'Apparently.'

'He must have been pretty seriously disturbed,' Anna said.

'I'd have thought so,' her husband agreed. 'But Marie won't have it. He was a bit gloomy and wouldn't talk, but he was always that way inclined. She had not been worried unduly by his behaviour during his last few weeks at home. The people in Stockport said much the same. At work he was quiet, but very efficient. In his lodgings he kept himself to himself, seemed to have no friends, but was no worse than many his landlady had seen. In his suicide note he wrote a P.S. to her, apologizing for the trouble his death might well cause her.'

'Did he bottle it up?' Felicity asked.

'It would appear so. Unless Marie and the landlady played it all down so that they didn't seem at all to blame. Marie's pretty much upset, as you'd imagine, but she's working away full time. Her parents are mucking in collecting children and so on.'

'How do you know all this?' Anna asked.

'It created some uproar in the office, and it's been in the local newspapers. One day I happened to call in when it was at a climax. Marie wasn't there. The principal told me all about it, and two of the girls. They knew more than he did, or were prepared to say more.'

'And are they back to normal now?' Anna asked.

'I expect so. I don't go into the place very often. It's your father's old headquarters, and though I've financial interest in the place I have very little to do with the day-to-day running. The principal's a bright man, younger than I am.'

'What sort of woman is this Marie?' Robert asked.

'She's worked there for some years. Before she was married. Had maternity leave when her children were born. I looked at her record, out of pure curiosity, and she seems eminently satisfactory. Not marvellous, but good enough. Reliable, dependable, willing to put in a bit extra in an emergency. Not given to hysterics or dramatics. Conscientious and accurate. Just what's wanted in an accountant's office.'

'Pretty?' Robert asked.

'I didn't think so.'

The party broke into pairs. Colin and Felicity left the room and climbed chatting together to the third storey, watched from the door by the other two.

'Odd story,' said Robert.

'There must have been something sadly wrong with the man. To leave job, home, children, wife to live in digs, however comfortable.'

Colin and Felicity stood on a small landing at the head of the stairs, waiting for the others. A shaft of sunlight from an open bedroom door struck the wall obliquely behind them.

'Are you coming up?' Felicity asked.

'We are.' Robert staring at them. He then stepped back into the shelter of the bedroom where Anna waited. 'They make a good-looking pair,' he said, surprising his companion.

'I suppose so.'

'Colourful. Unlike poor Marie.'

They moved upstairs, joined the others to look round. Remaining furniture had been labelled in three different hues, yellow, red, dark blue.

'Yellow is for us, red for Francis, blue for careful auction, unmarked to be cleared and sold any old how,' Robert explained.

'You're very well organised,' Colin, pleased with himself. 'Have you got it right?'

'Near enough.'

'Are you an expert on antique furniture then?'

'By no means,' Robert answered. 'But I've been about a bit. We attended sales regularly when we moved into our present house.'

'And we had this expert in to check our opinions,' Felicity said. 'He was a friend, and he'd been looking over a stately home in Derbyshire, and said he'd call in on us on his way back. Where was it, Bob?'

'He did tell us. Meant nothing to me. I've forgotten. I'd never heard of it.'

'And did his views coincide with yours?' Colin asked.

'On the whole. We'd missed one or two things. China. Pottery. That sort of thing. We didn't have to change our labels much. He didn't take long. Round the house in an hour and a half.'

'He greatly liked your watercolour,' Felicity said.

'So do I.'

'Best thing in the house?' Colin cheerfully gibed.

'No. Upstairs in a drawer was a Cotman. All wrapped up. It must have been handed down in my mother's family. Done in North Wales, I think. That was a real find.'

'And it never hung on the wall?'

'Never in its whole existence. Or so we guess. The colours are bright as day.'

Felicity and Colin had strolled out into the next room.

'I can't help thinking about that man and his suicide. Your husband soon got the story out of those girls in the office. He'd make a detective.'

'I never thought about that.'

'He's obviously a very big noise in the firm, and doesn't appear there very often. But they spilled the beans.' He grimaced at his turn. 'I should think that's a bit unusual. People don't confess too easily to their superiors, or at least that's what I've found.'

'They'd be upset, and ready to talk about it to anybody. And Colin's curious. He'd make himself pleasant to them. He likes women, and he'd soon have them giving their views.'

'He's interested in people?'

'Yes and no,' Anna replied. 'He's momentarily caught. As you might be by some unusual story in the newspapers. And then he forgets it, or puts it out of his mind. He'd remember it to raise it as a subject at the dinner table, or as he has done this morning. He'd be sympathetic, would say exactly the right thing while he was collecting the story, but it would never worry him.'

'Oh.'

'You think I'm criticising him,' Anna spoke apologetically. 'I suppose I am.'

'Have you ever put that to him?'

'Yes. Often enough. And he'll say, rightly enough, that it would do nobody, neither the injured or grieving parties nor him any good to be making a great fuss. I tell him that most of us couldn't help it.'

'And how would he answer that?'

'Shrug. Say he was different.'

'And is that true?'

'I think he's taught himself to stand back, not to become involved unless there was some advantage to himself.'

They stood at the window staring out across the village. The manor house could barely be seen among its surrounding trees.

'That's where your parents live?' Robert half-asked. 'Beautiful house. Eighteenth century?'

'Most of it. There's been some rebuilding and additions.'

'Mrs Johnson waxes eloquent on the subject. She's very keen.'

'More so than my parents, I'd think.'

'Don't they like it then?'

'Oh, yes,' Anna answered. 'I'm sure they do. But it takes some keeping up and as they grow older, it hardly seems worth the hassle.'

'It must be expensive. To keep it running properly.'

'I don't think that's the problem. My father's not been well. He

133

hates the cold and short days in winter, and a whole group of his contemporaries have died, all together. And it's left him with the feeling that life's hardly worth hanging on to.'

'Isn't a big and interesting house just the place for him. He can't or won't go out, then he can wander about from room to room, and keep himself from boredom.'

'His depression has been too severe,' Anna said. 'He sits in his office, and plays about with his investments, but that's no longer good enough. It's to be hoped the Spring will bring him round.'

'Why doesn't he go abroad to somewhere warmer at this time of year?'

'My mother's tried to persuade him, but she says he'd feel he was deserting his post. He was born in Germany, and came over as a schoolboy. He's propping England up, he thinks. He doesn't understand what's happening to the country, what with pop music, and pop government, football and alternative comedy, drugs and so on. He's holding old England firm. It takes a German to do it.'

'Does he speak German?'

'Yes. And loves to do so.'

'Does he speak English with a foreign accent?'

'Not at all. He takes all his holidays in Germany or Austria and at least twice every year.'

'And has this last winter been worse for him than any other?'

'From what I gather.'

Robert continued to stare out towards the manor house. Anna backed off to the door to look for the other two. She could hear their voices from downstairs. They must have passed the door, negotiated the uncarpeted stairs in silence, or at least unheard.

'And what are you going to do about it all?' Robert asked, joining Anna.

'There's very little I can. My guess is that Nancy Johnson keeps the ship afloat.'

'More so than your mother?'

'Yes. My mother has her own spheres of interest, but outside them she's been used to Kuno making all the decisions.'

They were descending the stairs together. Robert spoke slowly.

'I guess my father was in the same position. He'd given up all the jobs that gave him status, club secretaryships, examination marking, school governorship. He gave up playing chess because there was no-one here to take him on.' Robert held the stair-rail.

'He read a bit. Made up a game or two which he submitted to Waddington's, but they accepted only one after he retired. He kept the house clean, and the garden tidy. He never looked neglected in himself, bought clothes from time to time, cleaned his shoes every morning without fail, was one of the best ironers I've ever seen, quick but accurate.'

'I had a faint idea that Mrs Johnson might have fancied him as a husband. She was a grammar-school teacher as he was.' Anna advanced the hypothesis without conviction.

'She'd be too, well, I don't know the word I want. Interfering and noisy. She wasn't a mathematician, was she?' Robert sounded interested.

'Historian, as far as I remember.'

'There was about my father a kind of privacy. He had to take himself away from time to time. My mother understood this, and I think Francis and I did, even when we were quite small boys. That was good for him while he'd plenty of other irons in the fire. But when he retired, then he was lost, hadn't enough to fill his life. Had my mother lived it might have been different.'

They progressed along the tiled floor, black and red, into the kitchen. They pushed the door open. Felicity and Colin stood at the ready.

'Here come the philosophers,' Colin said.

'All sorted out?' Felicity asked.

'All, and more,' her husband answered.

'Right, Annie,' Colin spoke cheerfully. 'Time we skedaddled, and left these busy people to their work.' He kissed Felicity's cheek, shook Bob's hand; Anna touched fingers with both.

Colin rushed away, round the corner of the terrace while his wife followed more sedately. When they had settled in the car, fastening their seat-belts, she asked,

'Decent pair, don't you think?'

'She was bright,' he said. 'Clothes-wise.'

'And he was very handsome.'

'So we were both suited. Would you like to meet them again?'

'I wouldn't mind. I've no strong feelings. Robert didn't seem very like his father. In fact I didn't make him out at all. When he talked, it was all very sensible, but it was as if he was answering questions about characters in a book.'

'I don't follow you,' Colin said.

'They seemed cut-out figures. You could say half a dozen things

135

about them, and then that's it, done, finished. You can't do that with real people. And how did you find Felicity?'

'Good for an hour's company. As long as something else is going on. A round of golf, say.'

'Your rounds usually last longer than an hour.'

'We'll take them out for dinner while they're here. That is if they have time.'

'Where?'

'I'll think of some place.'

He was out in the afternoon, she did not know where, but was back by five. He seemed glum.

'I rang the Normans, but they won't be able to come out with us for dinner. Both of the evenings they'll spend here are already spoken for.'

She told him how she proposed to feed the children, and he said that it seemed satisfactory to him. Colin seemed preoccupied so that she wondered if the cancelled meal had disappointed him. Perhaps he'd picked out Felicity as someone worth charming or impressing, and now he regretted the lost opportunity. He hung about the kitchen, examining surfaces, frowning. She said nothing.

'How long before the meal's ready?' he asked as he moved towards the door.

'Six o'clock,' she said, 'if nothing interrupts me.'

He stopped at the door, gripping on to it, swinging it twelve inches backwards and forwards. He stared down at his shoes. She waited. In the end he looked up, smacked the door hard on the side of his right brogue, glanced down angrily.

'Do you remember the name James Glover?'

'No.' After a moment's thought. 'Should I?'

'I told you about him. I met him in town one morning. He was on his way to the General Hospital for tests.'

'He was at school with you. Had cancer. You invited him in to your office.'

'That's right. He's dead.'

'Did you keep in touch with him?'

'No. It was in this evening's *Post*.' He unwrapped the newspaper he carried. She had noticed it, neatly folded in his hand. 'Here. He laid the paper flat on the table and pointed. She read: 'GLOVER, James Arthur. In loving memory of James Glover, beloved husband of Marilyn, adored father of Frederica and

Samuela, who died peacefully in the City Hospital after a long illness, bravely borne.' There followed the date of the cremation ceremony, one week and one day ahead. 'Family flowers only. Donations to Cancer Research.'

'Are you going to the funeral?' she asked.

'I hadn't thought of it.'

'Have you seen him at all since that morning?'

'No, I haven't.'

'He didn't try to get in touch with you?'

'No. Not to my knowledge.' He wiped the clenched left fist savagely across his mouth. 'Do you think I should write to his wife? I could get the address from the 'phone-book.'

'That might be a good idea,' she answered.

'Would you,' he asked, 'would you sketch it out for me? I'm not very used to writing that sort of thing. I know you aren't either, but it's more your line. You could think up a good quotation or two. To comfort her. I should just be clumsy, and might very well put my foot in it.' He paused; she did not answer. 'Will you?'

'Yes,' she said. 'You'll need to tell me again about that morning you met. And also a bit about him as a schoolboy.'

He nodded agreement and relief as he re-folded his newspaper. 'Thanks.' Gruffly.

'I'll do it after dinner, and we can discuss it.'

'Good,' he said. 'Thanks, Anna.' He rarely used her Christian name. 'When I come to copy it out, should I do it in handwriting or get my secretary to put it on the w.p?'

'Up to you. It doesn't much matter these days. Some old-fashioned people might consider handwriting more polite or more, oh, heartfelt, sincere, but I don't think it makes much difference these days. Easier to read seems to be the criterion.' She smiled. 'I do think you ought to turn up at the crematorium.' She held his objection at bay with a finger. 'It comforts the family. Gives them something to talk about. Who was that tall man, and so on? It won't make any difference to him, but the sight of the pair of us might give them two minutes' relief.'

'You'll come with me?'

'Surely. But you're much more used to attending funerals than I am.'

'But this is different. I shan't know anybody.' He tapped the door. 'I've been thinking about Jim Glover. He'll be in his late forties, my age. He ought to be at the height of his powers. On top of his job.'

'If he's that sort of person,' Anna warned.

'Yes, oh, yes. But it made me wonder how I'd shape up if I were suddenly faced with terminal cancer. I'm the same age. His children are younger than ours. And there he is, condemned, frightened, thrashed about with horrible chemotherapy, sick as a dog.'

'Yes,' Anna said, dragging the word out, allowing him time to recover.

'He's like me, must have done things at work, had holidays with his family, is probably still paying his mortgage off, and then with next to no warning, the end. I don't know what I'd have done. He seemed moderately, y'know, composed in his mind when I saw him. Worried about getting there in time, not keeping anybody waiting.'

'I guess that your habits stay with you even in these dreadful circumstances. He'd probably not be the sort of man to kick up a fuss, to be polite, whatever the provocation. And that stood him in good stead.'

'But he was going to die.'

'I'm not saying he was not terrified, not disappointed at the things he'd be going to miss, not apprehensive about the future of his wife and family. He'd be all that, and more. Sick to the soul. But when he met a comparative stranger like you, he was able to put on this performance because he'd had so much practice.'

'Good God,' he said, in mock admiration.

'And another thing,' his wife riposted, 'why do you always stand at the door when you're going to talk seriously to me. Is it because you can run away?'

'Only if I don't like what you're telling me.'

'I'm willing to sit down and talk to you.'

'I know.' He left his door, made three quick strides towards her, put an arm about her waist and kissed her mouth. His face was smooth. He had recovered.

They attended the ceremony at the crematorium. As Colin had guessed they knew nobody amongst the thirty or forty people present. On the way out they shook hands with James Glover's wife, who stood dry-eyed and tense with her children in a flower-decked dark room off the main hall. She thanked them for their presence, as she did all the other mourners.

'I was at school with your husband,' Colin said, explaining himself. Mrs Glover bowed her head. Anna thought he might as well have spoken to her in Greek. They did not loiter after the service, but people looked at them with admiration. Colin's Daimler, chosen as suitable, outshone the undertaker's limousines.

'I don't know,' Colin said as he drove off.

That night they made violent love, and clung deliriously each to the other.

XI

Anna described James Glover's funeral to her parents over coffee at the manor house. Nancy Johnson was absent, visiting a sick friend in Essex. Kuno sat generously cheerful, though the weather gloomed. Hilda, always delighted to see her daughter, plied her with questions about Glover, his illness and his family.

'You seem surprised that Colin went?' Hilda pressed.

'I was.'

'Why? Surely in his line he must often attend funerals? Business people?'

'Yes, but they're social gatherings. Not much different from annual dinners, or conferences. They may be sorry that Old So-and-So has gone, but the interesting bit is the chitterchatter and the social drinks, and I guess more often than not the professional talk. That's so, isn't it?' she demanded of her father.

'You're right. I wish I had a tenner for every funeral I've attended. But the very odd thing is that in this part of the world accountants seem to manage their three score years and ten, if not more, without too much difficulty. Witness me. Seventy-eight this year and still going strong.'

'Not a stressful occupation?' asked Anna.

'I would have said so. And utterly sedentary. And much given to car-travel to save time.'

'And alcohol,' Hilda added.

'All that. And yet we do pretty well in the longevity stakes.'

'You've all married sensible wives who see to it that you eat in a healthy way. And take some exercise at weekends.'

'We keep you from extremes.'

'I don't know about sensible wives,' Kuno said. 'I can't think of one single woman amongst my colleagues and acquaintances I would have wanted to marry.'

'Get away,' Hilda said. 'You were quite dazzled at one time by John Stacey-Roche's gorgeous second wife.'

Kuno glowered, his usually pale face brick-red.

'She was a beautiful woman,' he answered. 'I'll allow you that.'

Hilda bit her lip, realising perhaps that this time she had gone beyond the bounds of propriety, and would pay for it.

'And Colin behaved himself?' she asked.

'Yes, he did. He was utterly modest, drew no attention to himself. He just said on the way out to Mrs Glover that he had been at school with her husband.'

'I would guess,' Kuno said, recovered now, 'that the pair of you stood out, head and shoulders above the rest. If not in height, in what the papers call charisma.'

'Colin's tall enough,' Hilda said. 'What is he, Anna?'

'Six, three.'

'Why did he go? Did he know the family? Or anybody.'

'No. Absolutely nobody. It was this chance meeting one morning when Glover was on the way up to the hospital for tests. Colin took him into his office for a few minutes.'

'And kept in touch thereafter?'

'No, he didn't. He read about his death in the local newspaper. He decided to write to the family, or at least got me to do it for him. I said he should turn up at the funeral service.'

'Why did you do that, Anna?' her father asked.

'I don't know, really. I was surprised, I suppose, that he raised the matter of James Glover's illness and death. Usually, if he thinks about such things, and I'm not so sure that he does, or not often, he doesn't share his conclusions with me. That might be that he's shielding me from his worries, or that he hasn't got any.'

'Your father was just the same.'

'I talked to you often enough,' Kuno objected.

'Yes. About what was going on at work, or bits of scandal, or music, occasionally, concerts, the theatre, holidays.'

'Isn't that enough?'

'When you told us that you were going to marry Colin, your father never gave me any idea of what he thought.'

'There was no need,' he said, defensively.

'There was. You worked with Colin. He was your employee and then your partner. You must have known what sort of man he was. You saw him every day of the week.'

'How a man shapes up at work doesn't of necessity indicate what he'll be like as a husband.'

'No, but it may. It was worth discussing. Whether he had a short temper or shouted his colleagues down or made passes at the secretaries. These might have given me some notion of what he was like.'

'You weren't marrying him. It was Anna.'

'But don't you think I was worried, or interested, or even curious?'

'It was no part of my business to interfere. Colin was Anna's choice.'

'You'd have been speaking your mind quickly enough if she'd announced she was marrying a drug-addict or a road sweeper or an unemployed immigrant.'

'Those would have entailed obvious drawbacks. I saw no such obstacles to successful partnership in Colin.'

His wife waited. Kuno looked uncomfortable.

'You knew he was a lady's man,' the mother said.

'I know people in the office said as much. That does not make it the truth. The girls there would have said as much about any young, handsome man. We never had a single complaint from any of them. About what they call sexual harassment nowadays.'

Kuno spoke with a flat voice, reciting what might have been reciprocally agreed facts. He did not seem to consider the effect of Hilda's accusation on her daughter. His wife gaped, unusually dumb. Anna looked from one to the other, a headmistress summing up two juvenile delinquents. She, she admitted it to herself, was shocked at their frankness in her hearing. Age had robbed them of tact and even of common courtesy.

'Don't mind me,' she said, icily.

'I'm sorry, Anna,' Hilda spoke at once. 'I raised the subject. I shouldn't.'

'Yes,' the father agreed, nodding apologetically. 'We aren't telling you anything you don't know, are we?'

'Kuno,' Hilda gasped. 'I'm sorry, Anna darling. We shouldn't be interfering. It's entirely my fault. My long tongue ran away with me again.'

'That's all right,' Anna said, not meaning it, angry.

'Oh, no, it isn't.'

'Look, mum,' Anna used this diminutive for the first time in her life, 'I know what Col's like. And I can say this.' She spoke sternly. 'Though we don't always see eye to eye, he's never totally embarrassed me. He has, I think I can say, my interests at heart.' She enjoyed the cliché.

'Provided they don't interfere with what he wants to do,' Kuno sharply.

'Daddy.' Hilda blushed.

'I've mulled this over quite a lot recently, because I thought, still think, that in the past few months he's shown signs of change.' Anna spoke calmly.

'For the better?' Hilda, recovering again.

'That depends. On the surface he's the same Colin I married. With plenty to do, money to make, totally occupied. Work takes precedence every time. If it's the dinner I'm preparing or some extended interview he's unexpectedly busy with, my meal takes second place. That's sensible, isn't it, Daddy? Annoying to me, but if the interview's important, too bad?'

'As long as he doesn't expect a full meal two hours later than the expected time,' Hilda said.

'I don't think Colin would mind. He'd make himself a sandwich or cut a piece of cake, and not complain. But that's not really what I'm talking about. I'm a bit hesitant to say this because I may be reading my own wishes into it, but I've noticed that he has recently been a bit more concerned about what I could call human, emotional matters. Oh, he's just as hard-working, out just as much coining money, but he thinks about other matters.'

'Such as?' Kuno, interested.

"Some natural sorrow, loss or pain'.' She smiled at the father. 'Wordsworth.' He did not return her smile. 'He liked the ladies. I know for certain of four affairs he's had. He knows I know. I'm not telling you I wasn't furious at the time. Angry and cast down. I lost my self-respect. For a while. And I kicked out against it. I let him know what I thought. We had some ferocious quarrels, I can tell you. The only thing I was careful about was not to have them in front of the children.'

'We guessed, from time to time, that you were not getting on well,' Hilda said, weakly.

'No. Twice I threatened to walk out on him.'

'Did that frighten him?'

'Not really. Colin thinks, or thought at the time, that if you have enough money you can pretty well arrange anything. If I'd have left, he'd have had somebody in to look after the children, to take them to and from school, to provide them with meals, to see to their clothes. And deal with his meals and laundry. That might

143

well have run to two even three people, but he'd have paid up and looked pleasant.'

'But what about mother-love?' Hilda blurted out.

'I don't think he was much concerned with such concepts. I also guess that if the matter had been raised he would have argued that some hardship, if hardship it was, early in their lives would have done the children no harm. Life was a rough business, and the sooner they learned this the better for them.'

'Did he have a bad time at home then?'

'Not as far as I know. He had two parents, and a brother thirteen years older than he was who must always have seemed like an adult, even a second parent, to him. Again they treated him decently. Both boys were clever, went to the grammar school. That entailed some sacrifice, but I don't believe the parents begrudged it. You must have known them.'

'Hardly at all,' her mother said. 'We met the mother from time to time. Well, after you became engaged to him.'

'My impression was,' her father continued, 'that Colin didn't always see eye to eye with old Mr Turnbull. I don't know why.'

'There we are,' Anna said pacifically. 'Nothing ran smoothly with the young Colin. He knew his mind too well.'

'That's true, certainly. After he'd qualified in London he joined us. And it wasn't very long before he was telling his seniors what they should do. And that did not make him altogether popular.'

'But were his ideas right?' Hilda questioned.

'No doubt. He was outstanding. Accountancy on the whole is a rather dull occupation, depends on conscientious hard work, long hours, care. If you ask an accountant whether you should take some unusual or out-of-the-way direction, he'll usually warn against it, and provide a plethora of figures to back his opinion.'

'And that wasn't Colin's way?'

'If he saw you had a dog's chance with a scheme, he'd point out the ways he'd try, and the costs. He'd encourage that sort of initiative rather than otherwise. He'd even invest his own money. Of course if it was a mad-brained scheme, without viability, he'd say so. He frightened some of his older colleagues.'

'But not you?' Anna asked.

'Yes, I must admit that at first he did. I thought he was too arrogant by half. But when I understood the convincing way he argued his case, and he could put it clearly and forcibly, he didn't suffer fools gladly, and when after an occasion or two he was

144

proved right I realised what a gift he had. By the time we'd made him a partner, and God knows he was young enough, it was before he married you, he was amassing a considerable amount of money on his own account.'

'Without ever slipping up?' Anna asked.

'Not that I can recall. He may have had minor set-backs, but I don't remember them. He was outstandingly gifted with the handling of money. That's why we made him a partner early, because we thought he'd leave us, go to some larger concern and chance his arm.'

'Should he have done so?' Anna again.

'No, I don't think so. Or I'm not sure. You can do it all with a computer in an attic if you were so minded these days.'

'I can remember the time,' Hilda said, 'when they weren't certain whether to spell computer, computer or computor.'

'They know now.'

The three talked on for another twenty minutes but at random. They had spoken out of turn, revealed themselves and were uncertain of the consequences. Both parents came penitently out to the car to say good-bye to their daughter, but Anna, composed, smiling, the perfect lady disregarded their efforts. She drove off effortlessly at speed leaving the two stranded, outside in the winter's chill without coats. Once in the warmth of the foyer Kuno, rubbing bony hands, said, though tentatively,

'Well, we spoke a few home truths this morning.'

'It was my fault,' Hilda answered. 'I don't know why I had to drag it up about Colin's love affairs.'

'Anna took it calmly enough.'

'Yes. She seemed to. You never can tell with some people. She may have been concealing it inside herself.'

'No. She's like you. If she wants to say something she'll out with it, and hang the consequences.'

His wife shook her head.

'She knows what she's doing,' Hilda declared, 'but that doesn't mean she can't be hurt. She's put up with Colin's fancywork, and probably used it to her advantage. She's more like you than me, secretive. If Colin's wounded her he's paid for it, at least in her judgement.'

'What's that mean?'

'I'm talking out of the back of my neck,' Hilda answered, 'but I'm not sure that Colin's the sort who considers what other people are feeling, or what the effect of his actions is on them. He's too concerned with himself is our son-in-law.'

'A narcissist?'

'Call it whatever fancy term you like. But yes. He's a high opinion of himself and of the things he does and brings off. Other matters he might consider if the others aren't concerning him too closely at the moment.'

'Anna said he was changing.'

'I'll believe that when I see it. But as long as Anna's managing to live with him, that's all that matters.'

Hilda guided her husband towards the kitchen. 'At least she knows we're on her side. If he goes beyond the acceptable we're here.'

'I don't know what old crocks like us can do,' he said.

'We're not short of money.'

'Not so rich as Colin,' Kuno warned.

'No, but if he left her, I imagine her lawyers would dispossess him of a fair amount of that in her direction. But that's not really it. She seemed emotionally steady. She knows she admits what sort of man he is, or was, but she can still put up with it.'

'When we talked to her this morning, and I admit it was unusual, and I can't quite say how it all happened, I felt really proud of her.' Kuno spoke slowly, like a judge. 'I thought to myself, what a wonderful woman she was.'

'Because she copes with Colin's philandering?' Hilda asked.

'No. It was because she could control herself so strongly. Some wives might have screamed and run in hysterics round to their lawyers, but not she. She overcame her feelings to her advantage.'

'You seem to assume,' Hilda argued, 'that Colin and his falls from grace are worth putting up with.'

'You don't think so?'

'He's an attractive man, and in some ways a good father and certainly very generous to his wife, but some women would have called a halt to it all, got rid of him, and then perhaps have looked round for somebody better. She's still very attractive.'

'Is that what you would have done?' he asked.

'Probably. Fortunately you weren't that sort of man. But if you had gone chasing some woman, I'd have collapsed emotionally, and then run away. I'd have employed an efficient lawyer to screw money out of you, but I depended on you, Kuno, and no monetary solutions could have set that right.'

'You think Anna is not so dependent?'

'I'm sure she isn't.'

'And is that because she's trained herself or is it genetic endowment?'

'I don't know. A thousand and one things for all I can guess. Genetic endowment. That's a fine flowing phrase. Where did you dig that one up from?'

'You feel worse about all this than you admit,' he said.

'I don't like anyone to take advantage of me and mine.'

'Do you like Colin?' he asked.

'I've told you already that he's an attractive man, and you admit he's outstandingly good at his job. He goes out of his way to be pleasant to me. He's never done me any harm. But all that counts as nothing when I think of the hurt he's giving Anna.'

'But it isn't.'

'It's a possibility that he should consider. And not take the risk.'

They talked on, repeating themselves, as though they did not trust their premises. They left the kitchen, walked three times along the entrance hall and back, and then as if in agreement opened the front door and stepped out on to the portico. The cold air stung, and Hilda clasped her husband's hand.

'Too cold out here,' he said, 'without overcoats.'

He bent to kiss her forehead before they turned indoors.

XII

The discussion at Ashby must have influenced Anna, she admitted wryly, because when the next day Colin told her that some new friends of his, unknown to her, had invited them to stay at their Tuscan villa she immediately agreed to go.

'When?' she had asked.

'Beginning this weekend.'

'I'll have to make arrangements for the children.'

'They're old enough to look after themselves.'

She teased him, not unseriously.

'Is it important?' she asked. 'This sudden visit?'

'Important? I don't know. They seemed keen to have you there.'

'They've never met me.'

'That demonstrates how well I speak of you to them.'

'What do you say their name is?'

'Gooch. James and Sarah Gooch. He's a learned sort of man, was a don at one time though he isn't now. So you'll be able to talk about literature to him, and walk round Florence pointing out its beauties to each other.'

'And what's in it for you?'

'A short break with interesting people. I'm not averse to pleasure.'

It appeared he had met them a time or two in London. Jim Gooch now did publicity, and his wife, even more highly paid, was a banker. They work like dogs, the pair of them, but take a rest every so often, and that's why they had bought this villa.

'They've no children, so they can work as long as they like, but every so often they arrange to spend a weekend, a week, a fortnight out there.'

'How old are they?'

'He's forty-five, fifty perhaps. She's much younger. Not much above thirty.'

They flew out to Pisa, found themselves in high Spring. The

148

Gooches were warmly welcoming. Jim stood smaller than Colin, thin, extremely quiet, jokily academic in his manner. Sarah, prettily plump, moved gracefully about the house. Both were learning Italian from a BBC video, trying out their bits and pieces of learning on the locals.

'Sarah wants to be able to instruct the gardener, and I want to be able to read Dante,' the husband explained.

The week seemed both frenetic and yet restful. They'd decide at the last minute to dash out for a meal. Twice Anna cooked dinner, English-style, helped slightly by James. He seemed especially delighted on both occasions.

'I'm always the English abroad,' he said. 'Beef and two veg. Dark gravy, that's me.'

'You should taste her jam-roly-poly,' Colin boasted. 'Melts in your mouth.' Anna could not remember the last time Colin had congratulated her on her cooking.

They drank wine, but in moderation. Only on one evening did they overdo it, became noisy and boisterous, singing. Sarah danced to them, hoisting her skirts high up her well-shaped legs. Next morning they were subdued, creeping about the rooms, touching their heads.

'Indulgence doesn't suit my style,' James groaned.

'I've never seen you so happy,' his wife chaffed him, wanly.

They drove into Florence and spent the afternoon in the Uffizi galleries.

'Have you a favourite?' Anna asked James. 'If you were only allowed to see one, which would it be?'

'The Portinari Altarpiece,' he answered without hesitation.

'Who's that by?' she asked.

'Hugo van der Goes.' His pronunciation of the Dutch 'g's baffled her.

Ignoring the other two he led her to the picture, and the pair sat down in front of it. They scrutinised it in a satisfied silence at first before he made one or two explanatory remarks, for which she was grateful. She asked questions; he answered immediately with confidence.

'How old was he when he painted it?' she asked.

'Mid-thirties. He died in his early forties. We aren't absolutely sure when he was born. He died 1482.'

'Do you know,' Anna said, 'I thought you'd choose the Botticellis, "Birth of Venus" or "Spring".'

'This is a northern picture. Perhaps that's why I think so highly of it, though I love those other two. Look at those clouds.'

'And the flowers. They're so accurate, and modern.'

'They're symbols.'

'Of what?'

'The columbines represent the sorrows of the Virgin, the scarlet lily the blood of Jesus, the iris the sword that pierces Mary's heart, and the sheaf of corn Bethlehem, the house of bread.'

'Goodness.'

'If you count there are fifteen angels. They represent the fifteen joys of the Virgin Mary.'

'Would viewers have recognised these?'

'Yes. Some. They were matters of importance.' He breathed deeply. 'Vasari mentioned it in his *Lives*. It was in the church of Santa Maria then.'

'Isn't that little girl beautiful?' Anna said. 'But her hands are wrong. They're not children's. They're overworked and bony.'

'You're right,' he replied, smiling, as if pleased she'd found fault with this high art. 'Where are the other two?' he suddenly demanded almost in alarm. They looked about. Sarah and Colin were nowhere to be seen. They retraced their steps, and were rewarded in the corridor by the sight of the others, in cheerful animated conversation.

'I wonder what they're talking about?' she asked. 'They're certainly immersed in it.'

'Making money,' he said. 'That's what they are good at.'

They stood, watching their delighted partners below the decorated ceiling.

'This is a different world,' Anna said.

'I think I would have hated to live in the fourteen-seventies. The pain, toothache or earache, the short life, the filth they lived in.'

'We don't notice our sort of pollution,' she argued.

'Perhaps you're right.'

James looked suddenly infinitely sad. Colin caught sight of them and pointed them out to his companion. He snatched at Sarah's plump hand and swinging arms together they advanced down the corridor, humming.

'You'll get us thrown out,' Sarah warned.

'Straight into the Arno,' Colin added.

'You two look pleased with yourselves,' Anna said. 'What are you talking about?'

'Money,' Colin answered, lightly.

'Love,' Sarah solemnly contradicted.

All four laughed, hesitantly delighted at the incongruity.

The holiday seemed packed with unexpected moments like this. The weather remained fine, even warm, the city relatively un- crowded, the hills blue, the air clear. Sarah said she had never enjoyed herself so much, nor eaten so well; she regretted that she and James had to return to their jobs. She looked momentarily sad before she modified his disappointment with, 'It's what we're good at, and it makes us a good deal of money.'

'That means you can buy what you like,' Colin said.

'There's nothing I could buy that will bring me as much pleasure as walking out of my front door on a morning like this.' Sarah shook her head. 'James doesn't quite see it like that. He's an artefacts man.'

'True.' James bowed his head in mock humility.

Back in England, colder than Italy, the Turnbulls drove up the Al from Stansted, talking like recently reunited old friends.

'That was a good holiday,' Anna said. 'Unusual.'

'Yes. Fine,' Colin agreed. 'A bit too much culture for me. Pictures and statuary and buildings. Still, we didn't go to any concerts.'

'You're a philistine,' she threatened her husband.

'You were well away with Jim Gooch. I knew you would be. He knows a great deal, and he doesn't throw his weight about.'

'And what about you and Sarah?' Anna asked, tempting providence.

'Not my type,' he said. 'She knows what she wants.'

'And that is?'

'Her job. She works for an American bank. She's on a fair salary, but the bonuses she makes are something.'

'Did she tell you about them? Boast?'

'I asked her.'

'Isn't it bad manners to ask people how much they earn.'

'You might think so. And you'd be right in most cases. But that's what she's obsessed with. She wanted to be pressed, though she answered modestly enough. I guess she brings home rather more than she said.'

'And what does she do with it?'

'Precious little, I guess. It's Jim who buys the villa in Italy and pictures to hang in their houses. To her the pleasure lies in

151

actually making the money. She knows, somewhere in the back of her mind, that you can, with that sort of earning, do all sorts of things that most people would give their eye-teeth for, but that's not important. She wants to make money as well as, or rather better than, other high fliers like herself.'

'It's like playing Monopoly to her?'

'The way I put it, that's perhaps what it sounds like, but she knows it's more important than that. You don't pack the money away in a box at the end of the game, and not think about until next time it's fetched out. She knows that one day she'll wake up to the real world and there stashed away is all this capital which she can use.'

'Is that what she says?'

'No, not exactly. She doesn't talk philosophically. Not like you. She's interested in the techniques of ordinary everyday work, of the personalities, of the fashions that she has to work with. It's marvellous to her, and even more so now that she is sure, as other people are, that she's so good at it.'

'Has she always been like that?'

'When she married Jim, oh, eight years or so ago, she started off by becoming pregnant in no time. She thought that's what he wanted. He was quite a bit older than she was and he earned a large enough salary to bring up a family comfortably. But it went wrong, there was a miscarriage, so badly wrong, the doctors said, that she wouldn't be able to have any more children.'

'That set her back?'

'Yes. She took up again with a bank, did well there, was head-hunted by her present concern, The New York and Boston, and began to make big money.'

'She told you all this?'

'Not really. I had it, in bits of pieces over the time I've known them, and mainly from Jim. He's much freer with confessions than she is. He's a human being in a way she isn't.'

'I found him interesting. You know we spent quite a long time looking at a painting by van der Goes in the Uffizi. Now when we got back, the next day really, he gave me a little lecture on why he could accept the convention in this picture that some figures should be bigger than others. The picture is realist even when it's depicting angels or dragons but in the wing-paintings the saints, Margaret and Mary Magdalene and on the other side St Thomas and St Anthony the Hermit are larger than the humans, the two

152

Portinaris and their children, whereas in the centre piece the humans, Mary and Joseph and the baby and the shepherds are bigger than the angels.'

'Well, what of it?'

'Exactly. I hadn't even noticed these differences, or, if I had, had dismissed them, but for James they seemed to offer difficulties that he'd only conquered by hard thinking. I'd have said the angels were small because he had to pack so many in, fifteen, for symbolic reasons. But Jim thought van der Goes could easily have got round that if he'd wanted to, but he chose not to.'

'Why?'

'I'm not sure. It seemed a strange combination of symbolism and aesthetics. The little Portinaris were living, but the others were dead, or in heaven, and so very different in status from people alive at that moment in Bruges, whom you could run across in the street. And once that was settled, in Jim's mind as well as Hugo's, it was only a question of choosing the most pleasing position and size.'

'Typical of Jim, fighting a battle for a man who's been dead five hundred years.'

'I tell you another thing,' Anna said.

'Go on.'

'It's lovely to talk to you like this. We're getting better at it. No, keep your hands on that wheel.'

'That's good,' he said without embarrassment. 'And you continue telling me so. I didn't think that the sort of things I talked about would be very interesting to you. You've never seemed very impressed when I've mentioned some particularly bright business killing I've made. You looked pleased, but clearly you thought that's what I was there for. As if a policeman in uniform walked to the middle of the road and held his hand up and the traffic stopped. No big shout. You'd expect it. That bobby in his uniform represents law and order, and his hand held up judges and parliaments and traditions and God knows what, not a human being with special powers within himself.'

'You're getting philosophical, my man.'

'Living with you. That's the reason.'

'It's taken a long time.'

'Don't you go spoiling it, my girl.'

When they reached home, Anna found she'd run out of both

153

Earl Gray and Darjeeling. She'd walk out and replenish the stocks.

'It'll take you three quarters of an hour,' he said.

'You sit down and read your mail.'

'The important stuff is along in my offices.'

'Has your computer here broken down then?'

'Neither of them.' He put himself into the stance of a bare-knuckle pugilist. 'I tell you what, I'll walk down with you.'

'Not run me down in your car?'

'If that's what you want.'

'No. I could do with stretching my legs.'

'Exactly.' He emptied his large glass of water in one virtuoso swallow. 'That's quenched my thirst. And when we come back I'll drink tea for the pleasure of it. Then I'll go down to the office. I've already told them I'm dropping in this evening.'

'Will Serena be there?'

'Not she. She'll know what I ought to see, and have made it handy. I shan't do anything really tonight. Just look what's been happening while we've been in Italy. It's tomorrow the work starts.'

'Why bother going tonight then?'

'I enjoy it. Gives me something to think about. Unless you want to do something special. I'd have thought you'd have seen enough of me at close quarters this last week.'

'But what if you find something important's happened?'

'It hasn't. They faxed me three times at the Gooches'. All's calm. And Tracey said when I rang just now that all was quiet. No panic.'

'But you'll still go in?'

'I shall.'

They put on their coats and set off down the hill, on the broad road between large houses and great limes and horse chestnuts, still bare. He came into the shop with her, unusually.

'That's more like the shops of my youth,' he said when they came out. 'More packaged goods, but still plenty of ham on the bone and whole cheeses.'

'You pay for your nostalgia, you know.'

'That's what money's for. To splash about on meals that are no better than those my mother cooked at home. Or you for that matter. My father would have hated wasting hard-earned wages on fancy table-cloths, and dim lights, and superior waiters. Food appeared on his table at exactly the time he stipulated, and he sat down and ate it heartily, and quickly. He did not want it to be accompanied by clever talk or subdued music. Good meat and vegetables excellently cooked. He didn't need foreign sauces, he said, to take the edge off the taste, though I do admit he'd have mustard or horseradish with his beef and mint with his lamb. I used to argue with him when I was growing up and away from home at university. 'Widen your experience,' I'd say. But he wouldn't hear of it. Good food is in no need of improvement. 'But you cook it, and put a bit of mint in your new potatoes. You don't eat it raw,' I'd argue. And he'd look at me and say, "Our Col, you always take everything to extremes."'

They laughed as they walked, he at his memories, she at his excellent imitation of the local twang. She had not known Horace Turnbull, who had died before she met Colin, but she deduced that this was an accurate portrayal.

As they tramped uphill, Colin carrying her shopping-bag, a painter in white overalls was loading his ladders on the top of his van, having finished for the day. As he roped them safe, he sang not loudly but in a baritone voice that carried,

> 'Then shall I bear a larger part
> When grace has well refined my heart.'

The man completed his verse as they drew level.

'You in a male-voice choir?' Colin asked pleasantly.

'No. Why do you ask?'

'"Deep Harmony." It's a great favourite. My father used to sing it.'

'And 'Comrades in Arms' and 'The Long Day Closes', the man said. 'What choir was your father in?'

'The Carlton.'

'Good choir. Had a couple of uncles in it. Keen. Well, I shall have to be off. I've told the missus I'd be home by five today. First time this week.'

'You'll be in her good books, then?'

'Hope so. You never know. She seemed content with life first thing this morning. It was a beautiful day early on. It's spoilt itself a bit since. But for a start it was perfect.'

'We were in Italy,' Colin said. 'In Tuscany.'

'What a wonderful world.' The workman changed his voice from nonconformist chorister to husky jazzman.

The pair left him to it, but they were smiling. The new Colin had shown himself again, chatting to a stranger in the street. She took his arm.

On the next day her mother rang up.

'You're back from Italy, then?'

'We are.'

'Did you have a good time?'

'Very.'

Her mother paused, unusually, as if lost for a topic or suitable words. She cleared her throat.

'This morning we had some bad news, very bad news.'

Again Anna did not help out. Her mother liked to prove her independence, to work through her difficulties herself.

'It's Nancy, Nancy Johnson. She's died in hospital in Essex. She was on holiday.'

'Was it unexpected?'

'It was an accident. She was knocked down three days earlier by a car. She was in a coma, never came round, died yesterday. She was staying with her sister, or sister-in-law, no, sister.'

'She couldn't have been all that old, could she?'

'Fifty-seven. But she was quick on her feet, and her eyesight was excellent. She was out shopping with this sister, and wanted to cross the road. There were cars parked on both sides of the street and the two of them wanted to get to the other side so stepped between two parked cars. Nancy called to her sister, a Mrs Corby, to join her, but the sister, who is older, I guess, hesitated. Nancy looked back, stepped out straight into the path of a car which was coming down the road, and far too fast. There were witnesses. The police are talking about a prosecution. The car smashed into her, knocked her flat. She never recovered, was never likely to, the doctors said. Her head hit the road. Skull fractured, blood clots on the brain. That's what killed her though there were a great number of other injuries.'

'There's a son, isn't there?'

'Yes. I don't know much about him. They kept in touch, I believe, but he rarely came to see her. I don't know what he does, or even if he's married. She did mention him from time to time, but not in any enlightening way. She didn't offer any lengthy comment or information. I thought, and this may be my suspicious nature, that he was a bit like his father.'

'What does that mean?'

156

'Again she spoke very infrequently about him. The marriage was a mistake. He ran through her money, so that when he died she'd not a great deal of capital left. She'd bought her cottage.'

'What did her husband do?'

'She claimed he was an inventor, though I don't know what he invented. He sounded a bit like a con-man. She married late. She taught history in a grammar school. She mentioned that from time to time, but she didn't talk a great deal about her past life. Mostly about what she was doing now. When I think about it, I guess her main interest was our house. It gave her something to do, and kept her solvent. It's all come as a great shock to us.'

'Yes. Are you all right? Do you want me to come over?'

'We'd be glad to see you.'

'How's daddy?'

'It's hit him harder than it has me. He doesn't say much. You know what he's like. If anything goes awry, he's very quiet, shrinks inside his shell. He talked to me for a few minutes, when we heard this morning, and then hid himself in his office. That's his way.'

'He was fond of her, wasn't he?' Anna asked.

'Fond? I don't know if that's the word. Daddy doesn't like change. Perhaps because what happened to his family when he was a boy. And Nancy represented continuity. He'd found a niche for himself in Ashby here. And Nancy saw to it that the house was properly looked after. It wasn't altogether my style. I did my bit, but there was always something extra needed doing and she did it. All the furniture moving for that nativity play you came to see. She organised it. She liked that. It gave her a sense of status, a purpose in life. I think that he saw her as keeping things going on an even keel if anything had happened to me. She was quite a lot younger than I am.'

'You think he'd have married her?'

'No, I don't. Unless that was the only way of keeping her at the manor. I don't think he had much concern with her as a human being. As long as she was efficient, and drew his attention to things that needed attending to, and made no out-of-the-way demands she could do as she liked. She ordered the girls about and Mrs King, the cook. I never quite made out what she thought of your father. I did consider, at one time, that she had cast a favourable eye on that Mr Norman of yours, the teacher who died.'

'Would they have been suited?'

157

'I doubt it. He was getting on. Twenty odd years older than she was. And eccentric. She didn't say so much about him recently. They might well have made something of it together, I don't know. She established her routines with us quickly enough, and she might have done so with him. Most men like being looked after, cosseted, as long as they have their own little corner of life where they can throw their weight about.'

'I'll come up and see you for an hour. After lunch.'

'Can't you come up for lunch?'

'It's difficult. I have three or four chores to get off my back this morning.'

'Is Colin well?'

'Yes. He went out at seven before I was up. He'll be back at twelve-thirty for lunch. Or so he said. That's one of my tasks. To provide a snack for my lord and master.'

Hilda made a slight noise of disparagement, but said she looked forward to Anna's arrival that afternoon.

'Two o'clock,' her daughter said. She wondered as she sat at her computer whether Nancy Johnson's death had had a greater effect than her mother let on. After lunch, as soon as she drove into the manor drive and parked her parents came out and stood under the portico. Obviously they had been waiting for her arrival.

'You shouldn't be out here,' Anna warned. 'It's really cold.'

'We're not altogether fragile,' Kuno answered.

'The March wind doth blow.'

'No snow I hope,' Hilda said. 'They didn't mention it on an forecasts. Where shall we sit?'

'In the kitchen. Anywhere. I could do with a cup of coffee.'

'That's good. Your mother wouldn't let us have one after lunch. "Wait until Anna's here. She'll want one".' Hilda opened the door of the smallest sitting room, and officiously ushered them into it. She switched on lights, before moving off to make the coffee.

'How are you?' Anna asked her father.

'Middling,' he said, comically grumbling with the help of local usage.

'I was sorry to hear about Nancy Johnson.' Anna took up the subject immediately, knowing that was why her mother had pushed them into this room together, so the pair could talk unhindered for a few minutes. 'It must have been a shock.'

158

'It was. It was also typical, the way she went. Rushing forward. I'm surprised she didn't look about her.'

'Was she a driver?'

'She had a licence, and a car. She'd occasionally drive your mother's Rover down to the village if there was something heavy to be carried. And now and again, she'd take your mother to the super-market in Beechnall. Hilda said how well she drove considering how little she did.'

'No trouble with her eyes?'

'Not at all. She wouldn't be looking. An impatient sort of woman very often. She'd be hurrying her sister along, or instructing her. That was the odd thing about Nancy. When she was in this house she was calm, utterly reasonable at least when she was talking to us. She'd blast the girls or the cook or the gardener, I reckon. But this house cooled her temper.'

'Why was that?'

'She loved this place. It suited her. She saw it as large and beautiful and needing looking after in ways we weren't able to manage. She knew how much I appreciated living here, and we often talked about it. Once a month, sometimes more often, she and I would make an inspection of the whole house, and discuss what had to be done. Your mother didn't care all that much. Hilda would have lived in a tent in the garden as long as it was waterproof and warm. With one or two small exceptions.'

'If anything happened to you would Mummy stay here?'

'I doubt it, but your mother often acts out of character. She'd have the necessary money. I've seen to that. On the other hand, I guess she'd probably offer you the house on tempting terms. That's what I think. Do you like the idea?'

'I've never considered it, and I hope I shan't have to for another twenty years. Besides, I'd have to consult Colin.'

'And what would he say?'

'The children will soon have left home, and he's never shown any interest in becoming a landowner. Our present half-acre's quite big enough. But you're never sure with him. Once he was faced with the possibility, God knows how he'd react.' Father and daughter smiled warmly at each other, real friends. 'What will you do now Nancy's gone?'

'Advertise for a housekeeper.'

'And how do you think that will work out?'

'I'm always optimistic. I don't much like change, and so I'm

159

sorry that the present régime has ended. Especially so tragically, I might say. But at work if ever we lost someone I thought was pretty well indispensable, we'd on the whole find somebody just as good. They wouldn't be the same; some things would have to be altered, but there was in the long run no great loss to the firm. Even the other way round.' There was a formality about Kuno's utterance.

The door was quietly opened and Hilda entered with a trolley.

'I'm sorry I've been so long. Our friend interrupted me, and I had to put a coat on to inspect some spot he'd chosen for another cool greenhouse.' 'Our friend' clearly designated the gardener who had been, Anna, surmised, under unfavourable discussion earlier in the day.

'All satisfactory, then?' Kuno asked.

'Oh, yes. There's no need for another glasshouse, but he's convinced himself he needs it, and it's not unsightly nor in the way.'

'So you yielded.'

'Yes. I'll keep him happy if I can. He's a good worker. And it was worth going out. The magnolias and camellias are almost in flower. There's going to be a good show this year.' She arranged, then filled, and then handed out their coffee cups. 'Would you like a biscuit, Anna? We're trying to do without.'

'You're both thin as rakes.' That was not exactly true.

'Did you talk about Nancy?' Hilda demanded, stirring vigorously.

'We did.' Kuno spoke easily. Anna nodded. Both assumed serious faces.

'It was sad. And so unnecessary. I suppose she crossed the main road there as she'd go over your village street.' Anna spoke as at a distance from both. 'It doesn't seem right.'

'She could have dodged back if that motorist hadn't have been exceeding the speed limit,' Hilda said.

'That's a thing I often feel,' Kuno commented thoughtfully. 'Whenever I've cut myself or knocked my head on something or tripped over I think, "If only I could have that last minute back." And yet I never learn from it. I suppose it's because we get away with it nine times out of ten.'

'Kuno thinks these last few years were the happiest part of Nancy's life. It made up for some of the disappointments she'd suffered.'

'Nothing succeeds like success,' he said. His two women stared

160

at him as if he'd come out with an esoteric oracle. 'I found that this last winter when I was so depressed. If some small thing went wrong, I expected it to have further unpleasant consequences. I'm an optimist on the whole by temperament, and from experience. But if some shop or department didn't do exactly what they said they would, I expected a week of 'phone calls and then a string of wrong deliveries. Before, before I was so down in the mouth I'd expect them there next day bright as buttons with a water-tight excuse and a full apology.'

'But how could your depression affect what they did?' Anna asked.

'It didn't. I expected a whole series of subsequent disappointments. And even when they came up to scratch on the next day I didn't feel much better. I nagged at myself. "They should have got it right first thing." My brain seemed programmed to disappointment.'

'It couldn't have happened very often, could it?' Anna asked.

'People can't take telephone messages these days,' he grumbled. Hilda supported him. 'We had a long struggle with a delivery firm. It went on for weeks. I laugh when I think about it now, but then I thought there was some vindictive devil there who waited for the order to be made up – it was for a series of shelves for the garden shed – and then deliberately removed some small, not very important but irreplaceable piece.'

'Three shelves,' he said, 'on wooden brackets. All very plain. No fancy decoration. We gave them exact measurements and a drawing, a plan, taken from a magazine. You couldn't go wrong. And Daddy wanted to do it himself that summer before we set off to New York.'

'And did you get it finished?'

'Just.' Kuno's face grew saturnine. 'The morning before we left.'

'He threatened not to go, though he was the one who'd wanted and arranged the trip. It was an accountants' conference. Very good as it turned out.'

'Yes, I remember your going.'

'I had no time to prepare myself,' Kuno said.

'Was that necessary?'

'Of course it wasn't, but it's half the fun, if that's the word, for the likes of your father to be looking this up or checking that. He loves it. Shall I need any summer shirts? How many pairs of shoes? It's better than actually going on holiday. And as to the hours tickling his computer, well.'

'Sometimes I think your mother doesn't altogether approve of me.'

'I don't think you're altogether perfect, if that's what you mean,' Hilda answered.

They finished their coffee, and pulling on coats walked out into the garden. The wind blew keen, even in the sunshine. Hilda spoke delightedly of the beginning of Spring, but Kuno seemed shrunken, as if he barely filled his overcoat. They came across the gardener, hoeing vigorously round a spreading clump of primroses, in a part-shaded nook.

'Beautiful, beautiful,' Hilda said.

'Ay, and them snowdrops. They bin lovely this year.'

'They always are,' Hilda said.

'Ay, but they're getting so thick now. Be like a mat next year.'

The gardener looked to Anna for approval, and she smiled in return so that he nodded and felt rewarded.

'We're having a new greenhouse, I hear,' Kuno said.

'It'll pay its way.'

'In flowers, fruit, vegetables?'

'The lot, the 'ole bag o' mashin'. Early planting. Beans, runners, y'know. Be ready to plant out as soon as th' danger o' frost's over. Same with tomatoes.'

'But what if we get a late frost?' Kuno made conversation.

'If they gi'e us warnin' on the TV, I'll be ready for it. Seasons are acting a bit funny these days, but there we are.'

'Will you build the greenhouse yourself?' Anna inquired.

'Oh, ay. They deliver the parts, metal and glass, and a plan an' I wo'k from that. Your dad gives me an 'and sometimes.'

'The weather will have to be warmer than this,' Kuno said.

'It's on'y March yet. Gi'e it a chance.'

They returned to the house. Kuno made for the lavatory.

'He's a different man altogether when you come,' Hilda told her daughter.

'Do you think he's over this depression or whatever it was that troubled him this winter?'

'I think so. There are signs. He just hadn't enough to occupy himself with.'

'He goes into his office every day, doesn't he, and has a secretary up three times a week?'

'Yes. But he's not lost his wits, and he realises that he's only playing at working. If he locked that office door and never opened it, it wouldn't make two pennorth of difference to his income. Honestly. And his letters and study of the markets don't have any effect.'

'But if he joined, let's say, a golf-club or a gymnasium or a club or society for recreation it would cost him money. From what you say this doesn't.'

'That's right. But it didn't seem satisfactory to him. Last winter, especially. He frightened me. In some ways your Father is rather like your Colin, in that he doesn't talk a great deal about his work. Kuno thinks I've no interest, and I wouldn't understand it, anyway. What he'd give me from time to time were bits of gossip, that somebody had done something silly, or that somebody else was proving a disappointment and would have to be warned. That sort of thing. As well as little boosts to my confidence: that the firm had done really well recently, that we could afford a world-cruise for six months every year, except I'd have to go on my own because he couldn't find the time. That sort of thing.'

'And you never took him up on it?'

'No. I'd no interest, either. I like it in Munich or Dresden or Vienna with him to see him shedding his Englishness. He becomes a different man.'

'And you approve of that?'

'I've seen it happen many times, and I quite enjoyed watching out for the form it would take. And it did him a power of good. I don't suppose he ever could forget his financial transactions or his property deals, but he was in a different theatre for two or three weeks. You'll remember, how chuffed he was when local people thought he was German.'

'I remember he used to read his German Bible at home just before we went on holiday. And sometimes a novel. Böll or Grass. It surprised me.'

'And the firm took a German newspaper every working day for him.' Hilda gently massaged her face. 'I used to laugh at him. He made the firm pay for it, though he was the only one who read it. How mean can you get?'

'And all that's over?'

'I hope not. We've fixed up a real tourists' trip, along the Rhine, in two months. I think I told you. And that'll whet his appetite so we'll spend quite a lot of time over there.

163

'He won't mind leaving Ashby? Now Nancy Johnson's no longer here to look after the place?'

'I hope not. When he was so down in the winter, so that nothing seemed to go right, I used to think he wouldn't have minded dying. I don't mean suicide. I don't think it ever got down to that level, though I don't know. He was pretty bad. But sometimes when he was very low (I found him in tears and incoherent more than once), he'd say something that made me think that somewhere inside himself he was clinging on to the old Kuno.'

'Such as what?'

'Well, he'd say, that is when he could talk, how comfortable we were compared with people abroad who were starving or being driven out of their homes or slaughtered and mutilated in civil wars. "And some of them look just like us," he'd claim. He meant Europeans, not Africans. Just imagine people in this village chasing about killing each other.'

'I used to argue a bit. I think it did him good, and anyway I was so apprehensive about him I wasn't myself and would come out with things that would have been better left unsaid. I used to tell him we weren't divided by religion or race as these poor souls were and so it was unlikely.'

'And?'

'He'd say that I'd be surprised how quickly societies could change. I imagine he was thinking of Vienna or Berlin before the War. They were by any standards the most cultivated, civilised places in the whole world and in history, and yet Jews and political opponents of the Nazis were barbarically hunted to death.'

'I suppose he couldn't forget it?' Anna asked.

'Yes.' Hilda mused. 'And yet it seemed a sign of reasonableness on his part that he could compare his troubles with others elsewhere. He wasn't so cocooned inside his own depression that he couldn't see that many other people were by any standard much worse off than he was. But he was bad. No doubt.'

'I hadn't realised . . .'

'No, he always put on a good show when you came. It made me suspicious at first because I thought if he could act normally when you were there he couldn't be as depressed as he made out. But I don't think that's right. We're more complicated than we appear to ourselves.'

'Do you think it's connected with his earlier life?'

'I guess it must be. Though Dr Coombes says it's mainly

chemical. But environmental factors trigger the adverse reactions off. Coombes is quite good and sympathetic. He was very interested in the form your father's depression took.'

'Oh?'

'Daddy said it was as if his whole world was made of thin cardboard. The walls of his office in town would buckle and crack and one could hear the slightest whisper through them. And it was the same with the house here.'

'But he'd only to walk across and feel them to know they were strong.'

'He couldn't believe the evidence of his everyday senses. It seemed, he said, that the whole of life was like a dream. He was cut off from the world and from himself. There was nothing substantial about him or anything else. It collapsed if he looked at it too hard.'

'I can't understand that,' Anna said soberly.

'Neither can I, but I believe him. He's not the imaginative kind. And he admired and loved the solidity of places. He didn't want tents or groundsheets or garden sheds. He needed well-built houses and strong doors and furniture that didn't look as if it would collapse. That's what he was working towards all his life.'

'I thought he wanted to be completely English.'

'So he did. Without his parents' foreign accents, and customs.'

'Why did he have to leave Germany?'

'His maternal grandmother was Jewish. Not that I think she had any religious beliefs. And both his father's partners were Jews. When they were arrested or harassed or whatever it was at first, they both died in concentration camps, he decided to settle in England and look after the branch there. Kuno would be sixteen. They took him on at St Paul's School. His father had a rough time in the war. I think he was interned for a time. Your father didn't talk to me about it very much.'

'What was the firm? I mean, what did they do? Weren't they goldsmiths?'

'Jewellers. Your grandfather did quite well, was quite a rich man by the time he died, though the German branch was closed, and I don't think there was any compensation paid to anybody. Not that there was anybody much left to claim it. It seems unbelievable to me, the atrocities that happened, and they happened to ordinary people like your grandfather and his partners. It's no wonder that they are so unsure.'

165

'If I had been well-to-do and Jewish,' Anna said, 'in Vienna, I think I'd have just have hung about until it was too late. I'd have convinced myself that such things don't happen.'

'I know. And when I see pictures of refugees I'm amazed. They're just carrying some little bundle. When we go on this Rhine jaunt I tell you I shan't be able to carry just my clothes. And these are leaving home for good. What would you take?'

'Depends on the weather.'

Kuno returned, cheerfully now.

'Who are you two running down?' he asked.

'You,' Hilda answered. 'What do you expect? Come in and talk to this beautiful daughter of yours.'

He obeyed, and with alacrity.

XIII

Colin arrived home soon after five. Anna made no comment on his early appearance.

'How were they all at Ashby?' he asked.

She gave her report, and they discussed the evening meal.

'Let's go out,' he suggested. 'There's a new Thai place that Charles Smart raved over.'

'Not unless you're very keen. You go and put your feet up for an hour.'

'The lawn could do with a cut by the look of it.'

'Jack's put weed-killer on it, and scarified it, and fed it again from what he was telling me yesterday, and I don't know if it would be altogether wise to start cutting yet. Next week, perhaps. It's early, only March.'

'Whose lawn it it?' he asked.

'Legally? Aesthetically?' She waited for him. 'If I were you I'd leave it to Jack.'

'I might get a bit of useful exercise out of mowing. I'll ask Jack's permission if I see him tomorrow. He'll be glad if I take a bit of work off his shoulders.'

'He's always pleased if you take an interest and talk to him about it.'

Colin seemed remarkably cheerful, almost garrulous, pursuing her into the kitchen, and pulling out a stool. She knew he'd tell her the cause of his pleasure before too long. He seemed, though, in no hurry.

'Jack was asking me about some shares he's acquired. From some building society pay-out. Would that be right?' Anna began.

'Sounds possible.'

'I told him to chase you. "He won't want to waste his time on my few hundred," he said. No, I told him. He loves problems. Even little ones.'

'Tell him to bring his paper-work along and I'll see what's what.'

167

He sat proudly, humming and spinning a knife.

'Come on, then,' she said. 'Let's hear all about it.'

'About what?'

'You come in like a dog with two tails, offering to take me out to dinner or do some gardening, and following me around the house. I deduce that you've done something you're pleased about.'

'Two things.'

'Congratulations.'

'You don't know what they are yet.'

After all these, nineteen, years of marriage he was not sure how to impress her, even when he wanted to. He began to explain. He had sold some large investments, and made himself huge money. Number two, he had got rid of some property he had only recently acquired. This transaction had impressed the manager of his local property office, a laconic man, not given to exaggeration, rarely praising a soul, but this time he had described the profit, through tight lips, as 'obscene'. 'I'd have said that it would have taken somethin' like five or six years of careful bits and pieces of selling off to make anything like a fair return for your money. And you've done it under a twelve month. Did you know something I didn't, because it's right against the run of the market?'

'No,' Colin had been taciturn to match his subordinate.

'Well?'

'Luck. The devil's luck.'

'I don't believe it.'

'You're probably right.'

The two men had parted straight-faced. Colin had displayed outwardly none of the pleasure he felt, and he had no idea exactly what his manager thought. He guessed that the man was envious of him, and cast about in his mind for excuses for his own inability to match the boss's enormous success.

Anna listened to her husband's account. He sounded off excitedly, like a schoolboy chosen for the football team.

'Are you a millionaire?' she asked, with assumed naivety.

'Yes. Even on these last two little bits of jiggery-pokery. A million's not all that much these days. Kuno will be a millionaire.'

'That's the way. You make it, and I'll spend it.'

'But you don't. You live very frugally. It surprises me, I can tell you.'

'Are you suggesting,' Anna asked, 'in a polite way that I'm not very well dressed?'

'No, but you don't pay the big prices some women do.'

'I derive as much pleasure from a bargain in the dress shops as you do out of your clever investments or property deals.'

He screwed his face comically awry, like a gurner.

'I don't know how to put this,' he began, 'but I always regard you as an educated person. At least, compared with me. You've read an enormous amount, and listened to music. Looked at pictures and sculpture. You knock off crossword puzzles in no time, and talk to the Cowlings as an equal.' (They were both professors.)

'The Cowlings don't talk to you because they're frightened of you. You a paid-up, admired member of the world of high finance, whereas they are simple souls concerned with their mycology and philology.'

'Never mind them,' he said. 'I sometimes wonder if I'm doing right by you.' He waited for her comment, but received none. 'I do what I want, and when I want. You just have to fall in with it.'

'Have I ever complained?' she asked.

'Yes. Occasionally. When I haven't turned up. Or have had to cancel some engagement we've made. Or once, a holiday. But you're solely concerned with the house and the children. You don't go to Oxford to study that.'

'I didn't regard university, even then, all those years ago, as a training for a career. Except incidentally.'

'Stop bloody well arguing,' he said pleasantly, 'and let me get on to the point.'

'Right,' she answered, 'I'm better educated than you, but spend my time as a mere domestic drudge. Is that the point?'

'One step further,' he said. 'Are you satisfied with that?'

'Why shouldn't I be?'

'I've been thinking these past few months, especially since I've been making so much money, and so easily, about what I should do with it. Do I move to a bigger house, or a second one abroad, or have two Rollers, or solid gold lace-holes on my shoes? Do I buy an aeroplane? Or present you with one? And the answer is "No". To all intents and purposes I'm no more than my father was. He made a bit of money, in rather slow time, I admit, so that he could live comfortably. He gave us boys a good start in life, perhaps not so easily for Terry as for me. And Terry is exactly the

169

same. He's a conscientious man, gives satisfaction, and has more than a couple of ha'pence to rub together in his pocket. But he's no big ambitions. Not like your father, for instance.'

'Go on.' "This night thy soul shall be required of thee."'

'Balls. I'm not talking about religion, but if you make money you should do something with it.'

'I thought the pleasure derived from the actual acquisition of wealth.'

'Something in that, I'll admit. More than something. But I'm coming round to see that your father's ambition to be a full-blown English gent, something of a landowner, was worthwhile.'

'Why should that be so?'

'You know as well as I do. He was a refugee of sorts. A German. A continental. And now he's settled amongst us, he wants to be distinguished from the rest by his high-class Englishness, milord of the manor. That's what his past led him to. And the desire's worth spending on.'

'And yet,' she said, 'he loves to go back and speak German and be taken for a native.'

'We all like our party-pieces. That's his.' He looked grim. 'But what puzzles me is that you, his daughter, a beautiful and gifted woman, seem quite content to potter about at home.'

'It's not very important to look after children full-time?' she asked.

'I wouldn't deny it. But youngsters who have nannies, or go to crèches, or are sent away to school when they're older don't seem much worse than those who have been supervised by their mothers.'

'Anecdotal,' she said. 'I'd like to see some supporting figures.'

'Agreed,' he said. 'But are you happy? Am I doing right by you?'

'We've been married nineteen years, and I've not threatened to walk out on you yet.'

'I'd be lost,' Colin said, 'if you did.'

He nodded gloomily over this.

'Linda,' he began, 'our sister-in-law, she built a Greek temple in her back garden.'

'And is that good?' Anna asked.

'She was doing her own thing. And she got Terry to help her. And he'd look on it as lunacy.'

'But you don't?'

170

'No. I don't think much of it. When it's built it's nothing much more than a garden hut. She can go and sit out there and drink her coffee if the weather's fine. It takes up more room than a practical bit of shed-building would, but the thing is it's what she wanted done, and she got the money together and the workmen and the ideas and she did it. Terry must have thought she was cracked, but he didn't try to stop her. He did the wiring for her, in fact.'

'And you approve?'

'I don't suppose . . . Yes. I do. She did her own thing.'

'But suppose instead of a temple of Diana, she'd have decided on a charity collecting-point for Oxfam, or Cancer Research or Children in Need so she had a long, dull storehouse spoiling the look of the place for Terry?'

'I don't care what it is. She, like your dad, had an ambition and achieved it.'

'Is it that, or isn't it rather the out-of-the-way nature of the project that impresses you?'

'You may well be right. I mightn't have noticed it otherwise with my head stuck so deep in my cash-book.'

'But,' Anna argued, 'you can't guarantee that your manor house or Greek temple will continue to bring satisfaction. My father, for whatever reason, had a bad winter, and neither his English house nor his continental holidays could drag him out of his depression. And then, circumstances change. Nancy Johnson gets herself run over. She's made herself a part of Daddy's ambition. Now she's gone, it's as if a wall or pillar has collapsed and thus threatens the whole structure. We can't plan for every eventuality.'

'Then we have to change. Your Dad knows that perfectly well from his work. If things weren't running smoothly, he'd alter them quick enough, I'll tell you. He was very astute at spotting weaknesses and setting them right.'

'I'm sure. But he's getting old now, and less confident.'

'He's only mid-seventies.'

'Seventy-seven,' she corrected him, smiled, and asked briskly, 'Just tell me what you're heading for. How are you going to comfort your old age?'

'Good question. I never thought I'd live to be old. My father died at sixty-six and was still working. I'd thought I'd die in my sixties, that's when I did think about it, which wasn't very often,

171

and leave you a great deal of money to spend as you liked.'

'And how did you imagine I'd spend it?'

'I never considered that. That would be your look-out. The children would be off your hands and Kuno and Hilda probably dead. You'd be perhaps in your early sixties and full of life still. The whole world your oyster, and money there in abundance to be enjoyed.'

'I'll begin to think about it,' Anna said laughing. 'I've enjoyed all that, but now it's away to the kitchen.'

'Don't bother. I'm putting on too much weight as it is.'

'Well, go out for a short jog. Dinner will be in an hour.'

She left the room and her husband in a daze of pleasure. If they had had such a discussion ten years ago, it would not have been long before they would have been at each other's throat, quarrelling, scoring mean points. Now they could talk over tricky matters, skirt difficulties, skate round them. The cynic in her suggested that they did not care now, that it did not matter. Their nineteen years of marriage had knocked the sensibility out of them. They'd put up with the set-backs, and snags, the sore and bloody wounds, even, of the relationship and grown carapaces to keep themselves intact from too deep a trauma. Besides, Colin had just done well for himself, excelled his usual marvellous performances and he had shared his joy with her in this way, by discussing their lives without rancour. She had not expected this. She went singing about the kitchen.

The next time, three days later, that she called in on her parents she found that they had been invited to a memorial service for Nancy Johnson.

'Where's that taking place?' Anna asked her mother.

'I've forgotten the name of the village. Your father has the letter. He'll show it you. It's where she was born and grew up.'

Kuno came in, all smiles, and was sent out to bring the invitation. When Anna had read it, he opened it up again and refreshed his memory.

'It's from her son. I thought she didn't get along with him?' Anna asked.

'No more she did,' her mother answered. 'He rarely came up to see her or wrote or 'phoned.'

'As far as we could make out,' Kuno said, 'he was like his father, something of a con-man.'

'He has a job of sorts,' Hilda objected.

'Good for him.' Kuno, dryly. 'We've been wondering why he's bothered.'

'He lives not far away from the place. Nancy left him her cottage up here, and the little house she lived in down there. So perhaps he felt grateful coming into property, and thought he'd be generous. It wouldn't cost him a great deal. Cups of coffee and a buffet lunch in the church hall.'

'But more than if he did nothing,' Anna said.

'I don't know,' her mother said.

'I'd say,' Kuno answered, 'it's typical behaviour. Of that sort of man. He can't resist putting on a show even if there's no advantage to him. He'll be doing the right thing, and lording it.'

'Will there be many people there?' Anna asked.

'I shouldn't think so. Some of the locals will remember her. But she never talked to us about great numbers of friends. A few old colleagues, perhaps. I just don't know.'

'Are you going?' she asked.

'I don't think so,' Hilda answered. 'It's too far for us to drive in one day, there and back. We'd be worn out. And I'm not so sure we're safe over any sort of distance. Your father's eyes aren't so good. As to me, I've lost my nerve.'

'I'll take you in my car,' Anna said, almost without thinking.

She had the impression that her parents enjoyed the day under her charge. They drove easily down to Ringfield where they were greeted by a chilly shower. The church, a modern brick-built place, low-roofed with mean gothic windows, was as disappointing as the service. They learnt little about Nancy Johnson; her son, a ubiquitous presence, made no public statements, took no formal part in the obsequies. An old colleague croaked about the conscientious nature of her teaching. An even older woman recalled Nancy as a girl in the village school, clever and pretty, always ready to lead, even in mischief. The vicar, who had never met her, made his dull catalogue of events and virtues with a flat voice and frequent recourse to his notes. The singing of two hymns, 'Morning has broken' and 'Be still for the presence of the Lord', was accompanied on a tinny piano.

They were conducted across to another building, not unlike the church in architectural drabness, set back in front of a pine plantation, the village hall for what Kuno, stimulated now by the tedious proceedings called 'carbohydrate and coffee'. Hilda, eating little, said that at least the coffee was hot, and the loos clean. Nancy's son, Gregory, descended two or three times on the Meyers, inquiring after their welfare. Obviously impressed by Anna, he boasted to her of one or two of his recent business successes; she listened with the smiling aloofness of an external examiner. Gregory realising that he had failed to excite his mother's closest acquaintances began to talk investments to Kuno who barely answered, vaguely professing his ignorance. He turned to Hilda and described a curious picture, or chart, which Frank Norman had left to his mother. The description of this 'valuable piece of work' was vague, as was his knowledge of its date of composition or its provenance. One thing, he said, he was convinced of. It was worth a great deal of money on account of its unique nature. The Meyers became more polite as their incredulity increased. On his last descent he invited them back to see his mother's old house before they left the village, but they refused saying that they wanted to arrive home while it was still light. He gave them up, but they could easily imagine how he would malign them in conversation with his cronies.

En route home Kuno, in the front seat, dissected Gregory's character over his shoulder with his wife who sat behind him. He could not imagine how anyone, he said, as straight as Nancy Johnson could have given birth to and reared so slippery a creature.

'Are we responsible for our children's failings?' Anna asked from the wheel.

'To some extent,' he answered.

'We take credit for their virtues,' Hilda said. 'So.'

'Whenever I look at you,' Kuno said to his daughter, voice ruffled with phlegm, 'I feel proud.'

'Steady,' Anna said. 'Not too many compliments, or I shall have us off the road.'

'He means it. He's admired you since the day you were born. That's why we decided on Anna for a name. It signifies Grace. My name is rather heavier. Hilda, a battle.'

'Very suitable,' Kuno answered pleasantly.

'What does that mean?' Anna asked.

'Your mother likes her own way. And is prepared to fight for it.'

'I never heard the two of you arguing when I was a girl. And that was unlike the parents of some of my friends. Do you

174

remember the Barnetts, Diana's mother and father. They used to shout and swear at each other, and one would comment adversely to me, a teenager, about the other partner. The father was especially bad.'

'Did you find it embarrassing?' Hilda wanted to know.

'Dreadful. And poor Diana didn't know where to put herself.'

'What sort of man was he?' Hilda asked.

'Ex-grammar school. He owned several businesses. He wasn't without money. He later had a partnership in Jim Accord's betting shops. That made them a pretty fortune when they sold them off. He was handsome, and spoke quite well. And when he was dressed up he really looked the part.'

'Do you ever hear from Diana?' Hilda asked.

'I run across her from time to time. Last week at Annette's fashion show.'

'What does she do?'

'She's married to a farmer in quite a big way. But she's always complaining how poor they are. Not that she looks it.'

'What happened to the parents?' Kuno demanded.

'They're still together, I believe; I haven't heard otherwise.'

'They didn't split up?'

'Not as far as I know.'

'And do they still quarrel? Publicly?'

'I'm not sure of that. I did just see them once about two or three years ago. It was at a charity bring-and-buy sale I helped organise. They looked much the same, or a bit older as you'd expect. They were no different from any other middle-aged or elderly couple. They talked to each other, and to me. Quite affably.'

'They don't quarrel any longer, then?'

'That I don't know. I saw them for perhaps five minutes at the outside.'

'Diana doesn't say anything?' Hilda, again.

'Not to me. But, then, she never did.'

'Perhaps they've grown out of it,' Kuno said. 'They've become more mellow as they've grown older.'

'That sometimes happens,' Hilda answered. 'My temper is less short than it was. Or perhaps I have realised at long last that however annoying Daddy's arrangements are, and however little he's consulted me, it won't matter a scrap in a month or two's time. We were lucky. I don't brood over slights and set-backs, and as long as Kuno's allowed a free hand with the one or two things he considers important, he lets me have my head. That's so, isn't it, darling?'

Kuno grunted muted agreement.

'But,' Hilda continued, 'it's not so with everybody. I know at least two couples in the village who have got worse as they've aged.'

'Who are they?' Kuno asked.

'If you don't recognise them from what I've already said, you could easily work it out for yourself. But in one case they can't do anything right for each other. If he brings her a cup of tea, let's say, while she's out in the garden, she goes for him, and says he knows damn' well she doesn't want tea out there. It wastes time. And gives her indigestion. If she wanted anything then it would be iced water. If the next day he took her a glass of water, she asked him what she would want with that on a cold day. It's almost as if they're programmed to take umbrage at whatever the other partner does.'

'Are they decent people?' Anna asked. 'Otherwise?'

'Yes. Very. And if you talk to them he always expresses admiration for his wife and what she's done. You get the impression it was a love match.'

'They're elderly, I take it?' Anna said.

'Yes. But, and this is sad, I hear from a neighbour who's in their house practically every day of the week, that she, the wife, has taken to violence, to hitting him.'

'Isn't it usually the other way round?' Kuno murmured.

'I'm no expert, but that's what you gather. Perhaps women are less free with their fists and feet, or more scared of being hurt. In this case, she took to pummelling him. He apparently did not hit her back, merely lashed her with his tongue. It seems such a pity.'

'Would you say they were educated people?' Kuno asked.

'Yes. Both are university graduates. I don't know whether that makes any difference.'

'I'm told,' Anna said, 'that solicitors are as likely to beat their wives as, say, miners.'

'Thank God I'm not a solicitor,' Kuno said.

They talked most of the way home, though Kuno dozed off from time to time. Hilda said he had been very much better these past few weeks, and had now taken to short, steady strolls, weather permitting, most afternoons of the week. He had left the

176

appointment of a house-keeper entirely to her, and had even said that perhaps it would be wise to quit the manor house, and live in a smaller place.

'And what do you think?' Anna asked.

'I'm like all old people. I don't like change, but I see that if we don't go now, I shan't be able in a couple of years' time to cope with the physical move, all the clearing out and clearing up.'

'So what are you doing?'

'We've advertised for a housekeeper, both locally and in the London press. If we get someone suitable, then we shall stay, and only leave when we're carried out feet first.'

'Have you had any takers?'

'Yes. More than I expected. Daddy says not to rush things. And another thing is that he'd like you to join me on the selection committee.'

'I'd only be a nuisance. If I supported you I'd be superfluous, and if I opposed you, wrong.'

'Will you join me? I'm serious about this.'

'Right-ho. Except I don't know what you want. You'll have to make it clear to me.'

'I will. You can be certain of that. One of the reasons that your father wished you to be involved was that he claimed it was one of the pleasures of his life to hear you and me talking together. We're like sisters, he says, not mother and daughter. We're mature equals. We can disagree without losing our heads, and laugh at each other. It's something he says he's not often met. We're satisfied with our status; there's no rivalry or scoring off each other. We talk for the pleasure of it and from what we can learn from each other.'

'Well, you could fool me,' Anna said.

'That's his line, often repeated now. I think he believes it, but as you see he's not so delighted with his dear ones' conversation that he can keep awake to enjoy it.'

'You'll have to tell me what a housekeeper does.'

'We'll discuss. Maturely. Like sisters.'

Anna experienced especial pleasure, tapping her hands on the steering wheel.

XIV

A week or so later, after two further chatty visits to her parents, Anna was preparing dinner and talking to her children. They had acquired the habit of coming occasionally into the kitchen when they arrived back from school, and spending half-an-hour with her. They were not nuisances, knew how to keep out of the way, how to lend an unobtrusive hand, did not inflict themselves on her too often and were invariably interesting. Thomas, seventeen, would help himself to things to eat, laughing out of court her objections that he'd spoil his appetite. If both were there they'd exchange ideas in what seemed to their mother a thoroughly grown-up way. They could be malicious about their friends, critical sometimes but less often about each other, but never extravagantly so, and always with the idea of entertaining their mother with their comments. They seemed to need her approbation. Alice, a year younger than her brother did not much like Tom's present girlfriend, who was in her tutor-set, though she made no great show of her disapproval. The words she chose to describe the girl were comically old-fashioned, 'a forward hussy', 'a pinhead', 'a painted dolly-bird' and were always accompanied by a warming smile. The insults were never delivered to Tom himself.

This evening as the three were talking they heard Colin come in, shout greetings, bang a door or two.

'Daddy's home early,' Alice said.

'No more money left for him to shovel up.' Tom.

'You shouldn't complain,' his sister answered.

'I wasn't just thinking about my allowance.'

'He'll be in here shortly,' Tom guessed.

'Five minutes?' Alice.

'Three,' Tom said, checking on his wrist-watch as the door handle rattled and Colin entered.

He looked them over.

'Hello, hello,' he said. 'Family conference? Who's feeling the lash now? I hope it's not me.'

'I'll have another rock-cake, if I may,' Tom said, ' and then get off and on with my physics.'

'Just pass me one while you're at it,' Colin said, 'if you please.'

'Is that all right, Mum?' Tom queried. His father looked affronted. 'Catch,' the boy called. He lobbed; father neatly caught.

'And how's my Ally?' Colin asked, pointing.

'At the peak of my powers,' she answered. They all laughed, appreciatively. Anna wondered from where the girl lifted these expressions. 'The very pinnacle.'

'Of perfection.' Tom completed the phrase for her.

The children went out together.

'They seem pleased with themselves,' Colin said. 'Are they in here often?'

'Fairly. One or the other or both. It depends what's on at school or elsewhere.'

'Did you go in and chat to Hilda when you were their age?'

'Not much. Very occasionally.'

'I could barely bring myself to talk to my father. And I expect the feeling was mutual. The old man thought I was a damn' sight too fond of the sound of my own voice to encourage me.'

'I'd have you down on my list of quiet people. One of the laconic, as Alice would say.'

'I've changed for the better.'

Colin laughed, not easily, but swooped over towards the tray of rock-buns. He raised an eye-brow in query, and she nodded permission. She thought how much Tom resembled his father in bodily movements, set of head; the boy had not yet learnt the successful man's two or three facial expressions; welcome; reflection; dismissal. Her husband strolled back across the room, stood a yard or two away, staring down at the unbitten cake in his hand. He had something to tell her or ask. She continued her chore, slicing beans, waiting for him. When she had finished she placed the tray conveniently for her next move.

'Have you seen Linda lately?' he asked. She noticed he had not yet started on his rock bun. Anna had ceased all pretence of working.

'No,' she said. 'Not for a few weeks. She's been busy. She's taken a full-time job. At Lewis Massey's. She's been working part-time with him for some time, as his computer expert. She'd been attending and teaching courses for long enough. I thought she wanted to help Terry out, to know what his machine were capable of. She doesn't boast, but Fred Tilley's wife said she was a wizard at it. 'Can you have a female wizard?' That might have been Alice.

'I believe she is.'

'And now Terry's sold up I suppose she thinks she'll not be needed there. Larry's is a really thriving concern. Plenty to do.'

'It was a toss up, I'm told, between him and one of the big banks, Nat West Central.'

'She must be an expert.'

'She's been quietly preparing herself over the past five or six years.'

Anna listened. This was an introduction to what? An announcement that Linda was about to be taken on by one of Colin's companies? He was making a meal of it all. Perhaps he was jealous that his children could come in to her so easily and demand her absolute attention, and then amuse her, give her something of real interest to mull over.

Colin seemed in no sort of hurry.

'So you haven't seen her or talked to her lately?'

'No.'

'Then you won't have heard?'

'Heard what?'

'That she's separated from Terry.'

'She doesn't live at home any more, you mean?'

'That's so. She's found herself a flat.'

'Why?'

He waved his arms about, helplessly short of information.

'That is the question.' He bit into his rock cake; crumbs spattered.

'Have you seen her or talked to her since it happened?' Anna asked.

'No.' Mouth full.

'Have you seen Terry, then?'

'Yes, I have. He's upset. It was bad enough for him that he's had the trauma of selling off his business, and settling to a new sort of life, without this.'

'Has he plenty to occupy himself with?'

'His consultancy? Nothing he can't easily manage. Enough to keep him interested. But he's sixty, and he doesn't like change. I'd have thought it was a very satisfactory arrangement as far as he

180

was concerned. It would bring in a nice little salary, and give him enough work to do to keep him from kicking his heels at home. He wouldn't feel left out. But you know Terry. He's riddled with anxiety. Had he done the right thing? For himself? For Linda? For Henry? For his work people? It had preyed on his mind.'

'And that affected them at home?'

'Pretty sure to.'

'Did you not press him?'

'Yes, I did. He as good as admitted he'd been a pain in the arse since these negotiations started. He knows what he's like, but he thought Linda could put up with it. She always had done. Whenever there had been trouble at the shops before he'd told her all about it.'

'And asked her advice?'

'I doubt it. It would help clear his mind if he set out for her what the problem was. Or so he thought.'

'But he didn't want her to solve it?'

'No. I guess not. I often said, "Have you talked it over with Linda?" when he came to me for my point of view. And when I asked, "What does she think?" there'd be no answer. She knew nothing about the running of such businesses. In spite of her work on the computer both for him and for Massey.'

'But he'd ask you?'

'I knew about money. Now in these last few years since Lin had begun working on computers he'd certainly ask her help there. She chose the right ones, for instance, for his business, and trained his managers and clerks for him.'

'And you think he didn't like this, he begrudged the fact that his wife knew things he didn't?'

'No. The opposite, I'd say. Not that I've discussed this at any length with him. But my impression was that he was pleased with her, proud, you know. And he praised himself in a roundabout way that she'd become such a wonder because he had up-to-date computers in the shop all ready for her to get the hang of and then to become an expert.'

'Is she?'

'It appears so. She not only does Massey's electronics or whatever, but that of two other firms, and teaches two or three nights a week at the W.E.A. and Bentinck College.'

'She'd hardly be at home, then?' Anna asked.

'That's right. But he's a man of some leisure now. She cooked the main meal four times a week, it appears. For the others he had to fend for himself. Pub lunches or sandwiches. But it didn't work out. It wasn't only the meals.'

'They quarrelled, you mean?'

'And the rows got more and more frequent.'

'With violence?'

'Not to the best of my knowledge. Terry's not like that. Nothing was right. They couldn't agree on anything. I'd guess that Terry would want Linda at his beck and call all the time, and when she wasn't he'd feel aggrieved. And when she started working full time it was worse.'

'That's unreasonable.'

'It's how it was. In the end she acquired this flat, small, quiet, place in the Lace Market. Said nothing to him, and when she was ready and knew he was out, moved all her things.'

'He'd no idea that this was going to happen?'

'He had not. I imagine she did it to cause as little trouble as possible. But you can imagine the effect on him. Right out of the blue. She left him a note. And apparently wrote to Harry who's working now in London.'

'When did all this happen?' she asked.

'As far as I can make out just over a week ago. I'm not sure about dates.'

'When did you first hear about it?'

'This morning. Terry came into my office at Meyer, Turnbull. He rang my secretary. I thought it would be about investments, but he came bursting out with all this.'

'How did he seem?'

'Beaten. Like a ruined man. He spoke in jerks and couldn't sit still. He didn't like confessing all this to me. He said as much. But he had to talk with somebody before he went to see a solicitor. And I was the only suitable person he could think of.'

'Has he tried to get in touch with Linda?'

'He's written to her, twice, at Lew Massey's office, but he'd had no answer.'

'He'd hadn't been down there to make contact?'

'I asked him that, but he said "No". He didn't want a public confrontation.'

'Does Lewis know about it?'

'Again, I don't know. Nor was he altogether explicit. She left him the note when she cleared off, and that was all. No 'phonecalls, not a word, nothing.'

'He was surprised?'

'Gob-smacked.'

'But if they'd been at loggerheads for some time?'

'I guess they had, but that was the order of the day. They'd have a row, and then get on with life. That was his idea.'

'She's younger than he is, isn't she?'

'Yes. She's my age. She was in my class at junior school.'

'Was she clever? Quicker than he was, for instance?'

'In many ways. Not that I'm making out that Terry's dim. He isn't. Linda did well at school and college, and then taught for some years. Longer than you. She was on the arts side like you. But I guess she would have been better studying maths. I don't know. But as soon as she started to look into computing, she was away. It really interested her. She'd got that sort of mind.'

'And Terry hadn't?'

'No. No more than I have. I've used computers long enough, but they're just useful tools to me, like 'phones or cars or lifts or 'planes or satellites. They allow me to do things more quickly. They save me time. And trouble. And now and again I have figured out a new use, but I guess from what I hear she's into new angles and suggestions all the time.'

'Like a poet with words,' Anna spoke hesitantly.

Colin started. He said nothing for a moment, as if she'd offered him something unusual in a language he barely understood. He made no answer but finished off the bun from his hand.

'If it's final,' Anna asked, 'will Terry get over it?'

'He'll have to, won't he?' He sounded unsympathetic.

'Do you think,' she sounded school-ma'amish, 'this constant niggling did him good, kept him on his toes?'

'I wouldn't be surprised. He was proud of her. She was a good-looking woman. She built Greek temples in her garden; she understood cybernetics. Men don't want wives who are copies of themselves. Terry was like my father, hard-working, conscientious, but he wouldn't take big risks. He'd try to weigh every side up before he did anything even slightly new.'

'And that's bad, is it?'

'No. But you'll never make enormous progress, unless you're very lucky. It sometimes happens like that. I've known one or two. He won't ever go bankrupt; he'll die solvent and even prosperous, but never stinking rich.'

'You've been thinking this out,' she said, with asperity.

'All day. Since he told me. In my view if anybody deserved a decent home-life and then retirement it was Terry. He worked like a black, and then, damn me, when that was over, with leisure and money to spare, she ups and leaves him.'

'But were they always quarrelling? She must have been pretty desperate to desert him after all this time.'

'Look.' Colin sounded slightly exasperated, as if she had missed some vital step in his reasoning. 'Terry never expects a straight run. He's had to struggle for what he's got. The same with married life. He expected Linda to be awkward sometimes. This Greek temple of hers seemed cracked, a complete waste of time and money. He thought he'd be a laughing-stock with the neighbours. But she wanted it, and kept on long enough saying so. In the end, he gave in, even helped her with it, saved her money on it. He saw to it that she always had the wherewithal to look after the house. She chose the furniture, the carpets, the pictures on the wall. She saw to the garden, and organised the holidays. He gave her a free hand. He didn't want a little woman doing as she was told every minute of the day. My mother wasn't like that. She ruled the roost at home. Terry was used to that, and it was the sort of wife he wanted. One with spirit, not just a cipher. It was his job to see he earned enough for them to live comfortably, and educate Henry properly. And she'd spend, within reason, the spare cash.'

'That's understandable,' she said, not altogether sure.

'But when he sold his business, even before that probably, when he first started thinking about it, it alarmed him. His place in the system had disappeared. He was going to be unemployed. Oh, you could argue he'd earned a rest; in fact, I often did. But he couldn't take it in once he began to feel fit again. He was a spare part. Linda still had her jobs to do: the house, the garden, the trips abroad, keeping in touch with Henry; she couldn't retire from that. And then she made it worse, by starting to go out to work, and spending more time than ever at it. She would always have put in a day or two at one of the shops for him if somebody was away or ill, and they were particularly busy. But now she was well-paid. Lew Massey and the others saw what she was worth, and Terry didn't like it. He felt left out. She had become the breadwinner, and he was just an idler.'

'I can see all that, but he must have made it unpleasant for her; she was the one who left home.'

184

'I expect he did. But I also suspect he didn't know how much he was getting on her nerves. There was such turmoil in his mind over the change at work that he never considered his behaviour at home. And she spent more and more time away.'

'Does he know now? And does he want her back?'

'He thinks he does. He said to me, "I love that woman", and that's not like him. He's not one to be flashing his feelings in front of the whole wide world.'

'Um.' She hummed the syllable.

'What's that mean?' he asked, ill-temperedly.

'There's no third party involved, is there? No other man or woman?'

'Not to the best of my knowledge. Terry didn't say so. Why? Have you heard rumours?'

'No. Except I thought at one time she was rather keen on you.'

Colin stared, giving nothing away.

'That's as may be,' he said. 'Unless you've heard something I haven't.'

'No,' she answered sweetly. 'Not a word.'

They preserved silence, though Anna moved about at her kitchen chores. It was as if this change of topic had caught them out, disturbed them. In the end Anna opening the oven-door, rather noisily, began again.

'What are you going to do about it?' she asked.

'What *can* I?'

'Did Terry ask you to try to see her?'

'No. I think he's waiting to find out what she'll do. He's had the one note she left when she cleared off. It didn't mention divorce or judicial separation. It just said she found him impossible to live with, and that therefore she'd gone off to live on her own. She'd told Henry, she said.'

'That was all?'

'That was all. As short as that. Nothing about hearing from her solicitor. Nothing about not trying to trace her. No address. She knew very well he could always contact her at Massey's. No. She was leaving him, and that was that.'

'She'd cleared out all her belongings?'

'She had. And one or two small pieces of furniture.'

'And it came as a complete surprise to him?'

'So he says, and I've no reason to believe he's lying.'

He paused for a long breath, then asked, diffidently, 'What are we going to do?'

'There's not much we can. We know too little of the background. We've only heard Terry's side, such as it is. Now if you don't mind, we'll stop there. As it is dinner will be at least a quarter of an hour later than it should have been. I'll talk to you again.'

Colin bowed his head. An unbroken conversation of this length between him and his wife was unusual; he wondered if the fact that she was working at the same time that she talked to him made a difference. When they next discussed the matter it would be from chairs, facing each other the whole time, with no excuse for turning away. It would be like a court or a police interview cell. He dismissed these ideas as fanciful.

They did not take up the subject again that evening. Colin received three long 'phone calls after dinner. He sat in his office upstairs. By the time he had finished Anna was in bed, and when he came up towards midnight he seemed preoccupied. He hugged her, almost in tenderness, made slight sexual overtures, but they came to nothing. He was asleep well before she was.

He left for work, early, before the children had finished breakfast and offered not a word about his brother or Linda.

'Might well be late tonight,' he muttered, his only farewell.

Anna drove over to see her parents in Ashby. Her father she found was not at home. He was in good health, Hilda reported, very cheerful, spending a great deal of time on the short list of prospective housekeepers, but today had decided to drive over to have lunch with an old friend, a retired regular Air-Force man, a group-captain, a widower of long standing.

'Will he cook for Daddy?' Anna asked.

'No. They'll go to a restaurant.'

'And what will they talk about?'

'I can't imagine. They haven't much in common. Or at least, that's my impression. When Jonathan comes over for a return visit they seem content to sit about saying nothing. Jonathan's years younger than Daddy. He teaches maths to engineers at the Poly; it's got a new name now it's a university, the Lindsey. I think when they're on their own they just mutter about themselves and what they do. When I'm about they daren't.'

'They boast, do they?'

'I'm not even sure of that. I expect they do. But mostly they say what they've done or are about to do. But they enjoy it. Or seem to. And these trips keep Daddy fully occupied while the weather's good. I don't know what'll happen when the winter comes. I dread it. I think Daddy'll be back to last year. Depressed.'

'Take him abroad.'

'He won't hear of it. Not until his first German holiday in Spring.'

They discussed Kuno's health, foibles and character, easily, in good temper as if concerned with a favourite child. Yes, admitted Hilda, he was stubborn some times, but never cruel. Depression brought an occasional tantrum when presumably he thought he was being pressed beyond bearing. But there was a kind of inability to make out what was good for him. 'There's no place like home', he said, 'especially in winter.' When she urged him to get away from the cold weather or 'flu, he shook his head. 'It's not the snow and ice that worry me,' he'd informed her.

'What is it then?'

'The inner man.'

'Your intestines?'

'My spirit. It dies on me.'

'That's a bit frightening,' Anna commented, 'because it doesn't sound much like him.'

'Retirement has changed him.'

'For the better?' Facetiously.

'His days aren't filled up as they were. Basically he's as he used to be, but begins to be afraid that there's nothing more to him than an accountant, what my grandfather used to call a daftar-wallah, an office-worker. I'm thinking about occupying him this winter, and I'd be grateful if you'd give it a thought.'

They talked to each other, and then walked the gardens. Over lunch, a boiled egg and two small buttered slices of brown bread for each, Anna asked, out of the blue, deliberately changing the subject.

'Have you heard anything about Linda Turnbull? Colin's brother's wife?'

'No. Should I?'

'She's left her husband.'

'Doesn't live with him any more?'

'Exactly. They've been, according to what Terry told Colin, uncomfortable with each other for some time now, since he decided to sell up. It was made worse because she had been taking up outside work on the computer. She's pretty well full-time now, and more, by the sound of it.'

187

'Who's to blame? In your opinion?'

'My opinion's not worth much. I've only heard Terry's story and that via Colin. Both could be awkward.'

'So they quarrelled and she flounced out?'

'No. Are you taking sides already?'

'I must admit I don't much like Linda.'

This surprised Anna. Her mother's tone spoke certainty.

'But you hardly know her. She's been up here a time or two with me, and I suppose you've seen her at most a dozen times over the years at family occasions.'

'Often enough for me to judge her as somebody who wants her own way.'

'Don't we all?'

'You can say that, but, no, we don't. Women don't like to give up careers just to stay at home and look after the children. But most of us put up with it.'

'Perhaps wrongly,' Anna said.

'I don't think you'd earn as much as Colin, now, would you?'

'Not at teaching, certainly.' Anna wheeled on her mother. 'Do you know I thought you got on rather well with Linda, the few times I've seen you together?'

'I don't go out of my way to pick quarrels with people. Why should I? But I just didn't take to Linda. I thought she was selfish. She dressed wrongly in my view. Too brightly.'

'No more showy than I am.'

'You can carry it off. She can't. Especially as her husband seems such a quiet man. He's praised by everybody as a good worker. He did some electrical work for Daddy's office, and it was excellent, and not over-priced. My guess is she led him a dance.'

'You know something, then, that I don't,' Anna objected.

'No, I don't. I'm guessing. They had only the one boy, didn't they? But she never went back to work.'

'I'm told she'd help out in the shop if they were pushed.'

'Good for her. I just didn't like her.'

'Because she'd ideas above her station? Is that it? A Greek temple in her back garden? Well, now she's found something that she can do really well.'

'What's that?'

'She knows all about computers.' Anna felt hot under the collar, in her defence of Linda. Wisely she let the conversation tail away. She felt uncomfortable and suspected she had spoilt her mother's morning. For a second time they walked round the garden and Hilda presented her with seedlings, peace-offerings, perhaps. Just as she was about to leave her father arrived. She saw him standing on the terrace in the sunshine. He seemed slim, delicate even, frail, his thin, longish hair blowing about in the wind. He barely filled his exquisite, grey suit, and his shoes gleamed. He raised a hand as Anna came up the steps from the upper garden. She kissed him on the cold cheek as she drew level.

'How are you?' she asked.

'All the better for seeing you. I'm sorry I had to go out, but this meeting with Jon Calder-Browne had been fixed for long enough. But I knew it would cheer your mother up to have you here with all the talk of the town.'

'Don't get cold out there, Kuno,' Hilda called.

'Come in for five minutes,' he begged. 'Your mother thinks I'm a tender plant.'

'And aren't you?'

'Getting old.'

'"We are not now that strength which in old days

   Moved earth and heaven".' She hammed the lines shamefully, voice artificially rising and falling.

'That's right. Who said that? Shakespeare?'

'Tennyson.'

He took her arm and led her indoors. Her efficient mother had lined up the plants she was taking away by her car. Hilda followed them in; they were still arm in arm.

'Colin's brother's wife has left him,' Hilda said bluntly. The two looked up at her. 'Had Anna not told you?'

'No,' Anna answered.

'That's Terry Turnbull.' Kuno said. 'I'm sorry.'

'He's retired, but she's working.' His wife's curt sentence was intended to explain.

'I liked him. He was a good workman. When he estimated for a job, he made a point of honour to keep within it, or offer a watertight excuse.'

Neither woman spoke for a moment.

'Do you remember Linda, his wife?' Hilda asked.

'Yes, I do. A tallish girl.'

'Did she make a favourable impression on you?'

Kuno frowned, brushing the back of his hand across his mouth.

'Yes. I think she did. She was smart, and well spoken.'

189

Terry, even when he was wearing a suit looked like an artisan. More at home in his overalls.'

'So you're not surprised they've parted?' Hilda asked.

'Surprised? Yes, I am surprised.'

'But if they were different? One well turned out, the other not?'

'I've known quite a few like that, and they didn't separate.'

'Who?' Hilda did not allow him to escape under cover of generalities.

'Horace Cousins, one of my office managers. His wife dressed like a peacock, and went out twice or three times a week to a dancing club.'

'On her own?'

'She made her own way there, I believe. She had a regular partner.'

'And didn't Horace mind?'

'No. Insofar as I am aware. He occupied his spare time studying local history. So he was happy as a king sitting at home every night with his papers and lists. He was secretary of the Willoughby Society for a time, and did their admin for them, arranged outings and had a hand in the publication of their journal.'

'And there was no scandal?'

'Not seriously. I believe some of the younger people made jokes about it, her dancing, I mean.'

'He was a dry as dust old fogey?'

'You've met him. And his wife. No, he was lively, and quite witty. And a bit of a disciplinarian in the office.'

'And the dancing-partner? Who was he?'

'As far as I remember, he was a teacher in a grammar school.'

'And what about *his* wife?'

'He was a widower.'

'Ah, ah,' Hilda crowed.

'Never mind "ah, ah",' Kuno laughed. 'It was never suggested that anything sexual happened between them.'

'Didn't they dance close together? Cheek-to-cheek?'

'I never saw them, but if that was what was required I expect they did.'

'That's the way you used to dance when you were young,' Hilda said.

'Yes, but unlike you and me they were entered for competitions, and sometimes won prizes. I'm not telling you they were world-beaters, but they were a good cut above the average.'

190

Anna listened to her parents. Hilda's questions kept Kuno stimulated. He was not allowed to slink away to his office, and waste all his time tapping at his keyboard.

'And when he retired?'

'He had more time for his history. He spent hours down at the County Archives.'

'Didn't she want to go out? With him? On holiday or abroad?'

'Yes, I expect she did. And he fitted in with her when he could. He had more time for it all, though he used to say on the few occasions we met and talked that the trouble with local history as a side-line was the more hours you had to spend on it, the more you wanted.'

'Had he a family?' Anna asked.

'Yes. Three boys. All doing well now.'

'And is he still alive?'

'No. Your mother and I went to his funeral a year or so ago.'

Hilda was tapping a table top impatiently.

'And what does all this go to prove?' she asked. 'That incompatibles needn't of necessity separate. I see. What will happen next?' Hilda asked Anna.

'What usually happens.' Anna spoke without force. 'They'll divorce.'

'And who's at fault?' Kuno.

'I don't know enough about it. I've only heard Terry's account via Colin. I'd guess he was more at fault than she was, but I don't know. I expect she can be awkward if she feels the need.'

They exhausted the subject inside the next ten minutes, when Anna rose to leave. Her mother pressed her to stay to lunch, but she said she was too busy. They all three went outside. Though the sun shone, a breeze ruffled their hair. As she drove off Anna noticed her parents stood together, hand in hand. She could not remember such an overt demonstration of affection from them, either in her childhood or more recently. Perhaps this morning's conversation had unsettled them, left them anxious about her own marriage. Her father waved with his unoccupied right hand. Again she was struck with his fragility.

She quickly touched the button to wind her window down.

'Look after yourselves, you two,' she said, speaking more loudly than she intended.

Her father nodded gentle agreement. Her mother stared elsewhere.

191

XV

In the next few weeks, Anna inquired about Terry and Linda from her husband, but he had seen neither.

'Have you tried to get in touch?' she demanded.

'No. If they need my help they'll ask for it soon enough.'

'Are you sure?'

'No. Of course I'm not bloody sure, but if I were in their trouble I wouldn't want every inquisitive Tom, Dick and Harry in the county poking noses in.'

'But Terry came to see you, didn't he?'

'And a fat lot of help he got from it.'

The subject seemed to annoy Colin, who was particularly busy according to him even though he was home soon after five-thirty each evening. He looked extremely handsome in a light-grey summer-suit, but serious as if faced with a problem he saw no way of solving.

'Are you all right?' she asked, the next evening.

'Yes. Fit. Flourishing.'

'Not worried?'

'No more than usual.' He grinned, wolfishly, teeth white. 'It did concern me when I began to think about Terry and the hash he made of retirement. He'd be unbearable.'

'And you think you'll be much the same?'

'I wouldn't be surprised. Of course Linda made it worse by becoming a success.'

'And I shan't do that?'

'You're a success already. I think it was the surprise of it that so knocked Terry about.'

'Have you seen either of them?'

'No. I rang Terry at home, but nobody was in. I'd like to know what Linda thinks about things.'

'Would she tell you?'

He pulled a sour face, but left the room singing to himself, waving fingers at his wife.

Two days later she met Linda. Anna went into town at least once a week, weather permitting, to do what she called idle shopping. She went in by bus, and walked about without any direct aims. When she was teaching, or when the children were young, she despised, she imagined, those women who had so little to do that they filled in their time staring into shop windows at garments they had no intention of trying on let alone buying. Even now, unconvinced, she comforted herself by suggesting that at least she got more physical benefit from tramping about the streets than she would by hunting out treasures in magazine-advertisements or on the Internet. At the end of such a morning so spent she certainly felt tired.

This morning she was looking at a dress in Cécile's where she made occasional excellent if expensive purchases. In the small right-hand window a single robe was displayed on a headless dressmaker's dummy. Of grey silk, three-quarter length, plain apart from almost invisible embroidery at the deeply-cut neck and on the short sleeves, it clearly represented elegance, at least in the eyes of its vendor. Anna had immediately taken against it, but held her ground trying hard to give some intellectual content to her dislike. The colour would not suit her, or most people; it was too modest, insipid perhaps, for her kind of attraction. It needed some beautifully arrogant plain Jane, with a flawless skin like that of a wax work. Plain and colourless but beautiful. That was a paradox for you. Anna frowned.

'Hello there. That would suit you.'

She wheeled about. Linda stood behind her, head cocked, matching tea-gown to human.

'I was just thinking how unattractive it was.'

'Sshh. Cécile will send one of her assistants out to mug you.'

'She'll be pleased we're looking at it. If we stand here staring for much longer we'll attract a crowd.'

Linda looked healthy, quite sunburnt. The small wrinkles about her eyes added to her attraction. She had dressed quietly as if for work, and conveyed an impression of controlled energy.

'Are you busy?' Anna asked.

'I just came back from Paris last evening.'

'Holiday?'

'No, work. Of sorts. No time for sight-seeing.'

'Bad luck.'

Linda smiled as if such considerations did not touch her.

193

'And how are the pair of you, then?' she asked.

'Well.'

'Colin's up to the eyes in it, I expect?'

'Yes, he is. He doesn't stop. I tell him he should start delegating, but he won't have it. "It would only give me more time to worry," he says.'

'Incorrigible.'

'And how are you?'

'You know I've left Terry, don't you?' This was lightly delivered.

'Colin said so. Terry had been to see him.'

'About my leaving?'

'Yes.'

'You surprise me.'

An awkward short pause lengthened as they were parted by a young mother, her push-chair, two walking pre-school children zigzagging through.

'I was sorry to hear about it,' Anna began again.

'Such things happen.'

Anna thought that was the end of the conversation but Linda seemed in no hurry to move away.

'Was Paris . . . ?'

'He was unbearable.' They had begun together, but it was Linda who continued. 'I couldn't do anything right for him. He had a pretext, I imagine. In his own mind. He'd sold off his business, and hadn't nearly as much to do as before, but that was no excuse for taking it out on me. He really was, well, let's say almost irrational.' Linda stopped, perhaps waiting for comment. 'Fortunately I was now in a position where I needn't put up with it, so I got out.'

'Did you warn him?'

'I did nothing else for weeks. I thought he'd improve, get over it all, but he grew worse.'

'Violent?'

'No. All verbal. Perhaps I wasn't exactly in my right mind, but he seemed to enjoy it in a tormented way. He wasn't in my company for above two minutes before he was off, complaining, shouting, snivelling, crying. Like a madman.'

'This was unlike him? His ordinary behaviour?'

'No, it wasn't. He'd always grumbled, been a grouser. But this was a thousand times worse. It was beyond all bearing. Whatever

I did was wrong. I tried to encourage him to try other distractions. To get meals, for instance. He's quite capable of that. He often did it when we were first married. His mother taught both boys to be independent.'

'Colin doesn't cook.'

'No. He wouldn't. But he wouldn't say, as Terry did, that it was an insult to his intelligence for me to suggest it.'

'And what about your intelligence?'

'I mentioned that. He flew off the handle.'

'So you think he'll be all right on his own?'

'He could be. But that's up to him.'

'You're not considering going back?'

'No. I'm off to America for three weeks on Saturday. For Club International.'

'So you're not lonely?' Anna asked.

'Occasionally. But that's not all that bad. I wasn't lonely in those last weeks in Templeton Avenue, but I often wished I was. I knew as soon as he opened the door the fur would start to fly. No. I've got used to the cramped spaces in my flat. I'd like a garden, but I see I can't have one now. Later, maybe.'

'Could you put Henry up if he visited you?'

'He doesn't. Not often. But yes, I could.' She sighed, histrionically. 'And my parents are still alive. I can drive round to see them. Not that I enjoy it. They're a miserable pair.'

'Why?'

'Immobility. My mother has had two hip replacements, and now needs another operation on one of her knees. My father's short of breath, and very hard of hearing. But they get on with each other. They have separate television sets and radios. And they have their own visitors. It can't be exactly the sort of life they'd choose, but they make something of it.'

'They're fond of each other?'

'It's hard to say. Neither's very open in expressing affection, but then they never have been. Dad's philosophical. "What have I to complain about when I compare myself with all these refugees of civil wars and political prisoners and people with AIDS?"'

'That's exactly my father's view. They'll be of an age, won't they?'

'Yes. I guess so. My father's seventy-nine.'

'Mine's seventy-seven.'

They suddenly laughed, like infants in the playground. My

dad's bigger than yours. My dad's got more money than yours.

'I don't think that would be much comfort to me,' Anna said. 'Especially as it can only grow worse. Was your father in the army? Perhaps they learnt to put up with things?'

'My dad doesn't say much. I got the impression that he thought a good number of his officers and n.c.o.s were unhinged.'

'We all like exaggeration.' Anna said.

'Do you think I'm exaggerating, then? About Terry?'

'Yes, quite possibly. Terry always seemed to me in the category of miserable sod rather than torturer in chief.'

'You're a cool customer,' Linda said, not unduly annoyed.

'You asked me.'

'I must get back to my office. Walk along with me, and I'll provide you with a cup of coffee.'

'Where is it?'

'Massey's. Goose Gate. Five minutes' walk.'

'You don't want me to, do you?'

'Want you?' Linda sounded genuinely puzzled.

'Need me? No, I don't mean that. Do you want me to walk along with you, take up valuable working time?'

'I wouldn't ask you. Come on now. Best foot forward.'

Linda's flat seemed cramped, sitting room, bedroom, bathroom and kitchen and was situated on the third floor of what had been in the eighteen-nineties a huge lace-making factory. Now part of the building had been taken over by Massey Exports, and the flat had once been the living quarters of one of the caretakers or night-watchmen. The room struck bleak with unplastered, painted brickwork only partially brightened by the carpets and furniture. Anna edged into a brilliantly crimson arm-chair. Linda obviously understood her friend's frankly critical scrutiny.

'This is temporary,' she said. 'It's handy for work; it costs me nothing, neither heat, light, water, 'phone or anything else.' She frowned smilingly. 'People write to me care of the firm, but they don't realise I live here.'

'Does Terry know?'

Linda shook her head.

'Does Colin?'

'No. He'd let it out to his brother. You know he would.'

'I don't. Colin can be as secretive as you like, if it suits his purposes.'

'Don't tell him, please.'

They drank their coffee in a hurry. Linda seemed now to regret her invitation, and when Anna made a move to go, the other took no steps to prevent her. Anna clacked along a corridor, down six flights of stone steps. She clung on to a cold metal hand-rail. At the bottom a man in shirt sleeves shuffled to the door of his small-paned office to sign her out.

'Mrs Turnbull?' he inquired. Linda had indicated, on the way in, that she should sign a register, though the doorman-porter was not to be seen. 'Our Mrs Turnbull's still in, is she? You'll be sisters, won't you? No, you can't be, if you're both Mrs Turnbulls.' The self-interrogation was kindly meant. He stared hard at the register.

'Sisters-in-law,' Anna said. The man came from his sentry-box and opened the door for her, even bowing slightly. It all seemed odd, old-fashioned, formal, suspicious. She was glad to be out in the street, even though she stood on the shadowed side. She crossed to the sunshine; even there a chill wind whipped down into the tall, narrow cleft of the street. It had been an odd, slightly unpleasant experience, even if she could not understand why she felt so uncomfortable about it.

At the weekend Colin glowered over a 'phone-call and then announced that his brother had been taken into hospital. Henry, Terry's son, had rung from London, because he could not come up to visit his father, and wondered if Colin or Anna could drop in on him.

'Is it serious?' she asked.

'I'd guess so. Henry was a bit vague. He'd only just heard. He wasn't sure, but they were doing tests.'

'Does Linda know?'

'Henry thought not. If he has his dates right she had gone off to America, yesterday, destination or address unknown.'

'Had Terry asked for her? Or for us?'

'Look, Henry had just heard, and was too shocked to quiz anybody. He couldn't get himself up here, so he rang me as the nearest available relative.'

'If it's serious, why doesn't Henry come up himself?'

'He has some sort of final professional examinations, today, Saturday, Monday and Tuesday. Don't ask me what it is he's training for. Architect, perhaps.'

'And if his father becomes worse.'

'Then he'll have to make his mind up whether he's going to miss these tests or whatever they are.'

'Is that what you'd do?' Anna asked.

'If he does them, he won't be at his best, worrying about his father. If he doesn't sit them, he'll be put back six months or so. That's if he bothers at all about his father.'

'What would you have done?'

'You think I'd just have followed my own advantage, don't you? I suppose I would. At Henry's age I wasn't exactly fond of my father. He'd seen me financially through university but once I'd joined the London branch of Kuno's firm, I had to pay my own way. When we met he spoke to me as if I was about nine. We were different people. We didn't seem to see eye-to-eye. When he told me about his business and I made suggestions he was furious, didn't want to hear them.'

'I expect you were brash about it.'

'I spoke to him as if he were a valued client at the office in need of advice. Politely, but putting things plainly.'

'I bet.'

'He didn't like it. He wouldn't have liked it if he'd consulted your father, professionally. He was a bit like Terry, not sure that he'd done as well as he might. I sometimes thought he feared my mother. Not that she ever made a great fuss. About anything much. But he used to quote a hymn about her.

'Thy kind but searching glance can scan
The very wounds that shame would hide.'

He died when I was twenty-three, not much older than Henry.'

'Did you come up to see him?'

'I did. But he was in a coma by the time I arrived and died next day. But at least I turned up. Your father insisted I took time off.'

'You told him?'

'I did. Mind you I should have come up whatever he said. But he was very sympathetic, and I wasn't doing anything very important.'

'Why did you visit your father, if the pair of you didn't get on?'

'It would have upset my mother if I hadn't.'

Colin spoke with conspicuous nonchalance about this, as if it was something he'd heard from a not very close acquaintance or read in a dull book. Once they had finished this conversation and as he turned to walk from the room, he said,

'Would you mind ringing the hospital to find out about visiting hours?' Anna, busy with preparations for their meal, touched with a twinge of annoyance, snapped,

'Can't you do it?'

'No.' The word was plain. 'I don't like hospitals, and I should be too brusque, and get nothing out of them. It's true. You'll soft soap them properly.' He looked up, feeling the excuse feeble or specious in her eyes. 'I can still see Jim Glover staggering up the road that bloody morning to receive his death sentence.' He shrugged, smiled wolfishly. 'It doesn't suit my style. He was my age. In my class at school.'

Anna caught her breath, suddenly vulnerable. She stepped forward and threw her arms round him, pressing her face against his. His surprise was palpable, but he squeezed her to him.

'Sorry, love,' he said, more awkward Terry than masterful Colin. She held her position for a moment or two longer, then released him.

'My hands are floury. I've spoilt your splendid suit,' she said.

He nodded his relief, and his thanks to her.

'Nothing a good brush won't cure. Oh, here's the name of his ward,' handing her a slip of paper.

Colin left the room, hurrying.

Anna cleaned up her hands, checked that the meal could be left on hold for a short time, then looked up the number of the hospital in the telephone directory. She rang, inquired about Terry; some nurse on Saxondale Ward reported him comfortable. Yes, he could be visited. Yes, that evening. The woman read out a list of times, pretty well all day from eleven to eight, but not Tuesday morning, please, not until two.

They ate ten minutes early, explaining to the children about Terry's illness and where they were bound that evening.

'Is he seriously ill?' Alice asked, eyes wide.

'We don't really know. It's a bit of a mystery. All we know is what your cousin Henry told us over the phone, and he seemed vague.'

'King of the anoraks,' Tom said.

'That's no way to talk of your relative,' Alice laughing.

'It's an Inuit word,' Anna offered.

'Meaning?' Tom again.

'An Eskimo,' said Colin. 'That's what we always called them when I was at school.'

199

'I believe it's the plural form of the word for a person.'

'That's the value of education,' Colin informed Alice. 'A prompt, accurate answer.'

'What's Eskimo mean, I wonder?' Anna said, and immediately jumped up to consult the dictionary she kept in the kitchen. 'Probably an Indian word meaning an eater of raw flesh,' she read out.

'And now you know,' Tom said.

Alice fiddled still with her dictionary.

'The singular of 'inuit' is 'inuk'.'

'How many "n"s?' Tom asked.

'Two or one, as you prefer.'

The parents drove down to the hospital sombrely dressed. Anna carried a small rose in a pot which she had recently fetched out of the greenhouse.

'That looks very neat,' Colin had commented as they walked from the car park.

'I hope it has time to flower,' she answered. 'Hospital wards are not the best place for rearing plants.'

They fell quiet as they followed direction boards along the corridors. Anna had rarely been in a hospital. Her friends and relatives had been healthy. As a schoolgirl she had once visited a new private medical palace where a class-mate who had been involved in a car accident lay, recovering, surrounded by flowers. Three of them had driven up to see Pamela; they had laughed after the initial five minutes of awkwardness, and eaten grapes and sweets, chattering and delighted to find their friend so unchanged. It was like a midnight feast in one of the girls' school stories she had occasionally read. Today seemed different, grimmer. They inquired after Terry from a nurse in the office at the end of Saxondale ward.

'Mr Turnbull?' Colin inquired. Anna understood what he had meant by brusque. The young nurse answered undeterred. She pointed. 'Alfred's third on the right.'

'Alfred?' Anna whispered as they set off.

'It's his first name,' Colin snapped.

Terry lay quietly in his bed, a big man, surprised. Other patients and visitors about the ward looked up gratefully at the smart newcomers.

They asked about his health. He said he couldn't grumble. They waited, received nothing for some seconds.

200

'Bad news travels fast.' Terry spoke breathily. 'How did you come to hear about me.'

'Henry rang,' Anna answered.

'I told him not to trouble you.'

'Yes, but he's got more sense than you have.' Colin, unsmiling. 'I don't suppose you know where Linda is, do you?'

'America.' Colin had left Anna to answer.

The pause while Colin rapidly organised two chairs allowed them to settle their minds. Terry did not look too ill, Anna thought. She began to ask questions. Yes, he'd been up and walking about, but they'd decided he'd had enough for one day. He squinted as he thanked them for the little rose-bush; he spoke carefully, but sounded genuinely embarrassed as if they had given him a present beyond his worth. He'd told Henry not to come up, as he had some important exams. 'I said to him to do well at them and that would be the best tonic he could give me.' On the way out Colin commented that was exactly what their mother would have said. He spoke disapprovingly. 'At first they treated him for a heart-attack, Terry had said. One young man had mentioned a stroke, but that was now ruled out. Now they were doing blood-tests and X-rays and God knows what and yet they seemed none the wiser. Or if they were they hadn't let on to him.'

'Don't you ask the big noise when he comes round?' Colin asked, pointing at the name above the bed: Professor H. R. Pennington.

'Yes. He says they're tracking it down, but the body is a complicated affair. They can't exactly put a finger on everything immediately. I thought,' Terry grimaced, "They'll know after the post-mortem." But he seemed nice enough.'

'Is he old?'

'No. About your age.'

They talked affably for half an hour until a bell signalled the time to leave. The patient sounded disgruntled, but neither ill nor abnormal. He asked Colin to chase up Lewis Massey to see if he knew where Linda was. 'I don't suppose he does. She can be secretive if she thinks fit.'

'You're not blaming her for whatever it is that's wrong with you?'

'She did me no good sloping off like that.'

'No,' Anna said.

201

'So what you're suffering from,' Colin commented grimly, 'is really a broken heart.'

'Bloody hell,' Terry wheezed.

Anna gulped at Colin's comment, which exactly mirrored her own idle thought. It seemed too nastily poetic for him, and even if it had been cynical she judged he'd have more sense than to blurt it out loud. By the time they left, and there seemed no urgency on the part of the authorities to get rid of them, they felt satisfied that Terry was not seriously ill.

'He seemed normal to me,' Colin grumbled.

'You think he's been here under false pretences, then?'

'I don't. He's not that sort. Too straight forward. He wouldn't know how to play-act.'

Back at home he asked Anna to ring Henry. She did so.

'Was he pleased?' Colin asked, when she had finished.

'I think he was. He'd done his first exam.'

Colin stiffly said he'd call on Lewis Massey the next day to see if he could find out anything of Linda's whereabouts.

Within four days Terry was discharged from hospital. A neighbour and a girl who had previously worked in his office called in to prepare meals and keep the house in order. Terry groused, at length.

'They're all right, but I'm capable of looking after myself. The district nurse or whatever they call her nowadays comes in and messes me about and takes samples for the hospital labs, she says.'

'And what's wrong with you?' Anna inquired.

'If they know they haven't told me.'

'Do you feel any ill effects? Pain? Or tiredness? Or nausea?'

'No.' He answered with a snap of satisfaction. 'I'm worn out sometimes.'

'What do you think?'

'My opinion's nothing, but if you want to know I guess it was a little stroke which knocked me out. And as I fell I gave my head a hell of a bang on the floor or wall or something that completed the unconsciousness.'

'Where did this take place?'

'At work. I keeled over suddenly, they tell me. They sent for the ambulance.'

'Were you suffering from a headache before it happened?'

'Now you mention it, I think I was. I certainly was when I came round.'

202

'Had you had any breakfast that morning?'

'Of course I bloody had.' He lifted his head in panic. 'I'm sorry. I beg your pardon.'

They left the house much reassured on the score of Terry's health. Whatever had afflicted him now seemed under control; tablets were being prescribed and swallowed in this period of common-sense, when he lived quietly, to order.

Lewis Massey tried to trace Linda, but she had moved around and was now reported to be in Canada. Colin sniffed suspiciously.

'I'm not sure about Lew. He'd be able to trace her all right these days, but I'd bet any money Linda's told him she wants nothing to do with Terry, and she wasn't coming back even if he was on the point of death.'

'What makes you think that?'

'Lewis Massey's efficient. He'd know where Linda was going, and even if she suddenly changed her mind he'd know how to make contact.'

'Not if she slipped off somewhere, told nobody, left no address.'

'Why should she do that? I bet Massey's are coughing up some of the money as well as Club International for this trip and she'll be looking into some things for him.'

'Then why doesn't he just tell you she doesn't want to have anything to do with Terry?' Anna asked.

'He's a good, sharp business man is Lewis, but he's old fashioned enough not to want to stir the water in personal matters he knows nothing about.'

Anna laughed at her husband, the amateur psychologist. In her view he came out well as a human being from the time of his brother's illness.

Over in Ashby, at the manor house, life seemed both settled and interesting. Kuno's health was excellent and he was preparing with relish for his first German holiday. Hilda had no choice here, she said. She supposed she could say outright that she was not going, but she saw no advantage in that. It would upset her husband who wouldn't understand her reasons, even if she had any, and besides the trips he arranged were always fascinating.

Kuno had appointed a new house-keeper in Nancy Johnson's place, or had half-completed the task. He had consulted wife and daughter, but had made up his own mind. The woman concerned a Mrs Emerson, a widow, years younger than Nancy, very smartly dressed, lived two villages away. Kuno had had a field-day with her. He made Mrs Johnson out to be such a paragon, that both he and Sandra, as he now called Mrs Emerson, had begun to believe it, so that neither could quite accept a permanent arrangement. They had decided on a three months' trial, to be accepted or rejected or extended by either.

'And is she any good?' Anna asked her mother.

'Yes. She's young. Your sort of age. Good family.'

'And her late husband?'

'He died abroad, working for some Arab sheik training his army, and was accidentally killed eighteen months ago. It was in all the papers.'

'Children?'

'No. None. They were married rather late. Or at least she was.'

'Is she going on holiday with you to Germany?'

'No. Why should she? She'll come into the house, as Nancy used to, to see all's well.'

'And you're pleased?'

'Yes. She seems sensible. And willing to learn. She'll suit us both, I guess.'

Anna met Sandra Emerson a day or two later, a tall, rather formidable woman who spoke quietly. She said she was looking forward to her new job, that she had never done anything like it before, but would get on well with the Meyers.

'Will you live in?' Anna asked.

'We'll decide that after the three months are up. It would be sensible, but I value my independence.'

Anna stared at this sudden defensive thrust.

Not a week later she received a phone call from Linda, her sister-in-law. Fresh from her month in the States and Canada, every minute of which she had enjoyed, she was now back at work; tasks had piled up while she was away and she was getting them out of the way. A challenge. That afternoon Colin was coming down to Massey's and she expected to meet him.

'You know Terry has been ill?' Anna asked, tentatively.

'Yes. Lewis told me, but not exactly what was wrong. Do you know?'

'No. Not really. Minor stroke or something like that. He didn't seem to know. We visited him a time or two. You've not seen him, then?'

'I've not. It's not a matter of principle. I shouldn't cross the road if I saw him approaching down my side of the street. Or at least, I don't think I should. But it's over and done with. I'm absolutely firm in my mind about that. I've recovered from the anger and frustration I felt when I walked out, but I don't want any more to do with him. I can't say I don't bear any grudges; I'm a human being. I shall have to meet him, I expect, over a divorce settlement, but that won't faze me. I'm busy, and that keeps me happy for the present. It's enough.'

'Will he be all right?'

'Terry? That's not my concern, is it? Why should it be?'

'You've been married a long time, nearly thirty years.'

'Twenty-five.'

'There you are then.'

'It's over, Anna. The decision's made. Irrevocably.' The last word spoke her firmness.

'Even if he's ill?'

'He isn't. Henry has been up to see him. By the way, he's qualified as an architect now. At least on paper. And he came up and stayed a couple of nights with his father.When I rang him he said Terry seemed perfectly well. And there were a couple of women looking after him. He'd had a nurse for a start, but she didn't visit any more.'

'Is he back at work?'

'I believe so. In some shape or form.'

'I'm sorry,' Anna spoke without force.

'Why do you say that?'

'I don't like change. Well, not of that sort.'

'That was Terry's trouble.'

Linda reiterated her grievances again. She spoke implacably. It would be useless, in her view, to begin the long haul of re-building the relationship. She did not want it. She saw no advantage. She and Terry had done their time together and now it was over. Anna noted that certain as she seemed, Linda spoke cheerfully, did not regret her decision. Henry, her son, was out of the way, wouldn't need his parents, she hoped, except on rare occasions, for a loan, perhaps, or a bed while he was in this part of the world.

'And Terry?'

'You do go on, don't you?' asked Linda in pseudo-impatience. 'It's all second hand, but as far as I can make out, he's doing perfectly well for himself.'

She rang off soon after this, saying she'd be in touch. 'Anyhow I shall see your better half this afternoon.'

Colin telephoned as soon as Linda had finished.

'You don't half have some long chats. I've been trying for the last thirty-five minutes to get in touch.'

'Linda.'

'Oh? And how does she seem?'

Anna summed up for him, but said she was waiting with interest to compare her impressions with his. He seemed uncertain. 'I may not speak to her on her own. It's a business meeting.'

'If you want to interrogate her, nothing's going to stop you,' she said.

'Would you like to go out to eat tonight?' he asked.

'No thanks. Tom and Ally are revising for exams, and I want to make sure they're well fed.'

'Quite right,' he said, sarcastically. She guessed, halfheartedly, that he was not altogether comfortable with himself.

The weather outside grew sunny after a misty start. Anna marched briskly into the nearby arboretum where she, prepared, fed the ducks, inspected flower-beds, talked for twenty minutes to a thin woman who complained about the television adaptation of *Pride and Prejudice* saying it tended to distort.

'My son and daughter watched it,' Anna said, 'and thoroughly enjoyed it, or at least that was the impression they gave.'

'How old are they?'

'Seventeen and sixteen.'

'Had either of them read it?'

'My daughter had. They're both scientists, mathematicians.'

The lady, thin, sixty perhaps, pursed her lips.

'Why,' Anna asked, breaking the silence, 'is Jane Austen so good?'

'It's the beautiful balance of her language. She was lucky to live in a good period for prose. As Shakespeare with poetry.' She spoke without hesitation. A former lecturer, Anna guessed.

Anna, delighted, left the lady of certainty on her bench. In contradiction to the warm weather, she wore lacy gloves, but without drawing attention to them. Anna wished she could often meet people with strong literary opinions to exchange.

Colin arrived home ten minutes before dinner was served. His secretary had rung to say he would be home for the meal, but they were not to wait for him. He arrived smiling, waved to the family who were already in the dining-room.

'Born in the vestry. Just in time,' he shouted, and rushed upstairs. Alice grimaced at his vulgarity. At table he seemed cheerfully talkative, inquiring about the scholars' revision, and his wife's day. The youngsters helped to clear the table without any pressure from the parents, but said they would do without coffee.

'We must return to our studies,' Thomas said. He sounded, Anna thought, just like his father. One was uncertain how serious he was.

'I'll make the coffee,' Colin said, when they had stacked the crockery and cutlery into the dish-washer. 'You go and sit yourself in comfort in the upstairs drawing room, and I'll bring it along.'

'News?' she asked.

'You wait and see.'

Upstairs he poured out and served with a slow formality quite unlike his usual dash. He offered her biscuits on a plate, and peppermints, which she refused. When he finally sat, he straightened the sharp seams of his trousers, and placing his shining brogues together drew himself upright, vigorously rubbing his hands.

'I spoke to Linda,' he began, 'as you may have guessed.'

She inclined her head, and delaying lifted her coffee from the table.

'The business part didn't take us long. Lewis and I were soon in complete agreement, and then he cleared off. Perhaps deliberately.'

'Was she friendly?' Anna asked.

'Very. But she started off as she meant to go on. 'If you've any ideas of talking me back into a reconciliation with Terry, then you can think again.''

'That was rude,' Anna commented.

'I don't know. She wanted me to understand where she stood. I quite like that. Then she went through the stuff she told you about Terry's unreasonable behaviour. I just listened.'

'"He's changed, Colin," she said. "He's not the man I married." She put it down to his selling up the business, and leaving himself with nothing of concern.' Colin tapped white teeth with a fingernail. 'I guess she's right. He's like my father. Work is all. It doesn't matter that Terry has plenty to retire on. That wouldn't seem important. He'd nothing to occupy himself with.' Again Colin paused, waiting for a comment she did not make. 'Your father had more sense. He bought his estate in Ashby, and that gave him plenty to think about. Moreover, he'd a second shot in his locker. The German connection. I remember when we went over to Munich how surprised the locals were that this typical Englishman, in his English suits, with his English manners could speak idiomatic German and with a German accent. Your dad loved the effect. They expected a monoglot stuttering out his orders and pointing and there he was speaking their language better than they could.'

'Yes, but he was very down last winter. He felt it was all going wrong.'

'We can't guarantee good health.'

'No?'

'That's what I'd like, when I knock off work, good health and plenty to do.' He scrubbed his chin. 'In my case I'm like Terry and my own father. We aren't born to do anything except work. My dad saved himself by dying.'

'So how are you going to find your salvation?'

'I'm depending on you.'

'Look what happened to your brother. His wife let him down. Not that I blame her.'

'No, she said you were sympathetic.'

'The trouble with your family is that you haven't thought about it early enough. You were all too independent. You all did too well. I know you think your father slaved away to impress your mother. And I guess Terry worked like a dog when he saw how much money you were beginning to make.'

'And what about me?'

'I often wondered. You had to beat everybody in sight. And I guess the best thing for you to do will be to go on doing what you do so well.'

'And hope I die young, like my dad?'

'I can't really think that's necessary. You might grow out of it. For one thing your father married too late. He never even saw Henry and Tom and Ally. Your mother lived long enough to get some pleasure out of all three.'

'Did she?'

'Colin Turnbull. I know Tom and Alice will shortly go away. And probably never again live permanently with us, but that doesn't mean we lose all connection with them. There are cars and trains, and telephones and aeroplanes even if they choose to live abroad. People often complain to me that they've lost touch with their families.'

'And you think it's their fault?'

'Who else? It's not like the good old days, when your mother and father and your children and grandchildren all lived in the same town, met often, laid the law down for each other, paid attention. It's not likely to be like that ever again except in very few cases.'

'Terry and I.'

'But that's no reason to lose touch. You have to work at it. Prepare yourself. Write and ring if you don't hear from them.'

'They may not want your interference.'

'If they're used to it, they won't mind too much, might even be grateful. If they know you're genuinely interested, not just curious and suddenly bossy after long stretches of indifference.'

'You've got it all worked out,' he said, in mock humility.

'I'm trying to suggest ways you can spend your retirement. But you see in this case you have to start now. There'll be no shortage of people wanting to pick your professional brains, and that's good; you can help the poor and needy. But you'll need to do things that stir you.'

'Such as?'

'Painting. Music. Travel. Classes. Clubs.' She spoke with un-disguised sarcasm.

'Oh, hell.' He groaned aloud in pseudo-horror, smiling with his eyes. 'I'm not your sociable man. When I meet people in my own line I think I could be spending my time better. And as to painting and bloody concerts, ughgh.'

'Start practising,' she mocked.

'Anyhow, it doesn't apply to me. I'm to work myself to death, and die in my prime.'

He gave a groan and collapsed back on his chair, hand on heart. It was not badly acted, and she watched the performance with smiling approval. He sat up, brushing his coat.

'Amateur dramatics,' she said. 'There you are. You choose for yourself.'

He bowed.

Anna, pleased that she and her husband had talked seriously, realised that her own choice of language had been too histrionic; true, she'd been neither whimsical nor hysterical, but more, simple word, flowery, expansive than was exactly necessary. She'd acted out her speeches, not only to impress Colin but to convince herself that she did not find herself too seriously engaged without an escape-route. If she could let words bounce and flow, he could take them lightly, act his death-scene. In her mind she had no doubt that they were engaged on a momentous enterprise, but neither must admit it to the other. They had been married nineteen years, yet they still needed these masks to discuss matters of real substance. It did not seem altogether satisfactory to her, but better than nothing.

She looked up from her conclusions, straight across at the human being opposite. Colin seemed to be studying her face, his head cocked to one side.

'What are we going to do about Terry?' she asked.

He straightened, shaking his head as if after a blow. 'Nothing much we can. We'll talk to him and to Linda. I hope he's got enough about him to keep himself going. He's got women chasing after him, or so you tell me. That'll have to do him.'

Anna suddenly realised that she was convinced that after she had married Colin, he had continued his affair with Linda. Apart from one letter she had no evidence. She did not know of other infidelities during the nineteen years, but there had been rumours: secretaries, a traveller for a jewellery firm, the daughter of titled aristocrats, people who had lived in the same village, to which they gave their name, since before the Norman Conquest. If there was any truth there, he'd kept his indiscretions well hidden from her. Even now, after all these years, their sex together was admirably satisfying. She shuddered with pleasure.

'It's not the end of the world,' he said.

'What isn't?'

'Terry's trouble.' He hung his head. 'I feel sorry for the poor sod, but he's only got himself to blame. You know, if you left me, I'd be lost. I wouldn't know which way to turn.'

'You'd manage,' she said. 'I know no-one better qualified to recover.'

'I'd be lost,' he said again, almost savagely. 'When I'm working I think of you getting on with the thousand and one things you do and seeing that the kids and house and that your old folks are well-looked after. When they need it. And my Ma when she was alive. It means I don't have to bother while I'm at work. It's a sort of base from which I . . .' He broke off.

Pleasure surged inside her, no, gradually overwhelmed her, with a calm, a wholeness, a holiness, almost. She did not rush away from it, sat astounded at its power and easy charm. Colin was stroking his chin again. Anna, the new mystic, recovered, and spoke humanly.

'You've never told me that before, in all the time we've been married.'

He grinned, yawned.

'I don't want your head swelling,' he said. 'It's such a good shape now.'

They sat too far away to touch, and neither left the armchairs on the edges of which they now perched.

'It's the nicest thing you've ever said to me.' She kept the language dull.

'You knew. You must have known.' That sounded slightly desperate.

'I hoped.'

He nodded vigorously, as if he'd convinced himself. He might well have received the news of some huge financial profit with such a movement of the head. Pick the bones out of that.

'I heard one thing from Linda that I forgot to tell you,' he said, and made her wait.

'Something important?' She pandered to him.

'Terry, someone told her, spent his time when he was going round the shops for the new owners, not so often now, mending television sets, the sort of thing he did earlier on in his career.'

'And is that good?' she asked.

'I'd think so.' He answered straight away. 'I mean it would be marvellous if he sat there inventing something which would make millions or save lives, but that's not our Terry's style. Well, not any of us.'

'Except you.'

'I've not made many millions today, I can tell you,' he said. 'Not millions of pence even.'

'How much is a million pence?' she asked.

'Knock two noughts off. Ten thousand pounds.'

'That wouldn't be bad for a day's work,' she said. They sat reduced to quiet, after this arithmetic, smiling up at the corners of the room, and sometimes, often, glancing at each other. Anna spoke first.

'That's the most we can expect,' Anna said, 'doing something that we hope's useful.'

'And a bloody good job.'

Anna stood, moved towards the tall bow-windows. Her husband, surprised perhaps by the breaking-off of the conversation, rose and quietly joined her there. He placed an arm gently round her shoulder and they looked out across freshly green trees, roof-tops, two spires, factory chimneys all gilded by the evening sun. In the far distance three ranges of low hills crouched seemingly one above the other, palely grey, touched with pink. A window, just one singleton, reflected the sunlight powerfully almost like a explosion.

A small knock and the door opened. Alice crept in.

'Hullo,' Colin said. 'Revision finished?'

'No. I've plenty more to do, but I thought I'd have ten minutes off, and I wondered what you two were doing in here. I could just hear your voices. I didn't know what you were talking about for so long.'

'And what did you guess?' Anna asked.

'I thought it might be holidays.' They were all going to the Dordogne as soon as examinations were over, perhaps, Anna had said, for the last time, the ending of childhood.

'No,' Anna answered.

'What then?'

'We were talking about Aunt Linda and Uncle Terry. They've separated.'

'I knew that.'

'And were you sorry?' Colin asked, out of character.

'No. Not if that's what they wanted.'

The door opened again and Thomas appeared.

'I heard you chatting, and then Ally's entrance, so I decided to find out what you were all up to. I'm curious.'

'You must have been revising hard, the pair of you. Dead to the world outside.' Their father sounded superior. 'Immersed in learning.'

The four stood looking over the tree-tops and out to the distant hills. No noise or movement disturbed the line of four. Tom stood by his mother, and Alice linked arms with her father, who still held Anna by the shoulder.

'And what were you doing?' Tom asked.

A small, awkward silence fell. They shifted their feet uncomfortably.

'Revision,' Colin said. 'How's that?'

They all burst out laughing, in confusion and relief.